PERFECT LIARS

Rebecca Reid

CORGI BOOKS

TRANSWORLD PUBLISHERS
61–63 Uxbridge Road, London W5 5SA
www.penguin.co.uk

Transworld is part of the Penguin Random House group of companies
whose addresses can be found at global.penguinrandomhouse.com

Penguin
Random House
UK

First published in Great Britain in 2018 by Transworld Digital
an imprint of Transworld Publishers
Corgi edition published 2019

A CIP catalogue record for this book
is available from the British Library.

ISBN
9780552175609

Typeset in 12/14.5pt Dante MT Std by Jouve (UK), Milton Keynes
Printed and bound in Great Britain by Clays Ltd, Elcograf S.p.A.

Penguin Random House is committed to a sustainable
future for our business, our readers and our planet. This book
is made from Forest Stewardship Council® certified paper.

MIX
Paper from
responsible sources
FSC® C018179

1 3 5 7 9 10 8 6 4 2

For my parents, who are so lucky to have me.

PERFECT LIARS

Peonies are out of season, so they were a nightmare to find.
Expensive, too – twice the price of almost any other flower. But
peonies were her favourite, so none of that mattered. After all,
you only do this once. It has to be perfect.

The room seems to sigh as the doors open at the back, filling
the church with icy air. The organ wheezes the strains of a
familiar song, one they've all sung a thousand times: at school,
at the weddings that used to fill their weekends and at the
christenings which had inevitably followed.

With one movement they are on their feet. Polished shoes on
wooden floorboards, angled uncomfortably to fit inside the nar-
row pews. When was the last time any of them had entered a
church?

Two hundred eyes flick to the entrance.

First, a priest.

Second, a man with a pale face and a badly knotted tie.

Then, the coffin.

It doesn't seem possible that she is inside that box, that the
person who was so real and alive so recently could be here, and
yet not here at all.

It's impossible not to wonder what she looks like. Would

she approve of the outfit they had agonized over? The task of picking those painfully final clothes – everything from her underwear to her favourite sky-high heels, to the slim gold chain around her neck – had fallen to them because no one else had wanted to.

The procession moves slowly. Finally, the music stops. The coffin is lowered.

They sit.

It's not a bad turnout for a Wednesday morning. A hundred or so people, all in neat black outfits. Winter coats in need of a dry-clean. Black dresses which lived in the back of wardrobes and were a little too tight around the arms. Dark work suits. White shirts. Ties.

It's a good photo, the one they've chosen for the order of service. It had felt ghoulish, clicking through her social media, scrolling past weddings and holidays and parties, hunting for a photo where she looked healthy and happy. But it's been worth it. The photo props up the lie that every person in the church has committed to. Such a shock. Such a tragic accident.

How long do these things usually go on for? It can't be more than an hour, surely?

And how long will they have to stay afterwards? It will be unrelentingly grim, so strained. All the makings of a party – decent food and good booze – yet none of the fun. It doesn't seem fair, to bring together people who haven't seen each other since the last big do and then make them feel guilty for laughing.

They're too young for all of this.

And then there's the question of what to say. None of the usual things apply.

No one can say she's lived a long life or that she's out of her pain. There isn't anything comforting to reach for.

Even calling it a tragedy seems inaccurate. No accident to talk about, no illness to blame it on – at least, not one that can be mentioned in polite company.

Nothing sounds right. Every platitude seems like an accusation – like it is someone's fault that she's gone. As though they could have done something. As though death could have been avoided.

NOW

Georgia

There was a chip in the polish on Georgia's left index fingernail.

Shellac wasn't supposed to chip. It had looked perfect when she left the salon earlier, or else she would have had them start all over again, but somehow, she had managed to spoil it. Nancy would notice, of course. She would pick her hand up on the pretence of admiring her eternity ring, and then raise her eyebrows with a smile. Nancy's own nails would be perfect. Dark-red, almost black lacquer, just as they always were.

Annoyed, Georgia pushed her fingers into the mixture in the bowl, relishing the wrongness of her hands in the meat, pressing it together with the onions and the sage. Would anyone eat it, she wondered. Certainly not Lila. She seemed to be on a liquid diet these days – Diet Coke by day and wine by night. Which increasingly meant tears, vomit and saying things she didn't mean. Georgia had started to worry that the liquid diet might be less about Lila trying to lose imaginary baby weight, and more about what was going on in her head.

They'd be here soon. She had meant to have the food

finished by the time they arrived, filling the house with delectable smells. It wouldn't be done in time now, unless they were late. She shouldn't have taken the test today. It was only supposed to take three minutes, but inevitably the whole miserable process took longer. The waiting, washing her hands, waiting again. Calling Charlie, pretending not to hear the accusation in his tone as he hurried her off the phone, rushing from one meeting to another, squeezing her wretched disappointment in between appointments with clients. It was always the same.

But she knew Nancy wouldn't be late. She never was. She was coming straight from the airport as no flight would ever dare be delayed with Nancy on board. Everything in her life, from the neat bobbed haircut she had worn since she was twenty-five to her patent shoes, was together. On time. Precise.

At least the kitchen looked good. Charlie had been horrified when she'd campaigned to knock half the ground floor into this huge, open-plan room. But now, with the twilight streaming through the huge French windows and the table set for six, laden with flowers and candles and crisp linen napkins, no one would be able to question her taste. Not even her friends. Georgia the scholarship girl with second-hand school uniform and Primark school shoes was dead and buried.

The sound of a key turning in the lock distracted her. She shook the stuffing off her hands and turned to the sink, knocking the tap on with her elbow and hurriedly rubbing her hands under the tepid water. Had Charlie snuck out of work early to come home and help her get ready?

She felt the corners of her mouth pulling into a smile. He could be quite sweet sometimes.

'Gee? It's me.' Lila's breathy voice came from the hall. 'Sorry I'm early.'

Lila had never been early in her life. She was the latest person Georgia had ever encountered. What did this mean? Surely Lila wasn't turning over a new leaf now, when Georgia had summoned Nancy all the way from Boston to talk some sense into her.

Georgia had only given Lila a set of house keys as a goodwill gesture, and because she lived a ten-minute drive away. They were meant for emergencies, not for letting herself into the house whenever she felt like it, but that message didn't seem to have got through. Nevertheless Georgia forced a grin and opened her arms to hug Lila.

'I thought you and Roo were coming at eight?'

Georgia had last seen Lila a few weeks ago. But she'd changed since then. Had she been ill? Her limbs had always been long and sinewy, but now her face looked entirely hollow, and while she still sported the kind of tan that only comes from spending eight weeks a year in blazing holiday sunshine, there was an almost yellow tinge to her skin. She looked, for the first time in as long as Georgia could remember, like shit.

She watched as Lila dragged up her jeans, jeans which should have been skin-tight but sagged around her thighs. The white top she wore was clearly designed to be loose and floaty, but it was slipping off one angular shoulder.

'I know, I'm sorry to surprise you, but I was coming past, and Roo was home early so he can do the babysitter and everything. Anyway, I wanted to see you on your own for a bit before everyone else got here. Is that OK?' Lila's face crumpled and for one horrible moment Georgia thought she might be about to cry. 'Am I a nightmare? Shall I go? I can call an Uber if you want, it's no big deal. I can go and come back – should I go and come back?'

Yes. She should. Early was coming at seven forty-five when the invitation had said eight. Not arriving at six while Georgia had stuffing all over her fingers and a coffee stain on the front of her T-shirt dress.

She parted her lips to say all that, but the needy, pinched look between Lila's eyebrows pulled at Georgia's chest.

'Don't be silly, it's fine. You can help.'

Lila immediately perked up.

'You're so cute, by the way,' said Lila, following her into the kitchen. 'Taking the day off to get dinner ready for Her Highness. What's this visit all about anyway? Are we in trouble?'

Georgia fixed her smile, wondering whether her tinted moisturizer would cover the flush in her cheeks. 'Of course not. And I haven't taken the day off for her, I didn't have to go into work today.'

'Why not?' asked Lila, heading towards the kitchen.

'The office is closed for the day. Some kind of training thing.'

The office was closed for staff training, so it had been wonderful luck that she could be home – that was the official party line. She'd made Charlie practise it that morning, and the previous night. She wasn't sure he would remember. He had rolled his eyes as if it was the stupidest thing he'd ever heard. 'Why can't they know the truth?' he had asked. 'There's no shame in it.'

Yet there was shame in it. There was always shame in failure. And whichever way you cut it, not being able to get pregnant was a failure.

'Lots of people take leave when they're doing this,' he had added. It simply wasn't true. She was the first person in the entire company ever to make use of their IVF leave scheme. Six weeks of unpaid holiday while she faced the worst of the injections and scans and invasive procedures and, worst of all, the crushing hope. Everyone knew that the scheme wasn't actually there to be used, that it was a nice-sounding, decorative bonus to lure the shiny young female graduates. It certainly wasn't meant to be used by people like her: admin staff. Replaceable people.

But she had done it anyway. She had booked a meeting with her thousand-year-old boss, reminded him that the scheme existed, quietly explained her situation, and announced that she'd be hiring a temp to cover herself in her absence. She'd left him blinking, but under no illusions that this was what was going to happen, whether he liked it or not. No one seemed to have found a way around the glaringly obvious problem that if you weren't pregnant on your return, everyone would be looking at you as if your entire family had died in a house fire. But that was an outcome she refused to contemplate.

Maybe she could have told Lila. It might have been nice, Lila might have understood. She'd had a baby, she knew what it was to crave a pregnancy. Lila could, when she was sober, be trusted to be understanding. But never discreet. She might tell Nancy.

Georgia tried not to wince at the mess as Lila chucked her huge leather handbag on to the side table, kicked her ballet pumps into the middle of the floor and headed towards the other end of the kitchen, not even pausing to sit down before she took a wine glass from one of the cupboards and pulled a bottle of wine from the double fridge. Georgia allowed herself an internal sigh of relief. Her concerns about Lila being on best behaviour, about Nancy thinking Georgia had exaggerated how bad things were, had been unfounded.

'Your fridge is so healthy,' Lila commented, standing with the door open, the rim of her wine glass resting against her lips. 'Ohh – bread. Do you eat carbs now?'

Georgia knew that Lila knew the answer to this question, because she asked it at least once a month, but it was their little routine, a routine which had been forged in their first year at school together, and was now nearly twenty years old.

'Nope. That's for Charlie.'

'So you still don't?'

'No, I usually just have a few berries or some Greek yogurt. I don't miss it,' Georgia lied.

'What about pizza?' asked Lila, in a pornographic voice. 'Don't you miss pizza?'

There was no way that Lila had eaten a pizza in the

last decade. She might have taken a nibble of Roo's while she sat on his lap talking in a baby voice and trying to look cute, but the chances that any notable quantity of refined carbohydrates had passed her lips were somewhere between slim and fuck-all.

'I miss pizza,' Georgia conceded. 'And I've missed you. I'm sorry I've been so busy.'

'It's OK,' said Lila, looking at the floor. 'It's just there's a lot going on at the moment. Inigo isn't sleeping, Roo is crazy busy at work, I've been thinking a lot about—'

'I thought Inigo was better now?' Georgia cut across Lila's words, not wanting to hear the end of that sentence. At least not until Nancy arrived. 'When we had dinner at yours with the Hendersons, you were saying he'd been perfect?'

That had been a weird night, looking back on it. Lila had opened the door with red eyes and a fake smile and spent the entire evening talking about how wonderful her son was. She'd served lukewarm soup and dry chicken and then Roo had announced that he had a work call he couldn't put off. They'd all left at eleven, saying that they'd had a lovely time but desperate to go home and pretend that the whole awkward, awful evening hadn't happened.

Lila pulled out one of the kitchen stools and seated herself at the island. The stool's legs made a painful scraping noise against the stone floor. Georgia tried not to wince.

'Guess we spoke too soon,' replied Lila, pouring more wine into her glass. If she was drunk by the time Nancy arrived then naturally it would all be Georgia's fault.

Typical Nancy, defecting to Boston for the last decade and leaving her completely responsible for Lila. 'He's a little twat most of the time.'

Georgia laughed. She'd learned from watching her friends procreate that it didn't do to look shocked when someone called their child a twat.

'Is he with the nanny now?'

'Babysitter. Anna quit. I don't think we're going to replace her.'

'Oh?'

'Yeah, Roo says there's no point. I wasn't working that much before anyway, and it doesn't pay well, so he feels I might as well be home with Inigo because it's cheaper and better for the baby.'

Silence hung between them. The question 'But what about what *you* want?' seemed the obvious one to ask, but it was Lila and Roo's business how they raised their children, and it was true, Lila's styling business had never taken off. A few shoots here and there, a couple of music videos for small-time singers. But nothing to write home about. Not enough to justify missing her son growing up. Anyway, once Georgia got pregnant and had her baby they'd be able to share childcare.

'I think that's lovely,' said Georgia resolutely. 'I bet most mothers would be so jealous of you, being able to be at home all day with Inigo. And you'll probably have another one before long, don't you think?'

Lila's face changed, as if Georgia had poked her finger into a bruise.

'What?'

'Nothing.' Lila's gaze fell to her wine glass.

'I was only asking, it's just . . . Inigo's nearly three, I assumed you'd be thinking about having another one.'

Lila stood up, her feet either side of the stool and reached over the counter, stretching for Georgia's phone. It lit up as she pressed the button at the bottom of the display. Georgia bristled at the invasion but said nothing. There was no point in scolding her, not this early in the evening.

Lila picked up the phone and pointed at the time. 'Are you ready?' she asked.

Georgia wanted to keep pressing. She wanted confirmation, to hear Lila say out loud that she and Roo weren't going to have another one. But the moment had passed.

'No, of course not. I'm not wearing this,' Georgia replied, gesturing at the T-shirt dress. 'I'm going to change. And shower.'

'Really? Nance will be here in like an hour and a half – you know what she's like. The earliest person in the world. She doesn't get that being super early is way worse than being late.'

So Lila did understand the theory of turning up on time. 'Do you mind if I go and get ready?' Georgia asked.

'I'll come with you,' said Lila. It was the happiest she'd sounded since she arrived. 'Let's get ready together. Why do people stop doing that when they get older? It's so fun.' She tipped more wine into her glass and got to her feet. 'Upstairs?'

People stop getting ready together when they're older because it's more time-efficient, Georgia thought to herself. And practical. And because it's nice to have some privacy when you're getting ready. Her mind moved to the bruises on her torso from the IVF injections. Every time Charlie stuck the needle into her stomach he winced at them, and then made the same joke: 'You bruise like a Georgia peach.' If Lila noticed, she'd ask questions. Sharing the innermost workings of her marriage wasn't Georgia's style at the best of times. And this certainly wasn't the best of times.

'I should totally style you,' said Lila, pulling the wardrobe door open and running her fingers over the fabrics. 'For tonight, I mean. Is this carpet new? It's insane, it's the softest thing I've ever felt.'

It was new. And the walls were newly painted, a soft, chalky grey which was apparently made from real shells. The room was perfect. The only reason she had let Lila come upstairs with her was because she loved walking into Charlie's and her bedroom and seeing the high ceilings and cream wood through someone else's eyes. It was like a hotel room.

Keeping her back to Lila, shielding her torso, Georgia peeled off her dress and tossed it on the bed, telling herself for the thousandth time that no, the bed wasn't too big for the room. Charlie still thought it was, even after Georgia and the woman who'd designed it had explained that it wasn't. When Charlie and Georgia had first got together they had slept in her single bed, in a shared house in Fulham, because his parents wouldn't let them share a room in their house. She'd believed at the time that his parents disapproved of sex before marriage. She knew now that it was her they disapproved of. If

Charlie had been sticking it to someone with the 'right' background, they'd probably have offered up their own bed. None of that had mattered back then, though.

They would tangle their limbs around each other and somehow manage to sleep soundly in the tiny space. These days he got home so late that he had perfected the art of slipping into bed long after she had fallen asleep. Or at least, when he thought she was asleep.

There had been a time when she would have forced herself to stay awake, drinking coffee and sitting on the sofa watching reruns of *Friends* until he got home. But she had learned eventually that he didn't want that. After a day of talking and shouting and arguing at work, he had used all of his words up, while she had used barely any of hers. Her desk was by the door of the office, so Georgia was first to greet anyone who arrived, but then everyone sat downstairs. Sometimes she would hear a roar of laughter from the basement and consider asking what was happening, but she knew from experience that by the time she made it downstairs everyone would have stopped laughing and no one would want to explain the joke.

After Charlie proposed, Georgia had seized her chance. The others had been asking for years why she wasn't auditioning any more and when she was going to start doing plays again. Now she had an excuse.

'I'm happy at Greenlowe for now,' she had told them, knowing that Nancy was just jealous because, well, who would have guessed it would be Georgia who got married first? 'I like it there,' she had lied. 'Anyway, soon there'll be babies. There's no point trying to get into a play or a film and then having to drop out because I'm pregnant. Actresses don't get maternity leave, you know.'

Nancy had made a face, implying that the position of office administrator at Greenlowe, a boutique estate agency, was below Georgia, as if working there somehow tarnished Nancy by association. It wasn't as if it had been Georgia's dream, either.

There was no baby. Not yet, at least. And Nancy had been right, as she always was. Georgia was bored. Painfully bored. So bored that she'd volunteered for charities, and redone rooms of the house which didn't need decorating.

'I don't really need styling,' she called across to Lila, who had disappeared into the walk-in wardrobe and was running her hands over Georgia's clothes.

'How do you keep it so tidy in here?' Lila laughed. She had her glass of wine in her hand. If she spilt it, she'd soak the carpet, and probably stain something expensive and cashmere at the same time.

'I don't know. I just do. Honestly, you don't need to do that, I've already picked a dress.'

Lila was pulling things off hangers and throwing them over the crook of her arm. 'You're not being fun. You used to love getting dressed. Remember the wardrobe at school?'

Of course she remembered it. They'd pooled all their clothes into one huge wardrobe – back then they'd all been the same tiny dress size – and shared everything. Even their uniforms were interchangeable. Georgia had hated it. Every garment she had chosen with her mother over the holidays, carefully sourced from charity shops, bought with money that was desperately needed elsewhere, would come back stretched, or shrunk or stained or burned with a cigarette hole. Lila and Nancy would wrinkle their noses at the labels in the back of Georgia's clothes and then borrow them anyway, filling the garments with themselves and, unused to the idea of valuing things, not being grateful for them or taking care of them, tainting them. They wouldn't be Georgia's any more. Like everything else in her world, they would be split three ways.

'Georgia doesn't like sharing,' Nancy would smirk whenever she tentatively suggested that they each have a few special items which were off limits. 'It's because she doesn't have sisters.'

'You don't have sisters either!' Georgia had retorted, her voice a bit higher than she had intended. 'You don't have any siblings at all.'

'That's different,' Nancy had said, clearly feeling no obligation to explain why. Which was Nancy's way, then and now. Except on this occasion. This time it was Georgia who had emailed Nancy, who had told her she needed to come home: *It's bad. I'm worried. I think you should come.*

And Nancy had, for the first time in her entire life, done as she was told. Lila would kill Georgia if she found out what she'd done, what tonight was really about.

Lila emerged from the cupboard and threw the pile of silky fabrics, assorted shades of white, cream, taupe and beige, on to the bed. 'Gee?'

'Yes?'

'We need to talk.'

Georgia's stomach tilted. Lila had been asking for

weeks, and Georgia had promised her that tonight they would finally talk, knowing that if she didn't there was a good chance Lila would text at the last minute with some flimsy excuse and Nancy's trip would be wasted. Nancy would be furious and disappear back to Boston, leaving Georgia with the entire mess still at her feet. Georgia had done everything she could to avoid having the conversation, short of putting her hands over her ears and screaming. Nancy was so nearly here to help, to deal with it together.

'We can. But I need to get dressed and shower first, OK?'

Lila looked disappointed. 'Please?'

Georgia picked up a silk dress and a fine knit jumper from the bed, and held them together. 'I was thinking I'd wear these?'

Lila was like a child. Distracting her was easier than it should have been. Her eyes widened in horror at the terrible combination Georgia had made. 'You can't do that! See? This is why you need me to style you.'

Georgia sighed inwardly, thinking of the neat printed J. Crew dress hanging in the wardrobe, which she had bought earlier in the week, expressly to wear tonight. The dress Nancy would have coveted.

'You're right. I don't know what I was thinking. Please will you pick me something?'

THEN

Lila

'Lila, please. Turn it down. Just a bit,' said Clarissa.

'My car, my rules,' Lila laughed, turning the dial again, so that Rihanna's voice drowned out the complaints. Her stepmother hadn't wanted to let her drive back to school, but as ever Lila had won the argument. 'That's why we bought her a car,' her father had reasoned over their last supper the night before, sealing the deal and making sure that Clarissa didn't stand a chance. Lila almost felt bad for her. She was clearly determined not to be a cliché, favouring Lila over her own children, desperate to avoid the label 'wicked stepmother'.

Lila swerved sharply into the drive, forgetting to indicate. She watched in her peripheral vision as Clarissa opened her mouth to complain and then seemed to think better of it. One of her hands was clinging to the handle above the car door, and the other was braced against the dashboard. If Lila accelerated hard and then did an emergency stop, Clarissa would probably break her arm. Tempting.

The car was the biggest perk of being old for her year. Driving up to the boarding house would make everyone else painfully jealous. Lila smiled sweetly at Clarissa and then took both hands off the wheel, feeling around for the button which would send the car's top down. Just as she put her hands back on the wheel, a battered green Volvo turned the corner and narrowly avoided Lila by swerving on to the grass. This was clearly too much for Clarissa, whose hand shot across the car. 'Camilla! You have to keep your hands on the wheel at all times. Both of them.'

Lila laughed, and put her hands on the wheel as the roof gave way to sky. Clarissa was full-naming her, it was sort of sweet how she tried to exert authority.

They were nearly at the top of the drive now, endless as it seemed. Lila suddenly remembered Nancy's theory that the drive was there to discourage anyone from trying to escape – it would be hours before you managed to walk from your boarding house to the road, and by the time you got there you'd have lost the will to live. But for Lila, driving over the gravel gave her a feeling of warmth, of coming home.

The hills, the fields, the lacrosse pitch, the tennis courts, the cluster of honey-coloured buildings. It was all the same, identical to how it had been two months ago when she'd gone home for the summer. The only difference was that when she had left in July it had felt tired, and now everything felt new. The air was cooler, all the clothes in her trunk still had the labels in, and there was a sense of potential in the air. Everything was ready to start again. New bedroom, new books, old friends. New, but old. School was trustworthy like that.

After an entire summer at home in the tall townhouse her father had filled with his new wife and new babies, she wanted her own territory back. She reached forward to press skip on the iPod, determined to pull up outside Reynolds House with the perfect soundtrack.

The car rasped against a speed bump, which she had accidentally accelerated into while playing with the sound system.

'Camilla, please. You focus on the driving and I'll sort the music.'

Lila sniggered. As if! In fairness, Clarissa wasn't old, old. She was thirty-six, which was the perfect age for a stepmother because she wasn't quite young enough to know how to talk to Lila, but she was so much younger than her dad or her mum had been, and she hated the idea of seeming old. Of all the clichés she tried to avoid, she failed at escaping this one. If Clarissa ever tried to meddle, all it took was a question from Lila about what it was like to grow up in the sixties to put her back in her place.

Clarissa needed to calm down. She was overreacting to every tiny driving mistake. Anyway, in twenty minutes she'd be in a nice air-conditioned car back to London where she could hang out with her real kids and forget that Lila even existed.

'Gee!' Lila squealed, jumping out of the car and slamming the door, the engine still running. Standing outside Reynolds House, perfectly framed by the wide yellow door, was Georgia. She wore a pair of navy tracksuit bottoms, rolled down at the waistband so that her tanned hip bones were on show, and a tiny white vest top. Her hair was blonder than ever, and her wrists were covered in bracelets.

Lila wrapped her arms around Georgia and they jumped up and down. Her chest felt tight and full, fizzing with the excitement of seeing her best friend again. Lila noted the streak of orange fake tan on Georgia's wrist. She tried not to think about how much it must suck to have spent an entire summer holiday in England. She and Nancy had already resolved not to say a single word about their week in Portugal together. And to keep pretending they believed the reason Georgia hadn't come was because she had a 'family wedding', when they both knew it was because her parents couldn't afford the flights.

'Who else is here?' asked Lila, looking around.

'Hardly anyone,' replied Georgia. 'I was first back.' Then, squealing, she pulled Lila into a hug. 'It's so good to see you!"

'Anyone would think you two hadn't seen each other for years,' came Clarissa's voice. She was dragging the bags out of the back of the Audi. Georgia glanced over and finally noticed the car. She looked at it, then back at Lila, cocking her head to one side.

'No!'

Lila tried not to grin. She didn't want to be that girl, but she'd clocked the new cars in the boarding house's car park, and she had definitely done the best so far.

'A convertible Audi?' Georgia was smiling broadly now.

'Yep.'

Georgia ran towards the car and climbed over the closed door into the passenger seat. 'You bitch. You actual bitch. How?'

'She has a very indulgent father,' Clarissa called, while dragging one of Lila's bags towards the door of Reynolds House. 'Who loves her very much.'

Georgia turned her mega-watt grin on Lila's step-mother. 'I wish my parents loved me this much!' Then she turned back to Lila. That was the good thing about Georgia. She never seemed to get jealous, even though she never had anything new or nice.

'When did you get here?' asked Lila, pulling the straps of her vest top down. No harm in trying to get a bit more tanned before the sun disappeared.

'Like, five minutes ago.'

'Where's your mum?' called Clarissa from the door of their boarding house. 'I was hoping to say hi.'

'She just left,' said Georgia, flushing. 'She wanted to stay, but she had to head back – she's got work.'

'I hope it wasn't her Lila nearly ran off the road on the way in!' laughed Clarissa. 'Which one's their car?'

'Clarissa, can you sign me in please?' Lila called across the drive. She turned to Georgia. 'Did Nance message you?'

'Yep. She's going to be back late. She said not to pick beds until she gets here.'

'Fuck that.'

'I know.'

'Have you checked the dorm list?'

'Not yet, I waited for you. But Cookie promised.'

'I know. Imagine if she went back on it? It's the only three-person dorm in the whole house, and this entire term will be ruined if we're not together.'

'We're the only trio in the house. It's ours, always has been.'

'Girls? Are you coming in?' came Clarissa's shout. Lila sighed theatrically.

'Stop,' said Georgia. 'She's not that bad.'

'Why are you so obsessed with her?'

'I'm not, I just don't hate her like you do.' Georgia twisted her hair up into a bun.

'I don't hate her. She's fine.'

'But she's not your mum.'

Lila bristled. This wasn't a place that Georgia usually went to. It wasn't somewhere she was welcome. Just like Lila didn't ask about Georgia's mum's job, or comment on her hand-me-down uniform. 'No. She's not.'

'You know she's pregnant?'

'What?'

'One hundred per cent. That's why he got you the car. Wait a couple of months. You'll see.'

Georgia stood up in the car, and climbed back over the door. 'Let me give you a hand, Clarissa, you shouldn't be carrying that,' she simpered.

Lila tipped her head back and stared at the sky. For fuck's sake! Georgia was right, of course. That was why Clarissa had been so whiny on the drive down, and why her father had held her so weirdly tight when he'd said goodbye to her the night before. Of fucking course.

Another one. They'd already popped out two kids who put their sticky hands on everything and made the whole house smell like mashed fruit. Did they really need another one? He was nearly fifty. Wouldn't he be embarrassed, doing the school run with a bald patch and wrinkles?

She pulled her biggest suitcase from the back seat of the car, where she'd wedged it earlier. She'd have to drag it up the stairs herself now, Clarissa wasn't in any state to help.

When she had started at Fairbridge Hall six years ago, they'd made a day of it. Her, her dad, her mum. They'd booked into a hotel the night before and raised a toast to her new school life. They'd made plans about what they'd do on her first weekend trip home. That morning her mother had blow-dried Lila's hair and let her wear mascara for the first time.

Her dad had dragged everything up the stairs to her dorm, and her mum had helped her decorate, sticking posters and pages from magazines that they'd carefully selected together on the walls. Everyone had thought her mum was cool because she'd left them with a box of Haribo and Freddos, and when she'd dropped her handbag she'd said fuck really loudly. Later, when Lila was lying in bed, trying to fall asleep on the strange mattress, she'd put her hand under the pillow and felt her mum's mascara there.

With these thoughts, the feeling – the bad feeling – was starting to come back, with its familiar burn in the back of her throat. That wasn't for now.

★

'Do you want to go up the back stairs, or the front ones?'
Lila called, surveying her pile of stuff, splayed over the
carpet of the entrance hall. 'I think this suitcase might
get stuck on the back ones. Why isn't there a lift in this
place?'

Georgia didn't respond.

'Gee? What's wrong?'

'You need to come and look at this,' said Georgia
quietly. Her eyes were cast down. 'The allocations.'

'What's going on?'

Georgia looked like she was about to say someone was
dead. Panic started to well inside Lila. Surely not? It
wasn't possible. Everything had been arranged. It had
practically been promised.

'The triple dorm?' Lila asked. 'You're fucking joking?'

The noticeboard was pimpled with holes where pins
had been. Next week it would be covered in notes about
auditions and practices and matches. For now it was
naked but for a huge piece of white paper with the dorm
allocations.

'I checked it while you were getting your stuff,' said
Georgia solemnly.

Lila reached forward and pulled the piece of paper off
the noticeboard, taking the pins with it. They pinged to
the carpet.

'Lila? What are you doing?' asked Georgia.

Lila said nothing. She stared at the piece of paper,
holding it between her hands, as if her eyes could
erase the Arial size-twelve font if she read it enough
times.

'Let me see it,' said Georgia, snatching the paper from Lila's hands. Lila yelped. 'Fuck off, Georgia, paper cuts!'

Lila held her hand up. There was an almost invisible slice between her thumb and index finger which had determinedly filled with blood.

'Sorry,' said Georgia. 'Accident.'

Lila put her hand to her lips and licked at the blood. It made her feel a bit sick.

'It's a mistake,' said Lila. 'That's all. It's a mistake.'

'Are our names on the door? We need to go and look.'

Lila took the stairs two at a time, her heart thudding in her body. She sprinted down the third-floor corridor, arriving outside the door of the triple dorm, the dorm they had known was theirs. Georgia's heavy breathing caught up with her. They stared at the names, mounted in little metal frames on the door.

'It's not a mistake,' whispered Lila.

'Nancy is going to murder someone,' panted Georgia. 'How the fuck could this happen?'

Nancy was always the last to arrive, every term. She didn't like the 'faffing' that came with unpacking and running around asking about other people's holidays. Lila and Georgia watched through the wide windows at the front of the boarding house as the people-carrier pulled up. Lila had clasped her knees to her chest and was pulling at the loose threads at the ankles of her tracksuit bottoms. It was cold in the hall, draughty. But they didn't know where else to go. The common room was full of giggling and chattering, and going to one of their rooms clearly wasn't an option. Their bags – Lila's trunks and bin bags, and Georgia's one neat suitcase – sat forlornly abandoned in the corridor outside their dorm. Or rather, not their dorm.

'She's here,' said Georgia unhelpfully.

Nancy stepped out, thinner than ever in her usual outfit – skinny jeans, a V-neck Ralph Lauren jumper and ballet pumps. They watched as she casually tipped the driver.

'Where's her stuff?' asked Lila.

'She has it sent on ahead usually,' said Georgia, who sounded in awe of this.

'What are we going to tell her?'

'I don't know,' replied Lila honestly. Not for the first time, it struck Lila how weird it was to be afraid of her friend. She'd never known anyone who could make her feel so nervous or so guilty as Nancy did. But then, she'd never known anyone like Nancy before.

'Why are you sitting here?' asked Nancy as she pushed through the doors. 'Let's go upstairs. Are my things in our room?'

Lila looked at Georgia, waiting for her to speak, but nothing came.

'Hello?' asked Nancy, standing above them. 'What's going on?'

Georgia clearly wasn't about to step up. 'It's the dorms,' Lila said quietly. 'We didn't get the triple.'

Nancy raised her eyebrows slightly, tipping her head to one side. 'What?'

Georgia finally spoke: 'They put Lila in it. With Heidi Bart and Jenny McGuckin.'

Both girls watched Nancy's face as she took in the information. What would happen next? With Nancy it was impossible to tell if she would laugh or scream. Or lash out.

'That,' said Nancy, 'is unacceptable.'

NOW

Nancy

Nancy tried to tune out the sound of Brett's breathing. He didn't mean to breathe loudly, she was aware of that, but that didn't make it any less annoying. He's perfect, she reminded herself. He's young, and beautiful, and funny and perfect and they will die of jealousy when they see him. That was the point of him. So, a little audible breathing could be forgiven.

'Can we have the radio on?' she said, leaning forward to catch their driver's attention. Perhaps Brett had picked up some bug on the flight over. She thought about reaching into her bag and covering her hands with sanitizer, but it didn't fit with the persona she'd created for him. He regarded her as more devil-may-care than that. A pleasing contrast to the uptight woman he had dated back in Boston. Her friends would think it was hilarious, the idea that anyone would think she was laid-back. But in the States not insisting on being picked up at her apartment before she went on a date made her happy go lucky. It was nice to be viewed that way. She'd never been seen as easy-going before.

People had teased her all the way through school and

university for being organized, for being 'OCD'. It was true, she liked to arrive promptly and complete tasks in good time. It was never entirely clear to her why that was such a laughable characteristic, or how it had anything in common with a disorder. Teachers had smiled indulgently at her early homework in the same way they'd laughed at Lila's chronic lateness.

'So this is London,' said Brett, watching the buildings flick past him through the window. 'I can't believe I'm actually here.' Nancy put her hand over his, trying to find his awe at the suburbs of West London endearing.

'It's the suburbs. It's pretty hideous actually.'

'I like it,' he said simply, and went back to leaning his perfect forehead on the window.

They were going to be late. Well, not late exactly – an invitation for eight meant eight thirty. But they weren't going to be prompt. They hadn't been able to find the car she had booked to collect them from the airport. Brett had sauntered around the terminal, looking for Nancy's name on a board, cheerfully carrying everything he needed for the entire trip – the weekend with Georgia and then their jaunt to Paris – in a small duffle bag. She had bitten her lip to stop herself from shouting at him. She'd been on best behaviour the entire time they had been together, but she had been able to feel it brewing, threatening to explode, his constant calm infuriating.

But she knew it wasn't the taxi situation which was the problem. The real problem was that Brett was about to meet her friends. He had asked her about it on the plane, even though she had put on an eye mask, hand cream and earplugs – as much of a *do not disturb* sign as anyone could provide. She had been worried he was going to ask her if she wanted to join the Mile-High club, which she absolutely didn't. Brett was young and he had never left America before. He'd barely even been on a plane. It was the kind of sweet, stupid thing he would like. But to her surprise, that hadn't been the question. Instead, he had managed to ask the right thing: 'Are you nervous about me meeting your friends?' She had said yes, and had found herself surprised by how much she enjoyed telling him the truth. Or at least, part of the truth.

He had spoiled it after that, though. 'Are you worried they're going to tell me all kinds of terrible stories about what you got up to at school?' And then he'd grinned, showing off two rows of perfect American orthodontics. Her stomach had tightened and she'd let out a nervous giggle, hoping he wouldn't realize quite how close to the truth he was. It was fine, she had told herself over and over again on the flight. It had been twelve years. There was no reason for it to come out now.

She had opened her mouth to try to explain and found, as she had every time she had ever tried to explain her friendship with Lila and Georgia, that the words wouldn't come. 'It's not a normal friendship,' she had managed, before running out of words.

'I get it,' Brett had replied. 'You went to boarding school together. You grew up together. That kind of thing has got to bond you for life.'

Nancy had almost laughed then. So close to the truth, and yet so, so far.

The crapness of the radio was pleasingly universal. Whether it was a cab from her apartment to the office in Boston, or from the airport to Georgia's house in Notting Hill, there would always be some unreasonably cheerful duo talking about things that couldn't matter less, interspersed with decades-old pop music. Brett ran his hand up her thigh.

'Baby?'

'Yes?'

'Are you OK?'

As if she was going to give any kind of honest answer to that question while they were sitting in the back of a car with a complete stranger driving. Even without the driver's presence, telling Brett how she felt in that moment seemed an unlikely prospect. He was not the type of man who could deal with a real conversation. His speciality was small, fixable problems. Nancy made sure to have a light bulb that needed changing, a low-level work dilemma or a faux friendship crisis about once a fortnight, so that Brett had something to get involved in. Like breadcrumbs, she left a trail for him, something for him to follow so that he felt he was moving towards her with each situation. That was the secret – seeming just vulnerable enough to keep a man interested, while remaining a challenge so that he didn't have a chance to get bored.

Brett's function was as a pleasant distraction, and a cure for her inconvenient desire for the physicality of sex.

Masturbation, which she had taken an almost scientific attitude towards, was disappointingly unfulfilling. Something inside her, something which didn't fit with the rest of her soul, needed the skin and sinew of another person. That was what Brett was. His body was reassuringly thick and he was beautiful enough not to be intimidated by Nancy's wealth. He had his own friends, and rarely complained about her working late. In short, he was the perfect concubine. She'd planned to let him go after six months, to follow her usual pattern, but then she'd received Georgia's email.

She had read it in bed. Brett had gone down on her, something he seemed to genuinely like doing, and then fallen asleep next to her. She'd pulled her phone from under the pillow for a final check and there it was. No subject line. Very few words; a plea to come home.

Nancy wasn't sure what was in the email that had convinced her. She wasn't in the habit of flying halfway across the world on the strength of one email. And Georgia had always been a drama queen. When they were at school, she was forever imagining scenarios involving the people around her; these mostly consisted of classmates' teenage pregnancies and lesbian romances between teachers.

But there had been something about the email, about Georgia's words. She'd deleted it, and then watched her fingers type in the words 'British Airways' and book two first-class tickets home.

'I'm fine,' Nancy replied, conscious of the pause she had left. 'Are you OK?'

'I can't wait to meet your friends. I want to hear everything about you.'

The truth was, there were no funny stories about her. No stories about getting drunk and shaving off eyebrows or pole-dancing in sleazy clubs. No mistaken one-night stands or drunken phone calls. Every story that she had told Brett, every pseudo embarrassing anecdote was stolen. Over the eighteen months they had been dating she had told him dozens of tales about her life in England, but they were all Georgia's or Lila's stories. She had lived, obviously. She'd got drunk, got high, fucked people she shouldn't have. But none of those things had been mistakes. It had all been thought through. Planned. That was how she worked. This light, easy, silly person that men seemed to like so much was a fiction.

She had almost shattered the illusion earlier, in the airport. Brett had offered to call an Uber when the car service hadn't turned up. 'Do you have Uber in London?' he had asked. She had missed the joke and snapped at him. Realizing her mistake, she'd immediately pulled it back, or hoped she had, winding her arms around his shoulders and pressing her body into his. He didn't seem to notice her racing heart against his chest. She didn't want an Uber. She had booked the sleek town car a week ago because arriving at Georgia's Notting Hill palace in a dirty Prius wasn't the sort of impression she was willing to give.

'Are you OK?' Brett repeated the question, his dark eyes full of concern. The consolation prize for having to come to Georgia and Lila's rescue would be watching them meet Brett. They were going to be sick when they saw him. It wasn't just that he was younger. It was the thickness of his arms, the width of his shoulders, the way that his lips were so full and so quick to laughter. He was objectively perfect. In the dark orange street light, Nancy reminded herself to look at him. She couldn't wait to see Brett, aggressively handsome, a cliché of good looks, standing next to their milky-pale English husbands with weak chins and navy-blue suits.

Brett had offered to change and, knowing Georgia would disapprove of his T-shirt and jeans, she had told him not to. She wanted the girls to watch his lean forearms and heavy biceps as he passed the salad. She wanted them to go to bed later and lie awake, thinking about what it would be like to wrap their arms around Brett's broad shoulders or twist their legs around his waist.

She thought of the sympathetic glances Lila had shot her during her wedding to Roo, and the painful blind dates Georgia had sent her on before she'd moved to America. Her lips formed a slow smile.

'I'm fine. I promise. It's strange to be back, that's all.'

'Are you excited to see your girlfriends?'

'So excited,' she lied. 'And a bit nervous. Do I look OK?'

Brett unclipped his seat belt so he could twist around and kiss Nancy full on her mouth. This was the kind of silly, dramatic gesture that she usually couldn't abide.

'You look amazing,' he murmured. 'I can't wait to tell them our news.'

Nancy looked down, her dark bob swinging around her face.

'Me neither,' she replied, her eyes fixed on the enormous stone which glittered from the ring finger of her left hand.

'Whoa,' said Brett, as he dragged Nancy's bag up the white steps of Georgia and Charlie's house. It was even bigger than Nancy had realized from the photos. 'Do they have an apartment in the building?' he asked.

Nancy pointed to the basement flat. 'That's an apartment. The rest of it is theirs.'

'Fuck! And I thought your place was big.'

Faking laughter, Nancy pressed the doorbell. She heard the click of heels on what would inevitably be a perfectly polished floor and pulled her lips into a smile. Nancy had presented to board members, secured billion-dollar deals – how was it possible that she was this nervous to see her friends from school?

Even as the thought formed, she knew the answer.

The huge duck-egg blue front door swung open and Georgia stood, framed by the hall, a wide smile on her face.

Georgia had hardly changed since they'd last seen each other. How long had it been? Eighteen months? Two years maybe. She'd gained weight, there was no questioning that. At least ten pounds. But her eyes were huge and green, and her heart-shaped face was still unquestionably pretty. She looked as if she should be presenting breakfast television.

'Nance!' Georgia cried. 'Come in!'

She stepped over the threshold, taking it all in. The Diptyque candles burning on the hall table. Polished marble floor. Double-height ceilings, the scent of flowers and cooking. It was like something from a magazine. Aware of a bitter feeling creeping from the back of her throat, she noticed Georgia looking at Brett, taking in his perfect body, perfect stubble, perfect face.

'Brett, this is Georgia,' Nancy performed the introductions. 'Georgia, this is Brett.'

'It's lovely to meet you,' breathed Georgia, leaning in to kiss him on either cheek. Was Nancy imagining it, or was Georgia blushing?

'You can come in and say a quick hi before you settle in,' Georgia said, 'or freshen up and then come down?' From the way that she was standing in front of the door to the kitchen, pointing up the stairs, Georgia was making it painfully obvious which she'd rather they did.

'Let's freshen up,' said Brett, always the gentleman.

'It's great of Georgia and Charlie to let us stay,' said Brett, dragging Nancy's suitcase up the stairs. The wheels were making grooves on the thick carpet, which pleased her. Not enough to actually damage it, but enough that Georgia would panic. 'Yes,' she replied. 'She's a babe like that.'

Brett whistled as he opened the door to the guest room. One of the guest rooms. No doubt this would be the best one. Georgia wasn't so much a social climber as a social mountaineer. She wasn't going to miss the chance to show off. Nancy had to admit it was beautiful. High sash windows were covered with silk curtains. The walls were a delicate, chalky pink, so pale it was almost white. Under her feet there were floorboards, ancient ones. They had been painted white, and in the middle of the room was a luxurious rug. The bed was enormous, drowning in throw pillows and spread with a velvet cover. The headboard must have been six-foot tall, mauve-grey linen and punctured by buttons. Everything was very big or very soft and very, very expensive. This was Georgia all over: tasteful excess. She'd come a long way since being Georgia Green, scholarship girl.

'This is bigger than my entire apartment,' said Brett, dropping his duffle bag on the floor and looking up at the double-height ceiling.

'Mmm,' Nancy muttered, wondering whether Georgia and Charlie's room was as big as this, or whether she had lived up to her lower-class convention and reserved the most impressive room for guests.

'Do you want to unpack?' she asked Brett, watching the awe on his face. In spite of herself, she found it endearing. He turned, heading into the bathroom with his little plastic bag of liquids from the plane.

He wasn't that much younger than her. Six years. But by the time she had turned twenty-six she had seen things, done things. All Brett had done was road trips to the beach and a sheltered, cushy liberal arts degree where his 'professors' would give their students time off if they needed a 'mental health day'. Brett thought he was worldly because he had escaped Idaho. He came from a world where just living in Boston made him somebody,

It didn't, obviously. But his enthusiasm, his confidence,

his conviction in everything he did – Nancy found that a pretty heady combination. He was hard to resist.

Which was how they had ended up together. Brett had asked her out seven times, always polite but somehow determined that eventually she would say yes. And he had been right. Not only had she agreed to a drink with him, she had surprised herself by enjoying his company.

'Sure thing,' he called back from the en-suite. 'Jesus, she's got hotel shampoos in here!' He bounded out of the bathroom with fistfuls of L'Occitane.

'You can steal them, if you like,' Nancy laughed as she stripped off her jeans and jumper and began to take neatly pressed dresses and blouses from her suitcase and hang them in the white wardrobe.

'How do you look so amazing after that flight?'

Nancy looked down at her body, pretending to be surprised that her nudity was having this effect. 'Do I?'

Brett nodded. 'Irresistible.'

She laughed again. Everything about Brett was so male. Her want for him was biological. 'Want to fuck?' she asked.

'We can't, can we?' he replied. 'They're all waiting for us downstairs.'

Nancy slipped her hand into her knickers by way of an answer. 'Well,' she said, 'I'm going to come, whether you help me or not.'

Brett didn't need to be asked twice. As Nancy ran her hand down his back and felt the tautness of his skin, she thought, for the hundredth time, how joyful it was to fuck someone younger than her. Someone full of aggression and life. He moaned into her ear and she writhed against his body, yelping.

'Shh,' Brett groaned. 'They'll hear us.' Nancy pretended to look horrified. 'Don't worry,' he whispered, kissing her neck. 'This place is huge. Hopefully they didn't hear.'

She practically screamed as she came.

Brett insisted on showering. While he did, Nancy inspected the room. Any missed spot of dust would mortify Georgia and probably mean her current cleaner got the axe. Luckily for the staff at least, there was nothing. Georgia had made an effort, she noticed. It pleased her. Bunches of identical flowers – fat pink ones – had been placed in the room, one either side of the bed on little bedside tables. White robes on the back of the door. Moisturizer on the dressing table. 'You're running a boutique hotel,' she would say when she went downstairs. And Georgia wouldn't quite know if it was a compliment or an insult.

Listening to the noise of the shower, she looked at the clock on the wall. Brett was always at least ten minutes in the shower, and he had only been in there for five. She had time. She slipped from the room, padding down the corridor and up another flight of stairs to Georgia's room. She pushed open the door, feeling it drag across the deep pile of the carpet. She shouldn't be in here. She knew that. If they were normal friends it would be impossibly strange. But they weren't. Nancy knew that too. She assumed the others did as well. They were like three strands of a vine which had been trained into one, bound together first with wire but then with nothing but time. Other people might have a few shared anecdotes and some amusing fragments of memory with their school friends. Nancy, Georgia and Lila had blood. So no, she shouldn't have been here, but there was nothing surprising about it, and she knew that Georgia would do the same, given half a chance.

Under the bed there was a box of ovulation sticks and a box of pregnancy tests, both half used. Nothing remarkable, other than that they were hidden. It would have been far less strange to keep them under the sink. The fact that they wanted children was no secret, nor was the idea that they were trying. This couldn't be the extent of it. There had to be more. She pulled open the bedside tables. Books, tissues, painkillers, bottles of water. Nothing. It was like Georgia was taunting her. Nothing else under the bed. Nothing in the chest at the end of the bed, just clean linens which smelt of roses and laundry. Pausing to listen for feet on the stairs, she went to the walk-in wardrobe. Her heart was quick in her chest, but she knew no one would come. They would be too busy downstairs grilling Georgia for details about Brett. There was a pile of shoeboxes on the top shelf. Noting the exact order that the boxes were stacked in, Nancy reached up and grappled to get purchase with her fingertips, and eventually they came down. This was going to be it, she knew it. She lifted the lid off the Ralph Lauren box. A pair of pumps. Excited, she yanked the lid off the Gucci box. A pair of heels.

The last box was a boot box – longer than the others. The corner of this box was wrinkled, like it had been opened hundreds of times. Nancy knew this was the one. She took a breath. The box was heavy. The wrong kind of heavy for boots. A solid, even sort of weight. What could it be? Booze? No. It wouldn't be booze. She could drink as much as she wanted in her kitchen, no one would notice, let alone question. This was something she didn't want Charlie to see. A thought entered Nancy's mind. Perhaps she should leave it. Maybe she didn't need to know what was inside? The thought was a nice one. It soothed the churning in her stomach. It reminded her that she was a good person. She had good thoughts. She had good instincts. Mollified by the knowledge that she didn't have to, that she could go without, her hands stretched out and she opened the lid.

Fifteen, maybe twenty Babygros, rolled into little cloth sausages. All in shades of white and yellow and cream. Bibs. Socks. Tiny jumpers. The box was packed full. There wasn't space for another single item, no matter how tiny. It was as if Georgia had promised herself one box, but no more than one. As if she believed that once one box was full she would be able to stop. Nancy put the lid back on the box, the crinkled corner in the same spot it had been before, and placed the boxes back. She sighed, trying to decide what to do with the information.

Later, perhaps, it would be of some use.

NOW

Lila

Lila had decided that Georgia was being weird. Every time Lila tried to speak to her, she found an excuse to get away. She had a skittish look about her, a bit like she used to when she was acting and would be nervous before she went on stage. After they'd bickered over an appropriate outfit – with Georgia turning down anything even slightly interesting and having a major freak-out at the idea of Lila slightly altering a skirt – she'd dressed Georgia in a green jumpsuit she'd apparently bought and never worn and a pair of heeled ankle boots. The boots had been a compromise – the outfit would have looked better with strappy heels, but Lila knew to pick her battles. Georgia had originally reached for a pair of very Kate Middleton nude heels and Lila had felt herself die a bit inside. She'd added a couple of long gold chain necklaces, and talked Georgia into letting her put her hair into a high bun, and stain her lips a dark plum colour. While her friend had seemed unconvinced by the transformation, Charlie had had a different reaction when he arrived home from work.

'You're a genius, Cammy!' he had told her, putting his arms around Georgia. 'She looks like a new woman.'

Georgia had done the wrinkled face thing and acted like she wasn't pleased, but she must have been. Her husband was saying how great she looked. What was not to like?

'Do you want another top-up, Lila?' asked Georgia. Lila heard the way she said 'another'. But that was just Georgia. Judgy-Georgia.

'Yes please,' she said, catching Charlie's eye as Georgia poured. 'A bit more than that. What are you, Methodist or something?'

Charlie laughed, maybe a bit too loud. They shouldn't flirt, at least not too much. They'd always got on well. At Charlie and Georgia's wedding they'd ended up dancing on the tables, Charlie pouring a bottle of Grey Goose into Lila's mouth, until she'd been sick all over her bridesmaid dress. But she never meant to be disloyal to Georgia. She loved coming over. The kitchen was long and warm and safe, with French windows and cooking smells, and everything you could need to make a room feel welcoming. Lila loved it here. She didn't want Georgia to stop inviting her to hang out.

She reached her arm out to Roo. 'Come here, baby,' she cooed, making her voice softer. He put his glass down on the counter and came to wrap his arms around her torso.

'What do you need, Cammy?'

'Nothing. Only you.'

Lila looked up at the ceiling above her. 'Did anyone hear that?'

'Hear what?' asked Georgia. 'What did you hear?'

The same high-pitched noise, again. Lila giggled. 'Is that . . . Nancy?'

Georgia's face drained. Lila's giggles turned into real laughter. She couldn't remember the last time anything had been this funny. 'It's Nancy and whatshisname!'

'Shhh,' said Roo, 'I want to hear!'

'You pervert!' laughed Charlie, who was also cocking his ear to the ceiling and listening out. 'Turn the music down, Georgia!'

Georgia rolled her eyes but she must have secretly wanted to know because she did as Charlie asked. They all stood, frozen in the centre of Georgia's massive kitchen, waiting.

'Maybe they've stopped?' said Georgia.

A long, high-pitched yelp made all four of them burst into laughter. 'Do you think that's her, or him?' asked Charlie as he regained his breath.

'If you'd seen him, you wouldn't need to ask,' grinned Georgia.

'Oh really?' said Charlie, pouring himself a beer and offering one to Roo. He looked tired, Lila thought. She didn't blame him. Twenty-four hours a day of Georgia must be exhausting.

'Are you sure you want beer, Charlie?' asked Georgia in a voice that was supposed to tell him how to answer. Lila giggled. Charlie was going to get in trouble. 'There's lovely white wine in the fridge.'

'Yes, I'm sure,' said Charlie, leaving no room for argument. Lila tried to catch his eye, to smile at him. 'Now, tell me about the man who finally managed to tame Nancy Greydon. Am I going to be jealous?'

'Is he fit?' asked Lila.

Everyone Lila had ever seen Nancy with had been good-looking, but never sexy. Lots of super-clean guys with heavyset jaws and Ken-doll hair. Lila had stayed with her in Boston before she'd got pregnant with Inigo and she'd been shocked by how amazingly boring all of Nancy's boys were. She'd asked about it once, in a taxi back from a bar where her dull boyfriend had plied them with drinks and talked about himself before picking up the bill. 'Huge cock,' Nancy had replied matter-of-factly.

'Yes,' said Georgia. 'I have to hand it to her. He's pretty special.'

'Urgh,' laughed Lila. 'Why did we settle for these two so early?'

'Hey!' said Charlie, smiling. 'I'm in peak physical condition, thank you very much. And so is Roo!'

Roo looked up from his phone. 'What?'

'What are you doing?' asked Lila. He did that a lot these days. Joined in for a few minutes and then got distracted and stopped, leaving the conversation, acting like everyone else in the room had ceased to exist.

'Work emails,' he said.

'On a Friday night?' Lila asked.

'Charlie's the same,' interjected Georgia. 'Doesn't matter if it's night, or weekends, or whatever, people are constantly emailing him. Do you remember, Charlie, I found you hiding in the bathroom on our honeymoon checking in with someone about a speech? Oh, Roo, I meant to say. Lila showed me a picture of Inigo earlier – he really is the spitting image of you.'

Georgia always did this. Defused the situation. Stuck

her hand in between Lila and Roo and pulled them apart so that they wouldn't have the row, they wouldn't say the bad things they wanted to say. Lila wouldn't force Roo to show her his phone and she wouldn't shout at him for being rude and not caring that she was talking. Georgia probably thought she was doing them a favour. She'd probably sit up in her bed later. 'Did I do the right thing with Lila and Roo earlier?' she'd ask. And Charlie would say yes because it would be stupid to say no, but he'd be wrong.

Lila and Roo needed the rows. Otherwise, it was like living in the days before a storm where everything was heavy and tense and hot and humid. They needed the weather between them to break. They needed screaming and shouting and raging at each other, to give air to all the things they'd been thinking and feeling and hating about each other. They used to fight. All the time, actually. Even at the beginning. Only, back then, fights would end with her legs wrapped around his waist and his hands twisted in her hair. Roo wasn't very good at sex, if Lila was honest, but the passion of it, the anger and frustration made it better.

Roo wouldn't fight with her now. He'd simply tell her that he wasn't in the mood, and if she pushed it he'd pick up his keys and walk out of the door. She'd have no idea where he was going and in the time it would have taken to wrap up the baby and wrestle with the pram, she'd have lost any chance of following him. Inigo was like a chain around her leg, staked in the middle of a patch of grass. She might have the illusion of movement but the truth was, she was trapped.

Lila picked up her glass and moved over to where Roo was sitting. 'Roople,' she said, using the nickname he used to like, once upon a time.

'What?'

'Can I sit on your lap?'

He softened a little bit then. He liked it when she sat on his lap. 'Go on then,' he said, like he was indulging her.

Georgia gave them a tight smile. She looked crosser now. Why? This was supposed to be a way of telling her not to worry, that she and Roo were happy together and she wasn't going to try and steal Charlie away for the evening like she might have done in the past.

But it had gone wrong. Georgia clearly thought she was rubbing their happiness in her face. If only Georgia knew. That had always been Gee's problem. She never looked any further than the surface – she accepted what people said and what they did as the truth. No suspicion in her, not like Lila had, or like Nancy had.

Sometimes Lila thought that if Georgia came out and asked, even once, she would tell her. Didn't other friends do that? Tell each other the truth? The mums at the baby groups seemed to, about their kids. All they did was complain, and talk about how hard everything was. About how their kids never slept and they never had any time to do anything. If she had kept trying, and stuck around with them, she might have got further than the baby conversations. And then what? Would they have been like the friends in films and on TV, sitting around their kitchens drinking cups of tea and asking each other how their marriages were going?

But Lila knew that Georgia didn't want to know. She liked living on the surface, ice skating through life and never touching any of the murky underneath things which might have punctured her lovely, perfect world. That was the deal of their friendship. Georgia would be there, calm and reliable and safe, so long as Lila never opened her mouth and broke the rules. Only, lately, Lila had started to wonder if that was how it was supposed to be.

'They'll be downstairs in a moment,' said Georgia from the stove. 'So for God's sake don't start talking about them again, OK?'

She'd been in a mood since the doorbell had rung – it was an old-fashioned, high-pitched one, sourced from a warehouse in the middle of nowhere that Georgia had driven four hours to find. Georgia had whisked them both up to their room in a murmur of voices. She hadn't even given them the chance to come and say hi first.

Lila shifted on her stool, putting the rim of her glass to her lips and staring into the pale-yellow liquid, trying to decide what she wanted to be doing when Nancy walked in.

'What's he called again?' asked Roo. 'Something ghastly like Duke or Caden, isn't it?'

'Oh, it's not as bad as that,' came a low, American voice from behind Lila. She jumped up from her husband's lap, her eyes finding the huge figure in the door frame. She laughed, too loud, trying to make it OK. Fucking hell, he was beautiful. How had Nancy managed that? He was huge. Dark-skinned. Bright-eyed. He made Roo look like wet pasta.

49

'Roo, you are so rude!' She skipped across the room and threw her arms around the stranger, feeling the warmth of his body through his T-shirt and inhaling gently, trying to catch some note of travel-worn staleness, some proof of imperfection. But it wasn't there. He smelt of nothing but clean. 'I'm Lila,' she said, trying to act as if Roo's comment was merely British humour, rather than her husband being incredibly bloody rude.

'I'm Brett,' he smiled down at her.

'So great to meet you,' she said. 'And this is Roo.'

Brett reached past her, offering his huge hand to Roo, who at least had the good grace to look ashamed of himself.

Roo puffed his chest out. 'I'm Lila's husband,' he said, putting an embarrassing emphasis on husband. He seemed annoyed. Like he had wanted to do the introductions himself. 'And this is Georgia's husband, Charles,' he added.

None of them called Charlie 'Charles', not ever. But apparently this was what they were doing now. Charlie and Roo took up their positions either side of Brett, practically sticking their chests out. Any minute now they'd start peeing on things. Lila's eyes travelled from Brett's crumpled easiness to Charlie and Roo's boring dry-cleaned perfection. Their shirts and chinos hadn't seemed ridiculous before, but now Lila looked at them properly she could see how silly this was; they might as well have put their prep school uniforms on and be done with it.

'Isn't anyone going to get Brett a drink?' Lila asked brightly.

'Brett doesn't drink,' Nancy said, pushing through the kitchen door behind Brett.

Lila stopped, her glass halfway to her lips, and greedily drank in every detail of Nancy. Skin-tight jeans gave way to heels that even Lila would have struggled to walk in. Her hair was mirror shiny. She had the tiny beginnings of lines around her eyes and there was a suspicious tautness to the skin of her neck, but otherwise she was the exact same Nancy. Unapologetic, unabashed. Unchanged.

Sitting in the same room as her was odd. Odder than Lila had expected. But then, it had been two years since they had last set eyes on each other. Lila had seen photos, of course. Daily updates on three different social media platforms, Nancy's dark hair alternately blow-dried or tied back for the gym, her long boyish body encased in a suit, which flattered her, and evening dresses, which did not. But those were filtered, angled, augmented for ultimate thinness and youth.

Lila had a choice. She could stay, standing where she was, and wait for Nancy to approach, which was what Nancy would want, or she could grasp the moment. She chose the latter. That was what a friend would do.

Bounding forward, she twisted her arms around Nancy's shoulders and pulled her body towards her. Her limbs were hard – toned rather than thin. Thinness was too easy for Nancy, all it required was not to eat. Exercise took effort, it was an achievement. Nancy had wanted to be toned and strong long before it was fashionable. The others had warned her about developing Madonna arms, but she had resolutely continued doing hundreds of press-ups and sit-ups beside her bed every night.

'Would you like a soft drink?' Georgia asked Brett. She

was doing that shy-sweet voice she always put on when she met someone new and wanted them to think that she was nice.

'Have a beer,' said Charlie, ice laced through his jovial tone.

Brett ignored Charlie and turned to Georgia. Lila felt a pang of jealousy for the wideness of the smile he gave her. 'Club soda, if you have it.'

'That's fizzy water,' said Nancy.

'Is it really, Nance?' Georgia replied, smiling. 'I would never have known that. You know we've got running water over here these days, too? And central heating.'

Nancy grinned and stuck her middle finger in the air at her. Georgia returned the gesture and they both laughed. Standing by the back door, blowing cigarette smoke into the garden (though garden was perhaps too flattering a term for it; Georgia had covered the lovely lawn with a kind of fake grass, which she claimed looked real but absolutely didn't), Roo shook his head. 'You lot. Nothing changes, does it? You're still like schoolboys.'

Georgia waited to see whether Nancy would correct him – tell him that their ability to tease didn't make them any less female. It would be their first row of the night. But before anyone could light the blue touch paper and stand well back, there was an interruption.

'You know,' announced Brett to the room, 'you made a little mistake when you introduced me earlier. I'm not actually Nancy's boyfriend.' He paused. 'I'm her fiancé.' He pronounced the word fee-on-say, with the emphasis on the last syllable.

No one said anything. The noise of Georgia's vege-tables frying was suddenly really, really loud. Lila jumped to her feet. Why was everyone being so awkward?

'That's amazing!' she cried. 'Nance! Rock?'

Nancy looked embarrassed, which Lila knew was completely fake because when anyone got engaged the only thing that they ever wanted to do was show off their ring. Nancy proffered her hand. The short, wine-red nails and fake tan that no one would ever know was fake had been the same for ten years. But the massive dia-mond glinting on her left ring finger was new. Very new.

'Fucking hell,' said Lila. 'It's enormous.'

Nancy looked embarrassed again. A more convincing embarrassed face than before. 'They do bigger stones for engagement in the US. It's a cultural thing.'

Georgia came skulking over. She took Nancy's hand in hers and looked at it. 'It's stunning, Nance,' she said.

'Yeah, stunning like if you punched someone with it they would probably die,' said Lila. Was she imagining it or did Georgia sneak a glance down at her own finger?

'It's cruelty-free,' said Nancy, doing a voice. 'Brett knew that was important to me.'

'Bloody hell,' said Roo, looking over at the ring and nudging Brett in his ribs. 'Did you sell a kidney or something?'

'Roo!' squeaked Georgia. 'Lila, tell your husband he can't say things like that.'

'It's fine,' said Brett. 'Though as we're amongst friends, I'm sure Nancy won't mind me saying that she bought it. I'm just a lowly writer and that thing is like, a year's rent.'

Lila couldn't remember having seen Nancy blush before, not properly. Her chest was suddenly covered in blotches. Lila didn't realize that a person could wear their shame on their skin like that.

'Well, I think that's lovely,' said Georgia brightly. Lila snorted. Of course Georgia was going to love this. Nancy had been raised up and then smacked back down. 'We're all feminists here,' she went on. 'And that clearly shows how secure Brett is in his masculinity.'

'If I'd known that I could save my overdraft by being more secure in my masculinity, I'd have done it!' laughed Charlie.

Nancy smiled. Her chest was still blotchy but it was dying down now. 'Weren't you getting everyone drinks, Georgia? I just took a seven-hour flight, I need a glass of wine – intravenously, if you can manage it.'

Lila laughed, and turned to see Georgia filling a glass with ice and a slice of lime, painstakingly pouring the San Pellegrino to avoid it fizzing over the top of the glass. The look of concentration on her face was mad. She was clearly trying to make a good first impression, pathetically invested in giving her guest a nice glass of water.

Her mother would have been proud. Lila remembered the first time she had met Georgia's mother. Suddenly everything had made sense: her house was the cleanest place she'd ever been, and she was wearing a full face of make-up even though she wasn't going anywhere. Everything about her had screamed 'striver'.

'The thing you'll learn about these girls,' Charlie

joined in, 'is that they're not girls. They take the piss out
of each other constantly, like a bunch of blokes.'

'Though unfortunately they very rarely wrestle,' said
Roo, winking at Nancy. Lila frowned. Roo hated Nancy.
What was going on?

Brett had gone to stand next to the boys as they
smoked out of the back door. He responded with a tight
smile.

'Do you mind if I smoke?' Brett leaned back to ask
Georgia.

'Everyone else is!' Lila heard herself say.

Georgia was grinning awkwardly. Was she blushing?
Did she fancy Nancy's boyfriend?

'Of course you can. You're sweet to ask.'

Brett took up a station by the doors, slotting in between
Charlie and Roo, almost a head taller than either of them.
Both men bristled at his proximity, but seemed to relax
slightly as Brett started to chat. What was he saying?
Charming them both, Lila supposed. She hoped Roo
would be nice. Sometimes he wasn't, especially with
men. It seemed to her that, after university, Roo had
decided he had already met every man he would ever
have a civil conversation with. If he hadn't met someone
through school or university – or under extreme suffer-
ance, work – then they weren't worth his time.

She could go and smoke by the door, stand by Roo and
be next to Brett. Or she could go and perch on one of the
kitchen stools where Georgia was chopping vegetables.
She wanted to go and stand with the boys, to ask Brett
more about America and his life. But if she went over

there, Georgia and Nancy would talk about her. She picked up her wine glass and examined the level. Someone else must have been drinking out of her glass.

'Who do you have to screw to get a drink around here?' she giggled, going to the fridge.

'I'll get it,' said Georgia. 'You sit down.'

'How's life as a mummy treating you?' Nancy asked Lila. Lila had learned from her baby group that there were rules for answering this question. You had to sound miserable enough that you weren't showing off, but not so miserable that they called social services.

'I mean, I've had about four hours' sleep in the last year. And he can be a little twat,' she replied, 'but he's the nicest boy I've ever had in my life.'

They all laughed. Not because it was funny but because she had followed the rule, and made them feel safe. They liked her when she did that.

'It's so beautiful in here, Gee,' said Lila, changing the subject. 'It should be in a magazine.'

Georgia basked in the praise.

'I love the flowers,' Lila added, gesturing at the short cylindrical vases full of heavy pink blooms. 'They're my favourite.'

'Peonies,' said Georgia. 'Mine too.'

'Where did you get them at this time of year?' asked Nancy, looking up from her phone.

'They're silk,' said Georgia.

'Fake?' asked Nancy.

'Silk,' Georgia repeated. 'We found them in an amazing interiors shop in Paris.'

Lila reached over the table and picked one up. 'Fuck, they look so real.'

Nancy was doing that wrinkled-nose thing that Lila knew made Georgia cross. 'Look, Nance,' Lila said, holding one out, 'see how real it looks.'

'You're dripping water on the floor,' said Georgia, dropping her knife abruptly and pulling the flower from Lila's hand and putting it back in the vase. Lila dropped her gaze, hurt. She'd been trying to help, to make Nancy see how nice the flowers were. Georgia rearranged the vase and went back to making her salad. Lila tried not to feel upset, tried not to think about how often Georgia snapped at her these days. Falling back on her usual routine, she picked up her wine glass and looked into it. She could see her own fingers warped through the needle-thin stem of the wine glass, the chipped pink polish shining through.

'Fake flowers just aren't my thing,' said Nancy. 'Sorry,' she added, in a voice that made her sound distinctly not sorry. 'The kitchen looks good though. I'd love to see the rest of the house. Give me the tour?'

Lila could have sworn she saw Georgia's knuckles go white as she gripped the knife. She was clearly annoyed, but never one to say no to Nancy, Georgia let the knife go and wiped her hands on a neatly pressed tea towel. 'Of course.'

A tour was a pretence, and not a very good one. If Nancy wasn't even going to try to hide her desire to talk to Georgia alone, then why should Lila make it easy for them? She knew what it was going to be about, anyway. Nancy would drag Georgia upstairs, make snide comments about Lila's drinking, as if it had anything to do with Georgia, and then tell her to fix it while she swanned back off to the States. As if Georgia could.

Georgia didn't even know about the baby.

'I'll come too,' Lila said.

'You've seen the house, like, a thousand times,' said Georgia, her face pinched.

'It's too dreamy, I want to see it again. And you can tell me that fascinating story about the hollow fibres in the carpets again.' She caught Nancy's eye, and felt gratified by Nancy's smirk.

'I can't wait to hear about the carpets,' said Nancy.

'I only mentioned it once,' Georgia replied. 'I don't know why you keep going on about it. Anyway, I need you to finish the salad. I'll whizz Nancy around the house, and then we'll eat.'

She held the knife out, the tiny beads of tomato seeds dripping off the shiny blade. Lila reached out her hand to take it, wondering momentarily what would happen if she gripped the blade in her hand, how much it would hurt. How much it would bleed.

She watched as her friends disappeared into the hall, and listened to them chatting as they mounted the stairs.

'I'm just going to find my cigs,' she called out to the boys at the other end of the kitchen, putting the knife down on the kitchen counter. They ignored her. Carefully she crept into the hall to look for her handbag. She'd thrown it down on to the floor, but someone, it would unquestionably have been Georgia, had hung it up on the coat rack. She reached up and slid her hand into the soft leather pocket. Her fingers closed quickly on the rectangle of the packet, but she continued the charade of looking for them, even throwing in a light 'Oh, for fuck's sake,' under her breath for no one's benefit. Then she heard it. Light feet, the flick of a light switch. They were on the landing.

'I just feel as if you brought me here under false pretences.'

'I didn't bring you anywhere, Nancy.'

'You told me it was an emergency. You scared me – you said she was a mess. I thought you were scared she was going to tell.'

'I am. Why would I bring you here if I wasn't?'

'Look, she seems fine. She's drinking a lot, but she's always drinking a lot. You could have handled it.'

'You've been here less than an hour! What the fuck would you know? Give it two more glasses of wine and you'll see.'

Their feet were on the stairs again now, so Lila went back to pretending to look for her cigarettes. She noted the moment of discomfort on her friends' faces as they reached the foot of the stairs and saw her standing there. They'd want to know if she had heard, but they wouldn't ask her. She pulled a smile across her face, and deliberately slurred her voice a little more.

'Trying to find my fags.'

THEN

Nancy

'Welcome to your penultimate autumn term, ladies. I trust you all had a productive break, and I hope that those of you I haven't spoken to yet had a wonderful summer and were pleased with your GCSE results.'

An assembly with their headmistress, Mrs Easton, on the first evening of the first day of the year was a tradition. Each year-group would troop into the concert hall and sit on the itchy wool-cushioned chairs and be welcomed back with a speech about how well they had done the year before and how this year, whichever year it was, was the most important year of their entire school career.

Mrs Easton paused to look around the hall. Nancy had been pleased, actually. She had pretended, when she opened the brown envelope in front of her father, that she was entirely calm. And when she'd read the long column of A*s she had smiled modestly. Jumping up and down and posing for photographs was tacky and it implied an element of surprise. Naturally, Nancy had done well. Girls like Nancy did well at exams. But inside she had been triumphant. Shortly after results day, her father had written a double-page spread for one of the broadsheets about how to support your child through their exams, how to maximize their chance of success. 'Send them to boarding school' hadn't been mentioned, obviously – that wasn't exactly 'on brand' for Nancy's parents. The piece had been covered with a veneer of self-deprecation, but the message was there: *My daughter is perfect. Your children should be more like her.* And Nancy had enjoyed it. It had been the culmination of a perfect summer.

'Now, I like to have this little assembly with you girls before the beginning of the term because there is sometimes a sense among the lower sixth that this is a year to take your foot off the pedal and relax.' Easton paused for dramatic effect. 'Wouldn't that be nice?'

The girls indulged her by laughing. This was the game they played with the teachers, this was how they kept them onside. How many times had the old bag stood at the front of the concert hall and addressed rows and rows of girls in identical navy kilts and powder-blue cardigans? Did she make the exact same joke every single time? Probably.

Behind Easton's podium sat a row of teachers. Among the various heads of departments was someone she didn't recognize. Could she be a teacher? She seemed far too young, far too pretty and far too well dressed. Her hair was long and red and looked like it had been blow-dried by someone who actually knew what a hot roller was. She couldn't have been much more than twenty-six. Maybe twenty-seven at a push. Her legs were crossed and she kept running her hand through her blow-dry while she listened to Mrs Easton. She was wearing cropped trousers and a skinny black polo neck under a fitted blazer. On her feet were coral-coloured shoes with pointed toes and high heels. Against the sea of beige and tweed, she looked like she came from another world.

Behind her, Nancy heard Isabella Brown whisper, 'Who's the chick with the shoes?' to whoever was sitting next to her. Nancy nudged Lila. 'Who's that?' she asked. 'Was she around before I got back last night?'

Lila shrugged. 'No idea. Good hair though.'

'This year is your opportunity to start work on your UCAS applications. Those of you who are applying for Oxbridge . . .' she paused, as if 'Oxbridge' was some magical kingdom, 'will be sending your forms off in December next year. That gives you three and a half terms to make sure that you are as rounded as you can possibly be.'

Not too rounded. There was a rumour that last year's head girl had failed her interview after exam stress saw her gain fifteen pounds. Fat, everyone knew, was a sign of weakness. A lack of self-control.

'Gee,' Nancy whispered, trying to get Georgia's attention from the front row. All of the scholarship girls had to sit together, wearing stupid robes.

Georgia was ignoring her. 'Georgia,' she whispered again, a little louder. The girls either side of Georgia turned around, and finally Georgia turned. Georgia was such a drip when it came to things like talking in assembly.

'What?' she hissed from behind her hymn book.

'Who's the redhead?'

'I don't know,' she replied. 'New teacher?'

Mrs Easton was still talking: 'I would like to see you girls starting your own societies. Suggesting trips. Last year's lower sixth organized a tennis trip to California to train at a top academy, a Geography trip to the Arctic Circle, and the Art History society completed a tour of Paris over the Easter holidays. Last year's biggest triumph was the anti-bullying petition which was eventually read in Parliament.'

Jesus. How many times would they have to hear about that fucking petition?

'More conventional activities are also important. I would urge all of you to recommit to your existing clubs. Those basic extracurriculars which will tick much-needed boxes. On that note, the community service sign-up sheet has been posted in the common room. We see no reason why you should not all be taking your silver level this year.'

Nancy felt Lila's elbow in her ribs. They had been working on their excuse to avoid community service for months. There was nothing appealing about the idea of wasting precious weekends digging through bags of other people's dirty clothing for charity shops or pouring tea for old people. They could raise ten times the amount of money over the course of a single evening. They knew every girl in the room would happily pay a hundred quid a ticket for a 'ball' if boys and booze were on offer.

'And that'll be all from me, girls. Welcome back, and

please do make this a productive and worthwhile term. Oh, and don't forget to have fun!'

A polite smattering of applause started to ring out across the hall, but as it did, there was some movement on the stage. Nancy cocked her head to one side, interested. The redhead was getting to her feet.

'Thank you so much, Mrs Easton, and don't worry, girls, I'm not going to keep you here much longer. I just wanted to take a moment to introduce myself, to speak to you all about the year ahead.' She spoke with an accent Nancy couldn't quite place.

Ballsy. Surely if Mrs Easton had wanted her to speak, she would have been invited to speak. 'I'm Miss Brandon,' she said abruptly, waiting for the name to sink in a moment before continuing. 'I'm the new housemistress for Reynolds House, and I'll be teaching History. I'm sorry I wasn't here yesterday to welcome you all back, but I was flying home from New York.' She brushed her hair self-consciously behind her ear. Was she trying not to look nervous? She had to be five years younger than any other teacher in the school, apart from maybe Georgia's pervy drama tutor. What was she doing here?

'I'm so looking forward to taking over the sixth-form boarding. I'm also going to be head of pastoral care for you all, so I'm your first port of call if you want to chat about anything, whether it's exam stress, uni applications . . . men.' Miss Brandon giggled and, to Nancy's shock, so did the girls in the rows around her.

It looked like she was getting comfortable now. Like the laughter had made her feel safe. She had propped her notes up on the lectern, the one Mrs Easton had been using, but she was standing at an angle, her hip popped to one side, her weight on one foot.

'To be serious though,' she went on, 'it wasn't that long ago that I was right where you guys are, dealing with the huge pressure which comes with being a young woman on the brink of entering higher education, so I truly do know how stressful it can be. My aim is to support you in any way that I can.

'And the one last thing that I wanted to say is that each week I'll be setting you a challenge. This week, I'd like you all to take some time to talk to someone you haven't spoken to much before. I know how easy it is to think that you're too busy to make new friends. That's simply not the case. And life is about getting on with everyone. You never know who you're going to end up networking with in the future, so it's good practice to start now.'

And suddenly, just like that, the dorm allocations made sense.

It was Miss Brandon who had taken the triple room away from them.

'Thanks so much!' Miss Brandon beamed, finally retreating to sit down. To Nancy's horror, the girls began to clap. Was Nancy being paranoid or were they clapping a little more enthusiastically for Miss Brandon than they had for Mrs Easton?

Mrs Easton stood. 'Thank you very much for that, Miss Brandon,' she said. Even she was smiling.

Every girl in the room got to her feet, and Mrs Easton descended the steps of the stage, followed close behind by her little grey deputy, and her cocker spaniel. Once the huge wooden door had closed behind them, a roar of chatter went up.

'Did you see her shoes?' said Lila. 'I'm pretty sure they were vintage Valentino.'

'Do you think I could get away with being a redhead?' Nancy heard Lydia, a painfully stupid blow-up doll of a girl who, rumour had it, had to have her father donate a science lab to be allowed to stay for sixth form, asking one of her friends. 'Like Kate Winslet in *Titanic* red, not ginger.'

'What's wrong?' Georgia asked.

'Nothing,' replied Nancy.

'You look really pissed off,' Georgia wheedled. 'Like, stabby levels of angry.'

'I'm fine,' Nancy snapped, too quickly.

'Really happy,' Lila screeched back.

'Over the moon,' hissed Georgia, trying their old joke. But their levity wasn't even touching the sides of Nancy's mood. The idiots, they had been taken in by a decent haircut and a load of hot air.

'Seriously, what's wrong?' asked Georgia, sidling up to her. There was something faintly desperate about the way that Georgia always wanted to 'be there for you' the second something went wrong. It wasn't about being nice, Nancy knew that perfectly well. It was about ingratiating herself. Being part of something. It was selfish.

'I told you, there's nothing wrong,' Nancy muttered. 'Jesus.'

'Are you still doing community service?' Lila asked

Georgia, clearly trying to change the subject. It wasn't like her to play the peacekeeper. 'Saint Georgia?'

'Oh, fuck off, Lila,' said Georgia, laughing to take away the sting. 'Not all of us are trying to go to art school.'

'You seriously think they care about it? At all?' asked Nancy. The crowd of girls ahead of them was slow-moving, everyone still swapping gossip about the holidays, no one desperate to get back to their lockers and start their lessons for the day.

'No idea, but my parents have decided it's important for my scholarship, so I've got to do it. No point arguing.'

A low note of panic registered in Nancy's stomach. She didn't approve of fear. 'Fear is the mind-killer,' her father always said. But it was there, nonetheless. What if Georgia's parents, uneducated as they were, happened to somehow be right? Everything they made Georgia do was aimed at getting her made a prefect, and then getting her into Oxford. Nancy might have university licked, but an embarrassing part of her yearned for the Head Girl badge. It would be tragic, mortifying to admit, but she liked the idea of addressing parents at speech day and being responsible for charming prospective students on open day. Her own parents hadn't said anything about volunteering or university applications, but they were unlikely to. Nancy had often turned to Georgia's parents for advice. Not directly, of course, that would be tragic. But occasionally she squirrelled away second-hand wisdom that Georgia would repeat. It was interesting to know what actual parenty parents thought.

Her own mother and father were wonderful, obviously, but it wouldn't do for them to be seen as helicopter parents. People were interested in them, their lives, their writing, the choices they made. Adults would quiz her on their more famous articles. Did her father really encourage her to try drinking and smoking at home? Had her mother really allowed her to choose her own schools from the age of four? Didn't she mind being written about in the supplements almost every weekend?

Of course she minded. Her parents took it in turns to sell stories about her, trying to one-up each other with how liberal their parenting was. After all, no one was going to commission either of them to write some long glossy feature, complete with photos of Nancy posing in her bedroom, about being a normal parent.

'Maybe we should all do community service,' Nancy announced.

Lila and Georgia stopped dead, slowing the queue of traffic even further. 'You are joking?' said Lila.

'No. I think we should do it.'

'Why the fuck would we want to?' Lila's eyebrows pinched together.

Nancy sighed. 'Don't make me say it.'

'Say what?' Georgia asked innocently.

'I hate you.'

'Ohhhh go on. Say it.'

'What is it, Nance?' Lila did not seem happy with Nancy's change of heart.

'Because Georgia might be right, OK?' She drew out the word OK, making it longer and higher pitched than the rest of her sentence. They loved it when she showed any kind of weakness. It was exciting to them. 'If we want to be prefects, we should probably show willing. Georgia's right! OK? Does that make you happy?!'

'Ecstatic,' beamed Lila, pushing Sophie Heilbron who was standing in front of her. 'Hey, Heilbron, move, we've got shit to do.' Nancy followed Lila's lead and shoved past Sophie. 'I'm not doing it,' Lila went on. 'I don't care if I'm a prefect.'

'You'll care when we get to eat at the prefects' table and we get late-night Thursdays to go to the village, and you're stuck on your own,' said Georgia.

'She's not wrong,' Nancy added.

Lila rolled her eyes and sighed, like she always did when she didn't get her own way. 'Fine,' she said, 'but I'm not touching anything gross, and I'm not wearing any kind of uniform at the weekend.'

'Deal,' said Georgia. 'Come on. We're signing up now,' she added, 'before you change your mind and I have to do it all on my own.'

Despite the fact that the common room was, technically speaking, crap, there was something deeply exciting about having a new space to make their own. It was a long, low room, partially below ground level under the oldest part of the school. The stone walls were damp to the touch, and the armchairs and sofas which lined the walls were torn and sagging. There was a kettle and a toaster and a decent set of speakers. The TV weighed about seven stone and was the size of a small fridge. It was fuzzy and only got four channels. But to the girls of the lower sixth, it was paradise. Already it was filled with screaming and laughing and bickering and the smell of toast.

'You're sure?' asked Georgia, pulling a biro from her bag. 'I'm writing you down. S'cuse me,' she said to Heidi Bart, who was holding her pen and standing by the sheet. Heidi looked affronted. Or maybe that was just the way that her squashed face always looked. Not for the first time, Nancy thought how tragic it was to have a name like Heidi – a name that conjured visions of blond plaits and milkmaid prettiness – when you looked like a pug.

Nancy watched as the blue ink filled the little black box on the piece of paper. Nancy Greydon. Camilla Knight. Georgia Green.

'I was doing that,' said Heidi in a small voice.

'Sorry,' said Georgia, not sounding sorry at all. 'I'm done now.'

Heidi's teeth were too small for her mouth, and there was something odd about the way that she held herself. She thrust her hips out too far, and her back curved oddly. Years ago Lila had informed everyone that the scars they saw on Heidi's back when they changed for bed were from an operation to correct a hunched back. Unimaginatively, everyone had called her Quasimodo for a year after that.

'You're not supposed to just push in,' said Heidi.

It was clearly costing Heidi a great deal to say this. Something about the effort Heidi was making to stand up for herself made Nancy irrationally irritated. 'Why do you care?' she asked. 'Does it actually matter?'

'It was rude,' said Heidi bluntly.

'Leave it, Heidi,' said Lila.

The three of them turned to walk away. Heidi had a habit of bursting into tears and then telling a teacher on whoever had upset her, despite the fact she was seventeen.

'I guess I'll see you all at Mrs Easton's lunch next week, then,' Nancy heard Heidi call to her turned back. Nancy picked up her backpack, trying to ignore the comment Heidi must be making it up. There was no lunch. If there was, she would have been invited. It was impossible that the school would overlook her as a prefect.

'What lunch?' snapped Georgia. Great. Georgia couldn't just freeze Heidi out, she had to engage. Her blond head was on the verge of spinning off with fear that she might have missed some vital prefect invitation.

Nancy shrugged. 'I have Spanish. Come on, let's go.'

'Aren't you invited?' said Heidi, following them.

Heidi's smug, ugly face made Nancy's stomach tighten. How dare she look so pleased with herself.

'Shut up, Heidi,' said Georgia.

Nancy took a deep, calming breath. What the hell had got into Heidi? She'd always been a crybaby, and she'd always been hideous, but she would never have dared start a fight with her and Georgia before. And where the hell was Lila?

'Georgia, are you coming?'

Georgia picked up her bag. 'Yeah, let's not be late. Also, there's a really weird smell around here.' She gave Heidi a pointed look. It was a petty, childish thing to say, and Nancy was annoyed with herself for being pleased by it.

'Jesus Christ,' muttered Georgia.

'What?'

'She's following us,' said Georgia. 'Heidi. What the hell is going on with her?'

Nancy turned around, still on the stairs which led up to the main corridor. 'We've made it pretty fucking clear that we don't want to speak to you. Will you take the hint and piss off?'

Nancy watched Heidi's face soften and followed her eyes, which were focused on something behind where she and Georgia stood. Turning slowly she saw, a few steps above them, the woman with the red hair from assembly. She was smiling the kind of isolated, frozen smile that didn't reach her eyes.

'Is everything all right, girls?'

'Fine,' Nancy ground out. 'It's a private discussion.'

'Is that true?' The woman was looking past Nancy, down to where Heidi was standing with a wounded expression on her face. Nancy pushed her nails into the palm of her hand, counting in her head. She couldn't lose her temper, not this early in the term, not while they were still petitioning to have their dorms reassigned.

'I'm OK,' said Heidi in a small voice. 'I was just going to Biology.'

The red-haired woman, Miss Brandon as they now knew her, looked unconvinced. 'All right,' she said, after a moment's pause. 'Off you go. And you,' she looked down at Nancy, 'might want to moderate your language. I'm sure you've got a far better vocabulary than that.'

Without a word, Nancy accelerated up the stairs, along the main corridor and towards her classroom, repeating the words 'head girl' over and over in her mind to prevent herself from punching a wall.

'Um, can you slow down, please?' came Lila's voice from behind them. 'I had to get my shoes.'

Lila's refusal to ever wear shoes if she didn't absolutely have to was precisely the kind of affectation that Nancy's mother adored. She'd made some reference to it in a column months ago and Lila had stuck it on her pinboard.

'Oh, you want to talk now? Why not before?' said Georgia. 'Trying to keep the peace with your new roomie, are you? Did you see what she just did?'

Lila's face clouded. 'You know it's not like that. I can't stand the bitch.'

'It didn't seem like that,' said Nancy.

'I couldn't think of anything to say.'

'Are you sure it's not just that you're so overjoyed to have your best friend back?' said Nancy. It was like pressing her finger into a heavy bruise. Lila's friendship with Heidi, best friendship even, might not have lasted beyond their second year at Fairbridge Hall but it went right back to junior school. They had been real, proper, playing together in the paddling pool friends. Until Heidi had grown stranger and stranger. For a time, she had been weirdly obsessed with Lila, trying to stop her from hanging out with the others.

'She's not my friend,' replied Lila, too quickly, her voice too high-pitched. 'OK? We used to be friends and now we're not, and I'm sorry she was being a bitch to you, OK?'

The bell rang, giving them a perfect excuse to decline to comment, to leave Lila wondering what had happened for the rest of the day.

NOW

Georgia

'Gee, I'm going upstairs for a wee – someone's in the downstairs loo,' called Lila from the corridor. Georgia steadied herself. She needed to make the salad dressing and put serving spoons on the table.

There was no need to panic. Larissa had emptied the bins. She was fastidious, that was why Georgia paid her twice as much as any other cleaner in the area got. And Georgia had double-checked the bins herself, polishing them until they shone. Charlie had always disliked the bins in the bathrooms. He had said they were a bit 'Weybridge' – a favoured expression of his to mean that they were a bit lower middle class. A bit new money. All things which it would apparently be disastrous to be. He would never have admitted his snobbery to anyone but Georgia. His career forbade it. Even letting it slip to a member of the press could bring his party into disrepute and ruin his ambitions. It was a well-guarded secret; most MPs had secret wives or second homes that they wanted to keep quiet, but Charlie's secret was his snobbery. These days the party that was all about having money and keeping money was supposed to pretend that it didn't care about money at all. As if it could be a surprise to anyone. Boarding school from the age of eight, Oxford and then the Army. Were people really so stupid to think that he was 'one of the boys'? It seemed so. He wouldn't be doing so well at work if he wasn't a master of the illusion. Georgia might not understand much else about what Charlie did, but she knew that.

Perhaps that was why he was so polite to her parents. It was good practice for talking to other people who he looked down on. They loved him, naturally. He always said it was because he had the same sense of humour as her dad. But she knew it was more than that. They kowtowed to Charlie because they admired him. They thought his smart education and smarter parents, his title and his easy accent made him a real catch. Every second Christmas when they packed up the car and went back to her parents' happy little house, she would watch her mother fawning over him, the way she would blush a deep pink when he complimented their taste, and wish that they knew how he took the piss out of them behind their backs, how he poked fun at their manners. She never said anything, though. They would be mortified. Heartbroken. They saw Charlie as another son (unlike Charlie's parents, who never seemed to regard Georgia as much more than a decorative accessory who once accidentally called the 'loo' the 'toilet').

But that was why she had been so upset, all those years ago, in Peter Jones, when she suggested they buy the chrome wastepaper bins. The words 'they're a bit Weybridge' had passed his lips and she had dissolved into hot, angry tears, stuttering to try and get words out but unable to make him see why she was so angry, gagged by her hurt. Charlie had been mortified. He had plied her with kisses and when she stopped crying he'd told her he was sorry, like he truly meant it. His eyes had been huge and he had looked terrified, as if he would do anything in the world to stop her from crying. Georgia had stopped because she couldn't bear to frighten him. They had bought the Weybridge bins and gone home in a taxi together, falling into bed the moment they got through the door. It was the first time they had tried to make a baby. Or rather, the first time they hadn't done anything to prevent it. They hadn't been ready, not really. She had been twenty-six at the time. Too young, or at least that was what she had told herself. Maybe that was the mistake. Maybe if she had started then, things would have been different now.

But back then it had been a relief when exactly two weeks later her period had arrived. She had celebrated – pouring herself a glass of wine and giggling with Lila that she had dodged a bullet. There were still holidays, parties, lines of coke that needed to happen before she relegated herself to the role of mum.

This afternoon she had trailed around the house, emptying every single bin, searching through with her bare hands to find every used ovulation stick and pregnancy test, wrapping it all in plastic bags and putting them in the bin at the end of the road. No risks could be taken. If someone, most likely nosy Lila, ended up in her en-suite and saw one it would be too much to bear. It was lucky that Charlie had been at work. He found the way she behaved around Nancy and Lila odd enough already. He couldn't understand why she wouldn't just tell them about the IVF. 'They're your friends,' he'd said. 'They want to support you.' He had no idea how wrong he was.

'George?' Lila was back. Georgia looked down at her hands, suddenly conscious that she had been distracted. 'Why are you being weird?' asked Lila.

'I'm not,' she said evenly, carrying a jug of water to the table even though no one would drink any.

For the starter, Georgia had roasted peaches. The idea had been to toss them with rocket and balsamic vinegar, and mix in sizzling hot halloumi. But the 'tour' Nancy had insisted on had taken longer than she'd anticipated and the peaches had overcooked. Some of them were OK. Others were an orange sludge. Carefully she lifted the better slices, earmarking them for Nancy and Brett. It didn't matter what she served Roo or Charlie, and Lila was too busy getting pissed to care.

'Does everyone want to sit down?' asked Georgia, trying to make her voice carry across the room.

'Where do you want us?' asked Roo.

'I don't mind,' replied Georgia evenly. Why hadn't she done a seating plan? It would have taken minutes and she could have kept Lila away from Roo, whom she would start a fight with after another glass, or Brett, whom she clearly wanted to lick.

'You two can't sit together,' said Charlie to Lila. 'Bad form to sit next to your wife. You go there, Brett, next to Nancy. She can look after you.'

Georgia's heart sank as Lila slid into the chair at the head of the table, leaving the only empty place at the far end, next to Roo. They would move around for pudding, she told herself. She wouldn't be stuck with him all night.

'There's no wine on the table,' came Lila's baby voice. Georgia didn't need to turn around to know that her words were accompanied by an exaggerated pout.

'I put a bottle out a minute ago,' said Charlie.

Georgia turned to see Lila, sitting with her legs crossed on the chair, holding the bottle of white wine upside down. A tiny dribble escaped the neck and beaded on the table.

'Bloody hell, chaps,' said Charlie, laughing. 'You'll drink us dry at this rate.' He laughed at his own joke as he went to the wine fridge to get more bottles. It wouldn't occur to him to make anyone feel bad, to mention that, at £48 a bottle, it was there to be savoured. Not used as petrol for Lila's latest meltdown.

As Georgia sat down, she remembered why she never wore the jumpsuit Lila had forced her into. It constricted her hips and stomach painfully, clinging to every ounce of flesh on her torso.

'This looks quite lovely,' said Brett loudly. His dedication to having a nice time was valiant, especially in the face of such an odd combination of guests. Perhaps he had some British blood in him.

'Quite means very in America,' said Nancy. 'I didn't realize when I first moved there. It led to some funny misunderstandings.'

'Quite funny ones?' teased Brett.

Do you live in America, Nancy? Georgia wanted to say. None of us could possibly have known. It's not like you talk about it at all.

'Like what?' asked Charlie.

Nancy cocked her head to one side. 'Sorry?'

'What kind of funny misunderstandings?'

Nancy looked affronted. 'I can't say, off the top of my head.'

Charlie said nothing, looking back down at his plate. Georgia felt, not for the first time, disloyally pleased at how much her husband disliked her best friend. He had barely ever made it known. But each time he got in a dig at her it felt like a tiny triumph over Nancy.

Charlie knew better than to suggest that Nancy be cut, or even to pry into why the two women remained friends. He realized that it was deep magic that he would never comprehend. Georgia liked that about him. He had only once questioned the relationship, when they had got engaged. They had been lying in bed together one evening, Charlie running his fingertip lazily over her stomach, when he said, 'Don't ask Nancy to be a bridesmaid.'

Georgia had been shocked. The idea that Charlie even cared who she was friends with had seemed unlikely.

'Why on earth not?' she had asked him.

'She won't want to,' he replied. 'And she won't be happy doing it.'

Georgia had claimed that it would break Nancy's heart, and that they were deeply bonded, tied together by mythology older than Charlie knew. He had smiled, apologized for even asking and thanked Nancy in his speech for being such a wonderful support. What he didn't know was that being a bridesmaid was Nancy's punishment. She had had to wear a dress, a beautiful, expensive dress which was whisper-light, floaty and pale pink. It was perfect on Lila and entirely wrong on Nancy, clashing with the severity of her haircut and the angles of her limbs. She had to stand next to Georgia all day, saying how beautiful she was and how much she deserved a lifetime of happiness, not allowed to be smart or sarcastic or anything other than a sweet handmaiden. There was no way out. To have said no would have looked as if she wasn't a real friend. Even worse, someone at the wedding might think that she hadn't been asked. So there she had stood. God, it had been satisfying.

'I had a terrible misunderstanding,' chimed in Roo, glass in hand, 'in America, when I wanted a packet of cigarettes and I asked the concierge where I could buy fags.'

Everyone laughed at Roo's joke, which probably wasn't true, or if it was true had likely happened to someone else rather than to him.

'So you're going on to Paris after this?' said Georgia, breaking the silence.

'Don't let Nancy order the wine,' laughed Lila.

'What?' laughed Brett. 'Why not?'

Nancy laughed an entirely fake laugh. Georgia knew she shouldn't enjoy this so much, forcing Nancy to embrace false humility in front of Brett, in front of everyone. But she did.

Nancy explained: 'I accidentally ordered the wrong bottle of wine on a school trip to Paris – my French wasn't so good back then – and it turned out it cost nearly seven hundred euros. We had to call my father and make him pay over the phone.'

Georgia forced herself to join in the laughter. It hadn't been funny at the time. They'd all checked their bank accounts, trying to scrape together the money to pay for the wine. Georgia's heart had nearly broken through her sternum at the thought of spending everything she'd saved in the last five years on a third of a bottle of wine.

'And what about your families?' Brett asked. 'Are all of your parents as cool as Nancy's? Is it just an English thing?'

'Mine are OK,' said Lila, waving a forkful of salad around. It would go near her mouth, but never in it. Georgia knew the routine. Lila would feed bits of her food to anyone who was sitting around her (even though they were all eating the same thing). Dogs or toddlers were especially useful. By the end of the meal she would have managed to make a decent dent in the plate without ingesting much more than a couple of leaves. 'My stepmother is about fifteen.'

It wasn't true. Clarissa was in her fifties now.

'She was furious when she found out we were making her a grandmother,' laughed Roo. 'I reckon we cost Lila's dad at least a grand in Botox that month.'

'My parents aren't "cool",' laughed Nancy, putting down her knife and fork. 'All parents are embarrassing in their own way.'

'Damn straight,' said Roo. 'My old man keeps touching up nurses at his home. Bloody nightmare. Can't stop sticking his hands up their skirts.'

Like father, like son, thought Georgia. Everyone knew that Roo couldn't resist anything with a single-digit dress size flashing a bit of leg.

'What about you, Georgia?' asked Brett. Georgia smiled. His voice was velvety. He was trying to draw her into the conversation. He cared if she was involved. 'Are your mom and dad embarrassing?'

What a question. If he hadn't seemed so easy with it, Georgia might have wondered whether Nancy had told him to ask. Certainly, she would say that the answer to that question was yes. But then Nancy thought it was shameful that her own parents didn't own a second home.

Usually, these days, Georgia liked telling people where she'd come from. It lent her a kind of cachet.

When people at work or at dinner parties, or Charlie's work friends, tried to brush her off as a posh piece of fluff, she liked being able to explain that she wasn't like that. That she hadn't grown up in a castle, no matter what her accent might suggest. Announcing, 'Not at all; my parents are working class and very strait-laced,' with a hint of superiority that came so easily to her now. How could it have been so impossible back then?

A teacher should have taken her aside on the first day, she had thought once, and told her how to tell her friends. Sitting in the front row in assembly and wearing the scholar's robe simply didn't cut it. Lots of Octavias and

Tabithas got a ten per cent Drama scholarship for the prestige. Georgia was different. It would have been better if the school had just posted a list of the scholarship girls, in order of how much discount they got. At least if everyone had known she was there for free then she wouldn't have to explain that, no, she couldn't come skiing this year even though she had missed out the year before, too.

She had invited Lila and Nancy back to her house once. After months of teasing from her brothers and a tearful exchange during which her mother asked if she was ashamed, she had capitulated and invited them.

If they were surprised by the cramped terraced house, the cul-de-sac or the fact that it was only half an hour from the school, they didn't say anything. Georgia thought she could remember a tiny twinge below Nancy's left eyebrow. Maybe a tightening around the corners of Lila's mouth. But not of judgement. More of surprise.

They had sat around the kitchen table and her parents had acted like her friends were visiting dignitaries. Georgia had felt embarrassed by the mismatched Ikea cutlery and the big TV left on in the next room, and then ashamed of herself for feeling embarrassed. Her mother had overcooked the green beans and Georgia remembered something Nancy had said years ago about how working-class people always overcooked their vegetables.

It hasn't been a total disaster. They'd eaten three tubs of Ben and Jerry's and watched a scary movie, screaming the house down. It had been fun, all of them sleeping on sofas in the living room, and if anyone had registered the fact that there wasn't a guest bedroom, they didn't say it. Nancy had mentioned her surprise not to have been offered wine with supper, but Georgia's mother had encouraged them to eat, something Lila and Nancy hadn't ever experienced. There was squirty cream, a complete novelty. They'd liked playing with Georgia's doughy littlest sister. But when Mr Green dropped them back at school the next day, all three of them knew that it had been a courtesy. The only visit that they would ever make.

'No.' Georgia beamed across the table, allowing herself a glance at Brett's right angle of a jawline. 'They're not cool at all. Old-fashioned would be the most accurate description.'

'They sound like my folks,' said Brett, leaning forward to top up her wine glass as he spoke. For a moment she wondered what it would be like if dinner was just the two of them, in some cosy restaurant with a flickering candle on the table between them.

'You haven't met Nancy's parents yet?' asked Charlie. 'Hope you manage to do it before the wedding!'

Georgia's fingers twisted in her napkin. She was horrified at the jolt of anger she felt towards Charlie for stealing Brett's attention, for giving it back to Nancy. What on earth was he playing at?

'I can't wait to meet them,' said Brett. He sounded genuinely excited. 'I've read a lot of their work. As a writer, I couldn't think of a better pair of in-laws.'

'Didn't Nancy's old man fancy Georgia?' said Roo, a

forkful of salad held aloft. 'Isn't that what you always said, Gee?' The table turned to look at Georgia.

No one said anything. Nancy chose that moment to take a slow, slow sip from her wine glass, her gaze deliberately avoiding Georgia. She could have saved it, thought Georgia bitterly. She could have laughed, brushed it off. Made it into no big deal. But in typical Nancy fashion she chose to make everyone else sweat.

'No,' Georgia said eventually. 'That was someone else's dad. Another girl in our year.'

It wasn't even a very good lie. Charlie said nothing, looking into the bottom of his glass. Chivalry really was dead, apparently.

'So, you three were at boarding school together?' asked Brett as the quiet resettled across the table. Georgia's shoulders relaxed. Thank God for Brett.

'Yes,' said Georgia. 'In Hampshire.'

'What was that like?' he asked.

Lila leaned forward, seizing the conversation. She loved this. Telling men what they had been like at school was her party trick. Usually she supplemented the story by angling herself to offer the listeners a peek down her top, her finger carelessly inserted into her mouth, her hands running through her hair. Clichés, but she performed them so beautifully. Or at least she used to. Tonight the wine had hit her harder than it should have done, probably because she wasn't eating anything. It was like watching an actress who was just a little too old to play the role she had been cast in and was desperately trying to overcompensate with a falsetto voice and too much make-up.

'Are you asking if we've ever kissed each other, Brett?' she husked.

Nancy smiled. She pretended she didn't like this routine, but Georgia knew she did. It gave her put-together-princess image a hint of an edge.

Brett did a comedy double-take. 'I wasn't, but now I am!'

The boys laughed. 'You'll never get it out of them,' chimed Charlie.

Lila giggled. 'Two of us have kissed each other. But we don't tell which two.'

'So, aside from kissing,' asked Brett, grinning, 'what did the three of you get up to at school?'

Georgia caught Nancy's expression across the table. The skin beneath her dark eyes had tightened slightly. It was fine. They didn't need to worry. Lila wasn't going to say anything. Not now, not here. She would tell the story of the time they broke into the pool and swam naked in the middle of the night, or one of her many stories about sneaking boys into the dorm and smuggling them back out in their uniforms.

'Well,' slurred Lila, 'we did all sorts of things. Naughty things.'

Her eyes were drooping now, just a bit, just at the corners. A sure sign that she was on her way to getting absolutely shit-faced.

'Georgia gave a teacher a blow-job.'

The table exploded into laughter. Georgia felt her neck

getting hot. It was strange how secrets aged. That one had seemed so vital at the time, and now it was a dinner-party anecdote. Why was it that one secret mattered so little and another had the power to come from the past and decimate the present?

Charlie, sitting across from her, smirked. He liked that story. He liked the idea of his wife on her knees in her tartan kilt, a man so desperate to feel her lips around the base of his cock that he would risk losing his job to have it. Brett and Roo were applauding. Georgia gave a little bow.

Sensing that she had the room, Lila went on, her voice growing louder: 'And then there was the time that Nancy had a coke dealer drive from London to drop off a gram of Colombia's finest on a Thursday night to win a dare.'

Brett grinned. 'Nancy? Surely not?'

Pretending to be annoyed, Nancy pinched the bridge of her nose, but there was a smile that she couldn't suppress. 'I was sixteen!' she said eventually, as the whole table laughed and cheered. 'Everyone's a nightmare at sixteen!'

'And then,' Lila went on, her voice raised over the hum of laughter and appreciation for Nancy, 'then there was that whole murder thing . . .'

Silence fell across the table, silence so loud that Georgia could hear the clock on the wall and the fan of the oven pressing their noise against her brain. What the fuck was Lila thinking? She searched across the table, trying to find Nancy's gaze.

'It was two grams, actually,' said Nancy. And then she laughed, a perfect replica of her real laugh. It took

Georgia a second, but she gave a laugh too. Hers was too loud and too high, but it was OK because everyone was laughing and the noise was washing her panic away. Even Lila joined in, as if she'd forgotten that the 'joke' was hers in the first place.

'I cannot believe you did coke at school,' Brett laughed.

'I'm telling you,' said Roo, who seemed to be warming to Brett, 'nightmares, the lot of them.'

Georgia stood and began gathering up the starter plates, desperately grateful for a chance to leave the table. Charlie got to his feet. He was being surprisingly helpful this evening. Together they carried the plates to the island. Lila's plate was almost untouched, and Nancy had pointedly picked out the two slices of burnt peach that had made it into her salad. Carefully she scraped the plates, the good ones from Harrods which would be a pain to replace if anyone broke one, and then stacked them on the side. She had organized for Larissa to come tomorrow morning to wash them by hand.

From the table came a roar of laughter. Lila was probably keeping them entertained with her ditzy blonde routine, asking if Dutch people were 'from Dutch' and earnestly explaining that she thought Wales was an island. Georgia never understood how Lila could enjoy embarrassing herself for laugh. It wasn't funny, it was excrutiating. But, Georgia consoled herself, if she was making a fool of herself then she was happy and distracted, and until she and Nancy had a chance to talk some sense into her, that mattered.

'You OK?' Charlie asked quietly, reaching into the

fridge for another beer. Why was he drinking beer? Why didn't he want the wine she'd chosen?

Georgia nodded. 'Yep. Do I not look OK?'

'You do, you do. It's just, I know you were upset about the test earlier.'

'I'm fine.' Georgia's lips closed tightly.

'Maybe you're taking on too much?'

Georgia half laughed. 'That's not usually your attitude.'

'What?'

'Well, you don't usually seem to think I'm doing enough,' she said tersely.

'That's not true.'

Georgia said nothing, raising her eyebrows and taking a cloth from the sink to wipe the surfaces down.

'That's not true,' he repeated. 'How many times have I said you can stop working if you want to? This matters to me too, you know.'

Georgia ran the cloth under the tap, twisting it to wring the water out, pulling it more forcefully than she needed to. 'No, I can't.'

'Why the hell not?' he held his hands out, gesturing around the huge room as if their high-ceilinged kitchen was proof that they were invincible. Georgia took his hands in hers, cloaking her desire to make him stop with affection. She couldn't bear for anyone to think that they were fighting.

'You know why not,' she murmured.

'So you're going to keep doing this forever? What about when we have a baby?'

'If.'

'What?'

'If we have a baby. Not when.'

Charlie rolled his eyes. 'If then. Will you keep doing this if we have a baby?'

Georgia dropped the cloth on to the side, sighing. 'I don't know, darling. I haven't got that far yet.

'It's fine,' she said. This was not the time to talk about it. 'Let's not talk about it now, OK? Love you.' She pressed her body into his, running her hands down his back. It was softer than it used to be when he was still rowing three times a week. His stomach curved into hers. After a big meal, he'd drum on it, saying, 'I'm getting fat.' Georgia would watch him and think about how wonderful it would be not to care.

'Bit of an off-colour joke from Cammy,' he said, sotto voce. 'After what happened with that teacher at your school.'

'I know,' Georgia said grimly. 'But that's Lila for you. She never knows where the line is.'

At that, Georgia drew herself away from her husband and turned her body towards the sink, lifting a glass to the tap. Angling it, she turned the tap on full force so that water sprayed off the glass, soaking her jumpsuit, which after eating her starter had become even tighter.

'Fuck!' she shouted, dropping the glass into the sink, carefully enough that it didn't shatter. 'Fucking fuck!'

The others looked up. Charlie was at her side in a second. 'Are you all right, darling?'

'Yes, yes fine,' she laughed. 'I can't believe I did that.'

'It's not like you to be so clumsy,' said Charlie.

'I know,' she shook her head in mock dismay. 'I'll have to go change. Can you keep an eye on the timer? If it beeps, just turn the oven off, don't do anything else.'

As she ran her fingers along the banister she could hardly believe her luck. She'd managed it. It would only be a moment's delay and the gloriously flattering J. Crew dress she'd been planning to wear before Lila had intervened would be shown off instead of left hanging sadly in her dark wardrobe.

Almost before she'd finished the thought she heard steps behind her and light breaths which quickly erupted into giggles.

'I'm just going upstairs to change,' she said, whipping around. 'You two stay and keep the boys company.'

Lila was half sitting, half lying on the stairs behind her, a wasted grin on her face. Nancy was standing, her face impassive, like she knew that this whole glass act had been an excuse, like she could see straight through Georgia, like she was wondering how, if things really were as bad as Georgia had said in her email, she could care what she was wearing.

The truth was that on any night with Nancy, Georgia would care what she was wearing. Because of the way Nancy had looked her up and down. Because she had watched Nancy's eyes linger on her waist and her neck and her arms. That was the thing about Nancy. She could make you feel like you were worthless, even when she had flown halfway around the world to help you. But it all happened under a cover, under a blanket of 'telling it how it is' and 'calling a spade a spade'. If you challenged her on it you found every point you wanted to make slipping away like water through your fingers. Suddenly it all seemed petty and intangible. So Georgia didn't say anything.

'Can we come with you?' simpered Lila. 'Please, Mummy?'

Lila's habit of calling her mummy never used to rankle.

'I'm only going to be two minutes,' Georgia protested.

'Mummy's cross,' said Nancy.

'I'm not cross,' Georgia snapped.

Nancy and Lila laughed. 'Not cross at all,' Nancy snapped back.

'Totally CALM,' Lila hissed.

'Loving life,' added Nancy, stamping her foot. Georgia forced herself to laugh.

'Fine, you can come upstairs and watch me take one outfit off and put another one on, since you're so obsessed with me.'

They trailed up the stairs to the top of the house. Georgia closed the bedroom door behind her and went straight through to the wardrobe, determined to change so quickly they wouldn't get bored, ignore the closed door, invade the bedroom and see the bruises on her stomach. If only Lila were a bit drunker, if only Nancy could get a snippet of what Lila was like. It was fine, Georgia told herself. They had only just finished their starter. Lila was drinking. It would happen, and then Nancy would do what she was here to do. Fix Lila.

Georgia twisted her arm, trying to get purchase on the slippery zip at the side of the jumpsuit which ran from her hip to under her arm. Her fingers couldn't seem to keep hold of the little metal tab. It was starting to feel even tighter and her armpits were pricking with sweat. Finally, Georgia dragged the zip down and desperately pulled the fabric away from her body. Awash with relief she dropped it into the laundry basket. Then, thinking better of it, she threw it into the bin. It had left a red ring around her waist, and the seams had imprinted painfully under her arms. It didn't fit her properly. And if things went the way she was praying they would, it would be far too small before long.

Slipping the dress off the hanger was delicious. The silk was cool against her flushed skin, and soft on the places where the jumpsuit had constricted around her. It was a blissful relief. Georgia had intended to keep the shoes on, the ones Lila had demanded she wore. But the comfortable nude heels, the ones which made her legs look miles long, were calling to her. It was no big deal. Lila wouldn't care.

'See? Thirty seconds of changing and I'm done—' Georgia stopped as she pulled the bedroom door open. 'What the fuck are you doing?'

Nancy was leaning against the banister, half of her torso perilously suspended over the air. She was laughing. Lila was cross-legged on the floor, convulsing with giggles.

'What's going on?' asked Georgia.

'Nothing,' smirked Nancy. 'It was stupid.'

'Tell me,' said Georgia.

Lila giggled again. 'It's too hard to explain. You look nice.'

'Thanks,' said Georgia. 'Were you talking about me?'

'No,' said Nancy. How could she lean against the banister like that? Georgia stepped forward and looked over. The staircase cut through the centre of the house, through all four floors. The marble floor of the hall reared up at her as she looked at it. The wine she'd drunk swirled in her stomach and her fingers twisted into each other.

'Can you come away from there, Nance?' asked Georgia.

'Why?' she said, still smiling. Her hair was so dark and so shiny under the hall light. How did she get it like that?

'I don't like it,' Georgia muttered.

'What?' she laughed. 'Is it even worse if I do this?' she swung herself even further over, her hands on the polished wooden banister.

'No, don't,' Georgia replied. 'Please.'

'Ohhh, you don't like heights, do you?' Lila laughed. 'Remember Florence?'

Years ago they'd gone on a History of Art trip to Florence. Their tour guide had taken them to the Duomo, a huge domed cathedral. The dome had a balcony around its interior rim. It was supposed to be some kind of treat to walk around the circumference of it, looking at the paintings on the ceiling, marvelling at how tiny the people on the ground were. Georgia's mother – who'd worked hours of overtime to pay for the trip – had gone on and on about the view, so when her stomach had twisted and every fibre of her being had told her not to step out on to the ledge, she'd done it anyway.

She had had a panic attack halfway around, collapsing to the floor with her back rooted to the wall and completely unable to move. It had taken two teachers half an hour to move her.

'Does it make you feel a bit funny?' Nancy asked. 'What about if I do this?'

Nancy looped one leg over the banister, then the other and stood, her arms holding on to it behind her, her bare heels on the ledge. 'I'm flying, Jack,' she giggled.

Georgia was going to be sick. She glanced down again, catching sight of the floor once more. The back of her neck was tight and cold and hot at the same time. 'Please, Nance,' she said quietly.

'Fucking hell, Nance,' said Lila, her eyes wide.

'OK, OK. You're such babies.' Nancy took one hand off the banister and spun herself around, but her fingers missed the banister and scrabbled at it, the polish too shiny. Her giggles became a sharp gasp as she reached out urgently. Georgia and Lila surged forward, grabbing at Nancy's arm. Georgia's mind filled with the image of Nancy's muscular body, contorted into an odd shape on the marble, a pool of maroon from her perfect skull. What would it sound like, her body hitting the ground?

'I'm fine,' Nancy snapped, dragging herself back over the rail and landing neatly on the floor. 'God, look at your faces!' she laughed.

Lila laughed, too. 'To be fair, it would have put a massive downer on the evening if you'd spilled your brains all over Georgia's nice clean floor.'

Nancy laughed, getting to her feet. 'It'll take a lot more than that to get rid of me.'

She looked Georgia up and down. 'Nice dress. I think I saw it the other day in J. Crew – on sale, right?'

THEN

Georgia

'I don't understand how it happened,' said Nancy, as she drew a cigarette out of the packet. Her voice was even and low. To a passer-by it might have seemed pleasant. Georgia searched for something to say, but came up empty-handed.

It had been twenty-four hours since they'd arrived at school, and Nancy clearly wasn't prepared to forgive the room allocations snub. More worryingly, she hadn't even mentioned the encounter with Heidi and the new teacher – the first telling off Nancy had had in years. It was a perfect storm of a black mood and it was Georgia and Lila who were going to have to weather it. It always was.

That morning Georgia had mentioned that she'd like to get the cartilage at the top of her ear pierced, like Miss Brandon had, and Nancy had practically thrown her cup of coffee across the table. 'She was actually pretty cool about you swearing,' Georgia had ventured. 'Some teachers would have given you a purple slip for that.' And now she was being punished, Nancy hadn't spoken to her in hours.

'It's not like we did this, Nance,' said Lila, whose patience was clearly also wearing thin. 'We got there, took our bags up to the room, and it had other people's names on the door. There wasn't a lot we could do. OK?'

It wasn't OK. This was what Nancy did. Most people either got angry, blew up and then calmed down, or they seethed below the surface. Nancy somehow did both. She'd be furious for the next couple of days – unless they got their own way, which Georgia thought seemed increasingly unlikely – and then she'd decide whose fault it was. That's who would be pushed out. Georgia had been on the wrong end of it before. Whichever of the two of them Nancy liked best at any given time was the princess to her queen. The deputy. Safe. Whoever she liked less would have to stand a few steps away, not quite close enough to be part of it. When they'd studied the Tudors last year, Georgia had let herself think how well Nancy would have done at court. Though she couldn't help but notice that it was the ones who reached too high who ended up with their heads cut off.

Georgia watched as Nancy leaned back on the wall, taking a long drag on her Marlboro Light. 'Why didn't you stop Heidi from unpacking?' she snarled at Lila. The question was so unfair that Lila couldn't find the words to answer it.

This had become their smoking spot last year. It was a gardener's shed, abandoned and half collapsed, at the bottom of a long hill, which sloped down from the school playing fields, right at the edge of the estate. Nancy and Lila loved it, they seemed to think it was ample protection from getting caught. Georgia disagreed. She leaned around the shelter and scoured the field for any signs of life, trying to force herself to stop worrying. It wasn't worth asking Nancy if they could walk the extra five minutes to the woods, where they would be totally out of sight. It would provoke a rant about how spineless and bourgeois (a word she'd heard at one of her parents' dinner parties and used a lot) Georgia was for caring about getting caught, or getting in trouble. It was easy for Nancy, she had parents who said stuff like 'children should be encouraged to swear if they feel it's the appropriate word for the situation at hand'. Georgia's parents would kill her if she got so much as a warning from one of her teachers. They lived in fear that she would lose her scholarship.

'I don't know why we're stressing about this,' Lila said. 'All we have to do is call our parents, then they'll call the school and the rooms will get changed around. Everyone knows we're the only three-group. I doubt Heidi and Jenny even want that room.'

Georgia bit her lip. Lila and Nancy's parents would call in, of course they would. But it was different for her. She couldn't imagine what her mother would say if Georgia asked her to make that phone call. She would be horrified. Mortified. She would say no.

Reynolds House was built over five floors. The top floor was for the sixth form, and was divided up into singles, doubles and a triple room. Most people wanted a single, for obvious reasons. Some girls, the ones who were close friends, or the pairs of girls who were sleeping together, liked the doubles. And then there was the triple, which ran almost the entire length of the house, with a huge window and its own bathroom. Back in their second year, when battle lines had been drawn and alliances decided, they had made an agreement. Whatever happened, for sixth form, they would have that room. They'd been pestering Cookie, their matron, the woman who had brought them up from the age of eleven, about it ever since. And while she had never said the exact words, it had been strongly implied the room was theirs.

'We shouldn't need to call our parents,' replied Nancy, her eyes narrowed. 'We're practically adults now. We had an agreement with them. They should respect that.'

'Exactly,' replied Georgia, too quickly. 'We're almost eighteen. We can't run to our parents for every tiny thing.'

'But Cookie isn't here,' Lila said.

'Why not?'

'She's ill,' said Lila, who was now sitting cross-legged on the ground and making a daisy chain.

'She broke her hip,' said Georgia. 'She's out for at least six weeks, but they don't know if she'll be able to come back at all.'

Nancy ground her finished cigarette into the grass. 'For fuck's sake. Cookie should have sorted the room allocations out before she went off. It would have taken ten minutes.'

Georgia caught Lila's eye and raised an eyebrow.

'Nancy, she broke her hip, it's not like she planned it,' Georgia said quietly. Nancy had taken this too far. They all loved Cookie. She had read to them when they were homesick in their first year, and chaperoned them to their first socials. She teased them about their little habits and indulged them with later bedtimes when they would get together to watch a particular TV programme. Everyone knew she was the nicest housemistress in the school. They'd lucked out.

'Yeah, stop being a dick, Nance,' said Lila, lightly. Lila always seemed to know how to handle Nancy, how to smack her down a bit without turning it into full-on warfare. There was something about her manner, her tiny blondeness maybe, or her soft voice, which people just seemed to like automatically. Why did people always treat you based on how you looked, Georgia wondered. Everyone thought Nancy was so sorted and capable and together, because she was tall and dark-haired and smartly dressed. Everyone was always so nice to Lila because she was all delicate and breakable. And her? No one seemed to notice her. Maybe that meant she looked unremarkable.

'I'm not being a dick, I'm saying I wanted that dorm.'

'We all wanted that dorm,' Georgia joined in, hearing the past tense in Nancy's words and hoping this was nearly over.

'We're going to get it,' said Lila. 'So calm down.'

Georgia's shoulders fell.

'I am calm. But we're not going to get that dorm, not for this term at least,' Nancy said.

'Why not?' said Lila. 'We'll have to call our parents, it's the only way. They'll insist we have to be together, they'll have to move us in there because it's the only three-bed. Sorted.'

Nancy snorted. 'You think they're going to make weird Heidi and her bean-flicking friend move out of that room, when they've already unpacked?'

'Maybe Lila could talk to her?' Georgia suggested.

Nancy caught her eye, and laughed. 'That's true. Fancy a catch-up with your bestie, Li? Ask her to give us our room back?'

Lila's face darkened. 'Fuck off, both of you.'

'Moody,' smirked Nancy. 'Shall we send you off to the san to get some mood stabilizers?'

Lila got to her feet. 'Not everyone likes to take handfuls of pills every day, Nance.' But her tone was lighter now, teasing. There wasn't going to be a row. Georgia felt relief at the realization. She plucked the newly lit cigarette from between Nancy's fingers and took a drag on it, then passed it to Lila.

'Ladies?' a voice called out from above them. Panic swelled up in Georgia's chest. Her mind clouded. It was the new teacher. Miss Brandon. Fuck, fuck, fuck. She turned her head a fraction, to see if Lila was still holding the cigarette. She wasn't. Nancy sprang into action, striding a few metres up the hill towards where the woman was standing, while Lila moved her heel over the cigarette butt and discreetly ground it into the floor, destroying any tendrils of smoke.

Georgia watched the back of Nancy's long body move rapidly up the hill. She reached Miss Brandon, who had tied her shiny red hair up into a jaunty ponytail. Georgia and Lila watched as Nancy reached Miss Brandon, stuck out her hand, and initiated a handshake. God, Nancy was good. The woman looked totally wrong-footed.

'I'm Nancy Greydon,' she said, in her Enid Blyton voice, the voice that she wheeled out when she gave tours to prospective parents and represented their year at the student council. 'We met briefly yesterday. You're new, aren't you?'

Georgia didn't catch what Miss Brandon said in answer. She stood still next to Lila, trying to guess what Nancy would want her to do, trying to guess what the official story might be.

'Georgia, Lila,' called Nancy. 'Come and meet Miss Brandon.'

It was time to mimic Nancy's jolly hockey sticks, then. Georgia bounded forward, pulling her vest top up to cover her chest, smiling widely. 'Oh, hello, Miss Brandon. I liked what you said in assembly yesterday. Are you all settled in? I'm Georgina Green and this is Camilla Knight.'

'Yes,' she replied. 'I am. What are you girls doing down here?'

To her left, Georgia could see Lila was looking downcast, and she realized what the line was going to be.

'I'm afraid Lila was feeling homesick,' said Nancy, gesturing at Lila.

'We came down here for a bit of privacy,' added Georgia, watching Nancy's face to make sure she was pitching it right. 'Some of the other girls can be a bit unsympathetic, they think we're too old for all that.'

Nancy gave her a tiny, almost invisible dip of the head,

telling her she had done well. Lila kept her distant, shadowy face on. 'It's not out of bounds,' she said softly. 'It's just that it's the quietest place in the school. Are we late for the house meeting?'

Miss Brandon's face was blank. She clearly didn't buy it, thought Georgia. All she needed to do was ask Nancy to empty her pockets and they'd be in trouble. They'd been caught once last year, so once more would mean a suspension. Georgia's heart was quickening. Her parents mustn't find out. They would be furious.

'That's a very nice story,' said Miss Brandon, a surprising hardness to her voice. 'But I saw you smoking.'

Georgia looked confused, as did Lila. Nancy looked affronted. 'I'm sorry, Miss Brandon, I hate to disagree with a member of staff, especially when you're new, but I think you were mistaken.'

Miss Brandon was smiling. Why wasn't she acting like a normal teacher? A normal teacher would tell them to run up to the dining hall and get there in time for supper, and save themselves the hassle of telling them off. Miss Brandon didn't seem like the telling-off type – she was young, and she'd made a joke in assembly. She was wearing Converse, for God's sake. She clearly wanted everyone to like her. What was she playing at?

'I'm going to need you to empty your pockets, girls,' said Miss Brandon, her smile still fixed on her lips, her eyes slightly squinted in the late evening sunshine.

'For what?' asked Lila, her voice a little too high. Nancy's face clouded at Lila's comment. She'd got it wrong. Nancy would be angry later.

'Cigarettes,' came the reply.

'Oh, I don't smoke,' said Lila, calmly, pulling things back. 'And I wouldn't spend time with people who do. You see, my mother died of cancer a few years ago.'

Georgia tried to keep the triumph out of her face. Lila's trump card. Her ace. She was careful about it, hardly ever using it so it didn't lose its power. But it left the teachers, especially the ones who'd seen her tearful white face in the months afterwards, eating out of her hands.

'I'm sorry to hear that – Camilla, was it? That's extremely sad.'

Georgia's head stopped swirling. Thank God. It was going to be OK.

'So you won't have any problem with turning out your pockets,' said Miss Brandon.

Georgia looked at Lila, and then to Nancy and felt the sinking realization that Nancy didn't have anything to suggest. Slowly the girls offered up the contents of their pockets – their mobile phones, a lip gloss, a packet of chewing gum, Lila's lighter and finally Nancy's packet of Marlboro Lights.

Miss Brandon smiled pleasantly at them. 'I think you had better go back to the boarding house. Don't you? I'd hate for you to miss supper.'

NOW

Georgia

'I think we're almost ready for the main,' Georgia called out, to the turned backs of her friends.

No one moved. Lila sat on Roo's lap, running her spindly fingers through his hair. She could have been a teenager from behind. Her head was swaying as if it was too heavy for her neck. They'd all given up on smoking out of the French windows and were happily smoking at the table now. The house would stink tomorrow, the curtains in the sitting room heavy with the tang of smoke.

'Guys?' she called again. Nothing. What the fuck was the point of making food? She should have just stuck a bottle of vodka on the table and left them to it.

'I think Georgia wants us to eat,' she heard Brett say gently. When he said 'Georgia' he somehow made the G soft and gentle. As the words left his lips, Charlie jumped up.

'Hop to it, team,' he barked, too loud.

'I LOVE this song!' exploded Lila, reaching across the table for the remote control. She pointed it at the speakers, mounted in each corner of the room and turned it up as loud as it would go. The music pulled at the speakers, making them vibrate, distorting the song.

There was a flat downstairs – the fact that they only owned four floors of their town house was a constant source of shame to Charlie. Would the people who lived there complain?

Roo at least had the good grace to look embarrassed, but said nothing to his wife. The ice in the water jug had melted. Georgia picked it up and turned away from the table, grateful for the excuse. For some stupid reason she felt like crying. She couldn't tell Lila to turn the music down, because that would mark her out as controlling and dull and everything else that they probably already thought she was. But she was hot, and tired, and it was painfully loud. She felt more aware than ever of the chemicals pumping around her body, heavy with hormones. As she reached into the freezer, relishing the coldness of it on her hands, the music stopped. She turned to look back over her shoulder.

Brett was holding the remote control. He was smiling and holding it just out of Lila's reach. She was giggling and reaching for it, like a child.

'Georgia said supper is ready,' he said, his tone light and friendly. 'So we should sit down. It smells amazing.'

She couldn't convey her gratitude towards Brett without seeming sycophantic, so instead she merely nodded her thanks as she watched everyone take their seats.

Georgia slid the oven door open and felt the wave of hot air hit her face. She knew as soon as she looked at the pork that it was overdone. She'd been so scared that it might be raw that she'd added fifteen minutes to the cooking time.

'Everything OK?' asked Brett quietly. Georgia turned around. Everyone else was still sitting at the table.

'Fine,' she replied, her voice making it clear that things were not fine.

'Sure?' he asked.

Something inside Georgia shifted. There was no way of getting out of this. She might as well tell him. 'It's overcooked,' she admitted.

'So?' asked Brett.

'So it'll be dry, and people won't like it.'

'But these are your friends,' Brett reminded her. 'They're here to see you, not the food.'

He was half right, thought Georgia. They weren't here for the food. 'I don't want everyone to think I'm a useless cook,' she laughed, trying to keep her voice light.

Brett grinned. 'The starter was the best thing I've eaten this year. You've got a sauce, right?'

Georgia nodded.

'Then we'll serve it up here, put a load of sauce on every plate and no one will notice if it's dry,' he reassured her. It took every ounce of self-control Georgia possessed not to throw her arms around him.

'I'll waiter for you,' he said, picking up four plates, deftly balancing them on his forearms. 'These look amazing.'

Gratefully she picked up the other two plates and carried them to the table.

'You're very good at that,' said Charlie. 'Almost professional.'

'I was a waiter for a long time,' he replied.

'You don't seem old enough to have done anything for a long time,' said Roo, shovelling a mouthful of potato into his mouth. 'Any salt, Gee?'

Georgia got up to get the salt and pepper grinders. Did he have to say that in front of everyone? Now they'd all notice, and they'd all cover their food in it. She placed the grinders down in front of Charlie with a little more force than necessary.

'I quit my waiting job last year,' Brett was saying to Lila. 'When my writing started to take off.'

'How's the renovation going?' Roo was asking Georgia. She wanted to shush him. They were only six – it was perfectly possible to have one conversation among six people. She didn't want to get stuck talking about carpets and paint samples at this end of the table while Lila ladled herself all over Brett. Lila's eyes were unfocused. A sign that she was about to lose control.

The drunker Lila got, the more of a liability she became and the harder it would be for her and Nancy to talk any sense into her. She and Nancy would have to bite the bullet and take her out alone tomorrow, to try and knock some sense into her. Why had Nancy suggested dinner in the first place? There were too many variables, too many temptations for Lila to resist. But as she pondered the question, Georgia knew the answer. This was what they did. They put on a performance. They wore costumes and said lines and they fooled everyone around them that they were normal, ordinary, childhood friends. Until recently, Lila could be relied upon to play her part.

'What kind of writing do you do, Brett?' she said, a little too loudly across Roo. She was being rude. Charlie would say something about it later.

'He's a freelance journalist,' replied Nancy, running her hand over his arm. 'Mostly for *Slate*, a couple of pieces for the *Atlantic*. He's rather good, actually.'

'Rather good,' Brett repeated, copying Nancy's accent. Lila laughed, far too loud.

'That's such a good accent,' she rasped. 'Do more! Say something else.'

'What do you want me to say?' Brett said, in the same faux-English tones. He wasn't very good, actually.

'He's not a performing monkey, Lila,' snapped Nancy. 'You're embarrassing him.'

'I'm not embarrassed,' Brett replied lightly. He had dropped the accent though.

Nancy's head jerked. That was interesting. No one ever disagreed with Nancy. He was brave. And she was clearly cross, but she wouldn't be cross with Brett, she'd blame Lila. And Georgia was grateful, because it would make the conversation easier, the conversation they were going to have when Lila had either passed out or gone home. Whichever happened first.

'What do you all do?' asked Brett to the table.

'Roo is in venture capital,' said Nancy.

'I have to ask,' Brett interrupted. 'Roo?'

Roo gave a smile, his lips closed. 'Short for Rupert. Like the bear.'

Brett looked blank.

'You don't have Rupert the Bear in America?'

Brett shook his head. 'At least, not as far as I know.'

'That is so sad. Don't you guys think that's so, so sad?' Lila lamented as she poured herself more wine. She didn't top up anyone else's glass.

No one said anything. Georgia knew she should, but she wanted to see how long this silence would carry on for, how long everyone would let her comment go unanswered.

Another beat, and then Nancy carried on. 'So, Roo is in venture capital.'

'For my sins,' he held his hands up.

'And Charlie is in Westminster.'

'That's government, right?'

'Trying to be,' Charlie replied, taking the bottle from next to Lila and offering it round the rest of the table. Georgia watched Lila's eyes follow it as Charlie poured for their guests. Don't you dare, she thought to herself. Don't you fucking dare pass out before I've even served the dessert.

'And what about you, ladies?'

'I'm an assistant. Part-time.' Georgia forced out the words, her lips tight. And now he wouldn't want to talk to her. It was the same stumbling block that came up at every dinner party. The asker would feel embarrassed at her answer, her boring embarrassing answer, and would turn to the person on their other side as soon as humanly possible to escape their initial blunder. How could anyone who went to Oxford end up as a PA, they'd whisper behind her back. No one ever bothered to ask any other questions, to find out whether her job was interesting or rewarding or fun. They just heard that she worked in admin, that she couldn't get their niece an internship at a film studio or help their husband's career in venture capital, and lost interest entirely.

Years ago, before she'd met Charlie, when she'd taken the job because she wasn't landing any of the parts she was auditioning for, and because she was sick of men sticking their hands down her jeans in dressing rooms, and making twenty quid a week performing in a show that only ever drew seven people a night, she used to justify it. Slip into the conversation that she had A levels. That she'd been to Oxford. That she'd been to drama school, too. But eventually she'd realized that all those accolades only made it sadder. She'd become a dab hand at avoiding the job question, at deflecting it before anyone got a chance to ask. She'd been too distracted this evening.

'She downplays it,' said Charlie, cutting through her thoughts. 'She does all their hiring, all the HR. Runs the place. Though I keep telling her that she should retrain to be an interior designer,' said Charlie. 'She practically did the whole of the house on her own. You should have seen it when we moved in.' She shot him a grateful look, her ribcage suddenly full of affection for him, a desire to tangle herself around him and listen to his heart beating. He could be kind sometimes. It was easy to forget. He had once carried her halfway home from a night out because her strappy high-heeled shoes had cut into her foot and made it bleed.

She used to try for him. She used to dress up and whimper embarrassing sentences into his ear when he was close to climax, foregoing her own orgasm, which hinged on staying in a specific position and concentrating really hard, in favour of wriggling and writhing in a way that made it seem like she was having fun. These days, Charlie hardly bothered to ask. She never said no, but sometimes she could feel herself punishing him with her indifference. Afterwards, when the first snores came from his side of the bed, she would kiss his cheek and then slip into the bathroom, where she would clamp a hand between her thighs and bring herself hot sharp pleasure, thinking about things which would shame her the next morning.

They should start trying again. Try for sex, rather than trying for a baby. Take a holiday. Go on a date. Do something, any of the things that magazines claimed made life easier. It was such a cliché, their mechanical sex life. She'd always assumed that they would be different, that even if they were trying for a baby, things would stay light and fun. But no. They were like every other semi-barren couple in the entire world. Driven apart by ovulation sticks and temperature taking.

'Georgia is amazing,' said Nancy, refilling her water glass. Georgia grabbed her wine, knowing what was coming. 'She signs over her entire salary to her parents.'

Doing her best to focus on the stem of her wine glass, Georgia consciously avoided Charlie's face. She knew he'd be scarlet. Furious.

'What?' asked Lila. 'I didn't know that.'

'It's not a big deal,' Georgia replied. 'Does anyone want more wine? Or bread? It's a homemade focaccia.'

'All of it?' asked Lila. 'Literally all of it?'

Georgia glanced up to see Nancy's face, illuminated by the candlelight and still somehow resolutely smiling. 'Yes, all of it,' Georgia replied. 'My dad can't work and my mum has to be home to look after him.'

'All of your money?' slurred Lila. 'God, you are so nice. I wouldn't give my dad ANY money.'

'You don't have any money,' laughed Roo.

'Not a topic for the table,' Charlie muttered. 'Politics, money and religion and all that.'

'Oh come on, Charlie,' Nancy chided. 'We're amongst friends. And I'm only saying how amazing your wife is.'

'Nancy—' Georgia started, not knowing what she was going to say next.

'That's beautiful,' said Brett. 'I wish I could help my parents out more. I try to send them something when I can.' He leaned across and put his hand over Georgia's. 'Really. That's amazing.' He stared across the table, gripping her hand. Georgia was torn between abject mortification and another, more confusing feeling. A nice one. It was like she could feel his kindness seeping through into her skin.

'And Lila is a stay-at-home mother,' announced Charlie, shattering the quiet between them. 'Aren't you, Lila?'

Brett lifted his hands away in a light movement, leaving the warmth of his long fingers on her skin. She looked up. At the other side of the table, Charlie's neck was red.

'How many kids do you have?' asked Brett.

'One,' said Roo, just as the word 'two' came from Lila's lips.

Brett looked confused. He said nothing.

Georgia's fingers slipped on her wine glass. Lila was pissed, yes, but not pissed enough to forget how many children she had.

Lila's face was set on Roo's. Georgia inched forward in her seat, trying to see Roo's face, to see what expression he was making.

'Don't do this now, Lila,' he said. His voice was quiet but inflexible.

'Fuck you,' came Lila's reply.

Roo stood up. 'I'm sorry, guys, my wife's had a bit too much to drink. We're going to step outside for a moment.'

He moved around the table and wrapped his hand around Lila's forearm. God, she was thin. His thumb and index finger were circled around her entire bicep, easily.

'I don't need to go outside.'

'Come on,' Roo smiled, a smile which wasn't convincing anyone.

'I am not a child, Roo.'

'Could have fooled me, the way you're acting. Get up. Let's go outside, you need to sober up. Sorry, everyone,' he added, rolling his eyes.

'I'm only trying to be honest,' she slurred. 'Why won't you let me be honest?'

The silence around the table was painful. Georgia wished the music was back on, even at the volume Lila had had it.

Roo had got her to her feet and was leading her towards the French windows. The group averted their eyes, determinedly pretending that nothing was happening as Roo yanked the door open and stepped outside, like Lila was a naughty puppy who had pissed on the carpet. Looking up, unable to stop her curiosity, Georgia stared after them. The lights in the kitchen were too bright to be able to see out properly into the twilight. Georgia could make out Lila's tiny figure slumped on the garden bench, and Roo's bulk standing nearby, smoking.

'Is she OK?' asked Brett. 'He seemed kind of rough with her.'

No one said anything.

'Do either of you know what that's about?' asked Charlie, ignoring Brett.

Georgia parted her lips to say that she had no idea, but as she did so, Nancy spoke.

'She had a miscarriage a few weeks ago.'

'What?' Georgia heard herself ask. 'How do you know that?'

Nancy had been in Boston. Nancy and Lila didn't even speak that much, a couple of times a month at the most. Georgia spoke to Lila every single day and she hadn't said anything, nothing at all. Most days, anyway. Things had been patchy lately, but usually they were insepar-able. Closer than Lila and Nancy. Far closer.

Nancy folded her napkin and placed it neatly on the table, next to her plate. 'I don't think it's fair to discuss it without her here, but clearly she's upset. I thought you knew.'

Should she say she had known? Could she pull it back from her expression of surprise – pretend that she was only blindsided by Nancy knowing? Probably not. Nancy would see straight through it. She'd probably interrogated Lila on the phone after she had got Georgia's email, that would be how she'd found out.

'When did she tell you?' She felt the words fall from her mouth, slippery.

'On Skype. Can you pass the water?'

Charlie passed the jug while Georgia sat, staring. 'When did you Skype?'

Nancy twisted in her seat. She looked annoyed. 'A week ago. Maybe ten days. I'm not sure. What does it matter?'

'We never Skype.'

'Well, when I get back we can start Skyping, if you like. Or I could go upstairs and Skype you from there, if you're that bothered about it?' Nancy smirked.

'That's not the point.'

Georgia knew she was being petulant. She was making a fool of herself in front of everyone. In front of Brett.

Would they talk about her later? She could see them lying in the smooth white bed in the guest room, rumpled from sex. 'What was with your friend?' Brett would say. And Nancy would talk about her. She'd keep her voice low, as if there was any risk of it carrying up two floors, and she would say that Georgia was jealous or paranoid or something equally damning. And then they'd laugh, and then they'd probably go and shower together, or slip into the bathrobes that hung on the back of the door and curl up to watch a film on the massive television concealed in the wardrobe, because their life hadn't been spoiled by all the smudgy messiness that came with being here and dealing with everything.

It was so easy for Nancy. She got to be a good friend simply by picking up the phone or shipping care packages. Lila would go into raptures about the parcels of Kate Spade and Laura Mercier which arrived every month or so. She was just as soppy about post now as she had been at school. Stupid, when she could order anything she wanted and have it delivered.

All the times that Georgia had held Lila's hair back while she was sick from boozing, or rubbed her feet when she was swollen with pregnancy, apparently meant nothing. Nor did helping to paint the nursery while Roo was away 'on business'.

All those times she had pretended that she couldn't smell the perfume on Roo's shirt or acted as if she thought the hairs in their bed could definitely be Lila's.

All useless.

It was clearly Nancy who she turned to for the important things. Nancy who had the inside track, leaving her to look stupid in front of everyone, like she was everyone's least favourite friend.

Nancy stood up, placing her napkin on the chair. 'I think we should get Lila to come back in and finish her food. She's barely eaten anything.'

Georgia pressed her fingernails into her palm, willing herself not to scream. It was her house. Her food. Her dinner party. Nancy was a guest here. She should act like a guest. Not that she ever had.

She'd offered Nancy and Brett a bed for the weekend,

thinking the offer would be declined. Nancy had never, ever stayed with her. She couldn't bear to be on the back foot. Not knowing where the glasses were or what time breakfast would be served was like a kind of torture to her. As soon as she turned sixteen, after a succession of parties where they had frozen all night on the floor of a marquee, or in the back of someone else's car, Nancy made an announcement. She would no longer be sleeping anywhere that wasn't her own bed, either at school or at home. She would call a taxi to any field, warehouse or suburban home where they had found themselves partying, charging hundreds of pounds of taxi fares to her parents' account. They'd never even ask why. There was a sense of serenity, the way that she would climb into the heated people carrier and let it sail her back to the safety of her own bed. There was nothing too distant or scary or big that she wouldn't be able to dial a number and rescue herself from. So the acceptance of the offer to stay the night had come as a surprise. An unwelcome one. Georgia could already feel the fluster rising as she imagined making Brett breakfast tomorrow morning. If she wore make-up, Nancy would comment on how much of an effort she'd made. If she didn't, she'd ask if she was tired. Tiny needle-pointed comments which on their own sounded ridiculous. But those things could add up.

Georgia took a breath, composing herself. It would be over soon. In thirty-six hours Nancy and Brett would be going and everything would be normal again. A few more hours of playing nice. That was it.

'Yes, of course,' she said. 'But I think we should give them a few minutes to sort things out.'

'I'll go and see if they're ready to come in.'

'We should probably—' she started, but Nancy was already opening the glass door.

'They won't want to come in,' she said, to no one in particular, crossing the kitchen to the huge oven.

To her surprise, Charlie followed her to the other side of the kitchen.

'Why did we do this?' she asked him, sotto voce. 'Nance is watching my every move, Lila is dribbling over Brett. Roo looks like murder. It's a car crash.' She buried her head in Charlie's shoulder and waited for him to comfort her, to praise her hostessing skills and say that it would be fine. But nothing came. He said nothing. On the subject of her friends, he had become cruelly reticent over time. 'You do realize,' he had said to her once, years ago, 'that you are actually supposed to like your friends?'

It had been a stupid thing to say. Georgia had swapped her focus to the bottom of her gin and tonic and stopped talking. Clearly her stories about her friends were making him think she was a bitch. The truth was, she knew that other people claimed to like their friends. But they, Georgia and Lila and Nancy, were different. Perhaps it was all the years of school or the secret that bonded them together, or maybe it was just something in their souls. In Lila's wedding vows she had used an Emily Brontë quote: 'Whatever our souls are made of, his and mine are the same.' Georgia had stood by the altar with a frozen smile, thinking that Roo's soul couldn't have been made of anything more different from Lila's. His was made from the flannel of his school trousers, his family's tartan, soaked in whisky and self-love. It was a selfish, indulgent fabric. The same stuff that all the boys they knew were made of.

Lila's soul was different. She might look like every other Arabella or India they had been at school with, but inside she was different. Roo would have been so much happier with any of the other well-mannered blondes he'd dated before her. But then, how was he supposed to know that he wasn't committing to someone sweet and unquestioning who would have walked two steps behind him for the rest of forever and never embarrass him at work events? Lila used to be as good at putting on a show as she and Nancy were.

Georgia scanned the plates which Charlie had placed on one of the counters, working out how much of their food each person had left. The boys had mostly finished. Nancy and Lila's plates were almost untouched.

Georgia pulled away from Charlie's hug. 'People will think there's something to be upset about,' she said, excusing herself.

'I've never met anyone who's so bothered about what other people think of them,' said Charlie. His tone was light but the words were still unquestionably nasty. Georgia looked across the room, to see Nancy closing the French windows behind her.

'They'll only be a minute,' she announced triumphantly. 'Lila's a bit emotional, which is understandable given everything that she's been through.'

'Yes, you have,' said Georgia to Charlie, under her breath. 'I'm just popping to the loo before we sit back down.'

Georgia never used the downstairs toilet. Loo. Charlie always winced when she forgot and called it the toilet. The bathroom on the first floor was far nicer. She locked the door behind her, turning the pretty brass key in the lock, and sat down on the loo, taking a deep breath. Everything was fine. Well, it wasn't, but everything was going to be. She inspected the white paper after she wiped herself, not because she was expecting to see anything but because it had become habit. She had to know where she was in her cycle at all times, writing down the dates, practically the times of every single bleed. She couldn't think about that tonight. Her head was far too full of Lila and Nancy and trying to decode the secret meaning behind every single thing either of them said. Did normal people live like this? Did they spend their lives trying to work out where the hidden insult was in every sentence their friends spoke? Probably not. But then, they weren't like ordinary friends.

Washing her hands, Georgia realized how pink her face was. It was the wine, and the hormones. Hot flushes were just one of the myriad joyful side effects she had to suffer through if she wanted to get pregnant. For the millionth time it struck her how wretchedly unfair it was that some people could do this on their own, without drugs and side effects and suffering. Without help. The heat swelled up inside her, it felt like it was stretching her skin. Desperately she grappled for the catch on the window, pushing it up and drinking in the cold air.

'. . . inside in a minute?' Georgia caught the tail end of a sentence. It was Nancy's voice.

'Fine,' Roo called back. 'Give us a couple of minutes – Lila was feeling a bit too hot.'

The door slammed. Georgia winced, wishing Nancy would be gentler with the door – the handles were antique.

'What the fuck do you think you're playing at?' said Roo. Now that Nancy had gone, his tone had changed from cheerful to absolute ice. Leaning forward, Georgia looked over the windowsill. Lila had her arms crossed over her chest. She was shivering and looking past Roo, into the distance. A cigarette was lit in one hand, but she seemed to have forgotten that it was there, leaving it burning. To her horror, Georgia watched Roo grab Lila's tiny arm in his fist and shake her. 'Lila? Answer me,' he said, his face centimetres from hers.

Georgia pulled the window shut, slowly and silently. She felt sick. She knew she had seen something that she wasn't supposed to see, something that wasn't for her. What happened between Lila and Roo was none of her business. It wasn't hers to fix.

Looking in the mirror, Georgia was relieved to see that the pinkness was gone from her face. She plucked a Chanel lipstick from the drawer of spare make-up, dusted powder over the bridge of her nose and smiled at her reflection in the window. There, she thought. Much better.

THEN

Nancy

'Did you call your parents?' Nancy asked, as Georgia closed the door behind her. Nancy and Lila were sitting on Nancy's bed, and Nancy was painting her toenails a bright coral colour. This room, the one they had been condemned to, was a floor below the triple dorm, and faced the wrong way, with a view of the school instead of across the fields. But at least Nancy was with Georgia. She could hardly imagine the stress, the humiliation of having to sleep and undress and live in front of a near stranger.

Lila's fate – sleeping in the triple dorm, the room that they'd been dreaming of, that they'd planned decorations for – was much worse. Sharing it with Heidi Bart and Jenny McGuckin was the ultimate insult. 'Couldn't I have at least been stuck with someone normal?' Lila whined every evening when it was time to go back to her room. The girls had tried to comfort her, seeing the redness in her cheeks and her hands balled into fists. They had told her that the room allocation had been a misunderstanding, that Jenny and Heidi would swap for the double room and that everything would go back to normal. Just as it should.

But Georgia had insisted on trying to make the double room look nice, tearing pages from *Vogue* and sticking them to the wall, blu-tacking fairy lights to the notice-board and putting her blue-checked blankets on both beds. Nancy had tried to be nice about it all, but hadn't been able to manage it. She had told Georgia that her efforts were pointless and unfair to Lila. Anyway, once their parents called Miss Brandon they'd be moving dorm in a matter of hours, and then they'd have to pack up and unpack all over again.

Nancy looked up from her toenails and screwed the brush back into the bottle. Georgia's face was flushed and swollen.

'What's wrong?'

'We're stuck here every weekend up until half-term.'

'She's barred us?' Nancy's voice dripped with disdain. 'No one gets barred in the sixth form.'

Georgia nodded.

Lila got up from the bed, her face ashen. 'You're joking?'

Georgia shook her head. 'She rang our parents and told them, and we're barred, we can't go out at all, and' – Georgia's voice started to wobble – 'it's Jamie's last weekend, next weekend.'

Pity stirred in Nancy's chest. Siblings seemed like a strange thing to have, and an even stranger thing to be bothered about, but Georgia had always been soppy about her older brothers. She couldn't even have the news on in the common room in case she heard about some accident at sea and convinced herself that Jamie had been involved.

Lila was tangling her arms around Georgia and stroking her hair. Should Nancy join them? Something about their intimacy was off-putting.

'You're not seriously saying that they're going to make you stay in next weekend and miss Jamie?'

Georgia nodded.

'He's going to be away for months. He's on a fucking submarine. That's ridiculous. Have your parents explained?'

'They asked if I could make up the weekend after half-term, and go home next weekend, so that I could see him and say goodbye and everything, and she said no. Mummy's furious. They said' – she broke off to sniff – 'that I've ruined his last weekend at home.'

'That cunt.' Lila knew how much it would have taken to get Georgia's parents to ask the school to make an exception. Her family worshipped Fairbridge Hall, they acted like it was fucking Hogwarts.

'Tell your mum to ring Mrs Easton,' said Lila, 'she'll overrule the new bitch.'

Georgia shook her head. 'My mum was so nervous even to talk to Miss Brandon. There's no way she'd ask Mrs Easton.'

Nancy got to her feet. It was too much. Georgia's mother shouldn't have been told no, even if she didn't exactly pay the fees. That wasn't how things worked. There was a hierarchy and parents, even scholarship students' parents, came above teachers. Miss Brandon needed to learn how things were done here.

'It's OK,' she said to the back of Georgia's head as she burrowed into Lila's shoulder. 'We'll sort it out. She's an employee. We pay her wages. She's not going to make any more trouble for us. Did you ask your parents about the room?'

Georgia looked confused. 'What?'

'Did they say they'd call about moving dorms so we're all together?'

The incredulity on Georgia's face told Nancy that she had said the wrong thing. 'No, Nance, I didn't. I didn't interrupt my mum when she was crying about my brother going to an actual fucking war zone, to ask her to ring up and get our dorms changed.'

Georgia's hysteria wasn't going to get them anywhere. 'I told you, I'm going to sort it out,' Nancy said, trying to stay calm. There was no point in rising to Georgia's silliness. 'But we need to present a united front. My parents are going to call. So are Lila's. We're getting our room back.'

Lila's eyes snapped away from hers, and with a rush, Nancy saw what had happened. 'You didn't ask yours either, did you?'

Lila at least tried to look ashamed of herself. 'Clarissa said she'd sign the slip and not tell my dad about the smoking. I didn't want to push my luck.'

Nancy had called her parents earlier. She had calmly discussed what had happened – that she and her friends had gone for a walk and found a packet of cigarettes on the ground, and now this new teacher was trying to assert dominance by making an example of them. Her mother had agreed that it was petty and unfair. Her father had told her he would complain about the dormitory immediately, noting that she had been talking about that room for years, and what incentive was there to stay on at a school like that into sixth form if it didn't come with any benefits? Someone of Nancy's academic calibre could get a place at Henrietta Barnett or St Paul's, without a moment's trouble. Fairbridge Hall should be happy. They should be grateful to have her.

'So neither of you asked your parents?' she repeated, frustration swelling in her chest. 'Thanks for telling me.'

Lila slid off the windowsill and stood up. 'My parents aren't like yours, OK?'

Georgia was playing with her nails, head down. 'Mine think if they make a fuss I'll lose my scholarship. It's different for them.'

Pathetic. It was like neither of them even cared that this was their penultimate year. They'd be gone before long. She'd be at Oxford, of course, and Georgia probably would too, assuming she could get her act together. But there was no way Lila was getting in, so, come next year they'd be scattered across the country. Why was she the only one who cared enough to try and give them a perfect last few terms together?

She got to her feet. This was ridiculous. They needed to take things into their own hands.

'I'm going to speak to her.'

'What?' Georgia looked worried.

'To Brandon?' asked Lila, who at least looked excited. Lila loved a good fight.

'Yes. Come on.'

Lila got to her feet. For a moment Nancy thought

Georgia was going to argue, but she didn't. Her face was impassive as she got to her feet.

'What are you going to say to her?'

'I'll be nice.'

'As if,' snorted Lila.

'I will. I'm just going to explain it to her. She's new, and she probably isn't aware, but she needs to respect the system. Sticking Lila in that room with disgusting Heidi and Jenny isn't going to make them friends. We pay her salary. She has to listen to us.'

'You can't say that to her,' whined Georgia.

'I know I can't,' said Nancy. 'I'm not stupid.'

'We should come up with a story,' said Georgia, fiddling with her hair. 'Tell them we need to keep an eye on Lila because of her mum and everything. Sorry, Li.'

'It's fine,' said Lila. 'But she didn't buy it before, with the smoking. I don't think she'll buy it now.'

'Well, let's say it's because of Nancy's eating then. They're shit scared she'll stop again.'

Georgia was right. The best thing to do would be to bring up that little black spot from the third year and act as if getting the right bedroom was the only way she'd be able to avoid a slip back into trouble. A complete lie, obviously. She was fine. Totally fine. It had been years. But a useful option. Yet something about it felt wrong. As if she would be cheating. She didn't want to beat Miss Brandon by using her trump card or telling a lie. She wanted the little bitch to realize that she couldn't play God with their lives. She was new, and she needed to learn. Nancy wanted to be the one to teach her that lesson.

'No. We're not doing that. We're doing it my way.'

'What makes you think she's going to listen to you?' asked Lila.

'She will,' said Nancy, as they tramped down the stairs towards the front office. 'If she doesn't listen, she'll regret it.'

Nancy raised her hand and knocked on the white door, her knuckles stinging as they hit the wood.

'Come in,' said the voice.

Nancy pushed the door open. It was wrong to see that woman sitting in her housemistress's place. Everything was the same, the green carpet, the rows and rows of books, the big white cupboards with all their labelled medications. But she looked wrong. She was too young, and too shiny. Her face was smug. Unlined. Not knowing how old she was irked Nancy. There could only be six or seven years separating them. Somehow, knowing exactly how many years it was seemed important. Like it would help Nancy better sum her up.

'How can I help?'

Nancy pulled out a chair and sat down. 'I feel like we got off on the wrong foot.'

Miss Brandon shifted in her chair, leaning her elbows on the desk. 'Oh?'

'Yesterday. Before term started. I think you might have the wrong impression of me, and my friends.'

'And what's that?'

Nancy smiled. 'We don't get in trouble. Not usually. We like to toe the line. We're all pretty set on going to good universities, we love the school. That kind of thing, it's just not us.'

Miss Brandon said nothing, so Nancy went on. 'Now I'm totally aware that we messed up. I shouldn't have been carrying cigarettes. It's something of an adjustment, coming back to school, having been at home for so long.'

'I can imagine that would be a strange transition.'

'Did you go to boarding school yourself?' she asked, knowing the answer. No one with an accent like that could possibly have been publicly educated.

'I went to grammar school.'

Nancy feigned sympathy. 'I think it's so sad that they're losing support. Grammar schools are so important.'

'You think so?'

Wrong-footed, Nancy went on. 'Well, they provide a wonderful education based on merit.'

'And you think that's important?'

Nancy wasn't sure what to say. This woman was not reacting like she was supposed to. She brushed her hair behind her ears and took a deep breath.

'Miss Brandon, you must be hugely busy, so I'll get to the point. I think there was some confusion about our room allocations. We had been promised the three-person room at the back of Reynolds. We've been waiting for it for years. It's quite important that we're with Lila, we're sort of like her family now.'

Miss Brandon said nothing, appearing to be considering her next move. Nancy appraised her figure. Her legs were long, her arms thin and her fingers, studded with gold rings, were long and slender. It was a far better body than she deserved. Nancy doubted that she had much use for it.

'The other girls didn't want to say anything?'

'They feel the same way,' said Nancy, resenting the implication.

'But you came in to talk to me?'

'I think they're a bit intimidated, with you being a new teacher and all.'

'Perhaps they don't share your feelings?' Miss Brandon raised her eyebrows high and her eyes sparkled just a little. She was taunting Nancy.

'They do.'

'Do you often find yourself speaking for them?'

'Is that relevant?'

'Watch your tone, Nancy.'

She had to keep calm. She must not explode. She must not let this woman get to her.

Nancy held her hands up. 'I apologize.'

Miss Brandon sat back down at the desk. 'I will tell you the same thing that I told your parents. The room allocations are final. We will take note of any requests for when everyone changes dormitory after the autumn term. If your behaviour has been adequate, I will consider putting all three of you together. But for now, why not let Lila enjoy her new room-mates? Changing things up is good. You should be doing the same. It's not healthy to be stuck in one small friendship group for the whole of school.'

Nancy took a deep breath. This bitch wasn't getting it.

'I'm doing my Oxbridge prep, Miss Brandon. I have an incredibly full schedule. I'm doing five AS levels. I don't have time for the drama of new friends. I need a solid support system around me.'

Brandon was smiling now. 'Amazingly, that's exactly what your parents said to me. Almost word for word. But surely even a busy girl like you can make some time for a bit of chatting with other girls in your year.'

'If you've spoken to my parents you'll be aware of how strongly they feel that my education shouldn't be disrupted.'

'I don't want to have to ask you to watch your tone again, Nancy.'

Her lips were moving before her brain could engage. 'My parents pay your salary, Miss Brandon. You should listen to their wishes.'

All she could do was listen as those words echoed around the room. The words that so many Fairbridge Hall girls had said in private before, but that no one – no matter how bold – ever dared say out loud to a member of staff.

Miss Brandon opened her mouth to speak, stopped herself and pursed her lips tight for a moment. 'You're hoping for Oxford, aren't you, Nancy?' she eventually said.

Nancy nodded, her eyes focused on a spot just above Miss Brandon's left shoulder. Brandon's unflinching calmness was unnerving.

'Go and stand outside my office.'

'I'm sorry?'

'Go and stand outside my office until I tell you that you can go.'

'I don't understand?'

'What's confusing you? I am punishing you. Go and stand outside my office. I'd suggest you take the time to reflect on how you came to have such a terrible attitude, until I dismiss you.'

She was joking. She had to be joking. She would laugh in a moment and tell Nancy that it was all a joke, she wasn't really sending her to stand outside the office, because she was in sixth form and no one would ever tell a sixth former to do something so humiliatingly juvenile.

'If I have to repeat myself once more, I will be taking your comments forward to the head. I hate to think how disciplinary actions might affect your university reference.'

Nancy stood up, mustering as much dignity as she could. Miss Brandon couldn't make her stand there, of course she couldn't. And one little disciplinary issue shouldn't interfere with her Oxford acceptance. But, she paused on the threshold. Imagine. Imagine if it did. If it was the reason she didn't get in, the reason that she had to spend three years at Durham or even worse, Bristol. Nancy crossed the threshold and took a smart step to the left and leaned her back against the wall.

Miss Brandon's office was just off the staircase that ran from the ground floor, up to the sixth-form dining room and then up to all the rooms of Reynolds House. There was no way of getting from your bedroom to the sixth-form supper without going down it. She looked at the clock. In six minutes they would come streaming down that staircase, running, pushing, sometimes sliding if no one was looking. If she was still here in six minutes, when the ancient bell started shrieking, then every single girl in Reynolds House would see her, and would know that, despite being in the sixth form, despite being Nancy Greydon who went to the BAFTAs last year, she had been forced to stand outside a teacher's office. And if that happened – if this new bitch was stupid enough to let that happen, Nancy would not stop until she felt Miss Brandon had been suitably punished in return.

She focused on the cold of the wall seeping through her back. If she leaned back like this it didn't look so much like she was standing here on instruction. Could she pass it off as being casual? Like she was waiting for someone?

The big hand on the clock seemed to click as it hit the six. The bell above it shrieked. Footsteps stirred. Nancy squeezed her eyes shut for a moment, trying to pretend that this wasn't happening, that it wasn't real.

But it was. She could hear mounting chatter now. Laughing. Shouting. By the end of supper, everyone would know.

There was nothing else for it. Nancy was going to ruin that smug little bitch's life.

NOW

Lila

'We should go inside,' said Lila, trying again to stand up. Nancy had told her to come inside, so they had to go inside.

'You're not going back in there until you've sobered up,' said Roo.

Roo was cross. He was cross all the time but he seemed extra cross now. He was grabbing her arm and talking way too close to her face. There was a fleck of spit on his chin and he was giving her those weird staring eyes he did sometimes. The garden felt warm. Could it be warm? It was February. It should have been the fourth month. Looking down at her arms she saw that they were tight with goose pimples. Maybe she wasn't warm. She tried to stand up but her legs didn't seem plugged in. She stumbled backwards on to the bench, feeling the dampness of the wood underneath her legs again. Her arse was wet. Why was the bench wet? It wasn't raining.

They used to have fun in the rain. But then, Roo used to be fun.

They'd met on a photo shoot. Roo had been dating one of the models. He'd been standing around on the sidelines looking bored while she pranced around, thigh deep in a pond in Clapham, wearing a fur coat. The setup was supposed to be 'all fur coat and no knickers' so the model was facing away from the camera, raising the coat to show her bare arse. Lila had styled it, and the budget was tight, so she was doing make-up as well, which meant constantly reapplying foundation to the girl's arse, which was pink from the cold. At some point, while Lila was calf-deep in water, trying to apply more without pulling the model out of the pond (where she might realize her feet had gone dead and push for a break) she had some- how fallen over, flat into the water. Her clothes were soaked, her hair was soaked, she hadn't even known it was possible to be that cold. Everyone else had been hor- rified but she and Roo had laughed until they were nearly sick. He'd taken her to look for a hot drink, leaving the shoot going on. They didn't go back. 'I've left all my shit there,' Lila had said, worried. Roo had merely laughed and said, 'I'll buy you new shit.'

'You're going to replace all of my make-up?' she had asked. So he hailed a taxi and took her to a department store. First of all, he bought her dry clothes, a pair of soft Seven for All Mankind jeans, a warm jumper – had it been Theory? Or maybe Sandro? She couldn't remember. And some ankle boots. Beautiful black ones with gold stars embroidered all over them. Her eyes had widened as the cashier rang them up, but Roo hadn't blinked. He'd just handed over his shiny black card and asked her where the make-up department was. He hadn't even seemed bored while she spent the next hour testing brushes and trying out different shades. He didn't know how much new make-up would cost, thought Lila to herself. And he didn't know how much she had had in her kit. The truth was, it was pretty skeletal, because her father had switched off the money tap six months before and she kept getting fired from temping jobs because temping was stupid and a waste of her time. But Rupert didn't know that. And if he was stupid enough to say he'd buy her an entire kit, he could buy her an entire kit.

When she handed over her basket, laden with expensive make-up, he looked surprised. 'Is that it?' he had asked. 'I thought you'd need more than that, as a professional.'

He had taken her job seriously back then. Or pretended to, at least. These days he didn't bother. There was no point in pretending. She knew he thought it was a sweet little hobby that she had indulged in until she became a wife and mother. Perhaps he was right. Maybe it wasn't a proper job. It wasn't like she'd ever made any money out of it.

He didn't have money like that any more. Lila wished she'd known then how much poorer they would be later, how Roo's job would go to shit because of that nasty business with a lying PA at his old office. That she wouldn't be the next Grace Coddington. Actually, she wouldn't be the next anything, other than maybe a nursery class rep in a year's time. Sometimes she looked around the room at playgroup, the one she dragged Inigo to once a week because it gave her something to tell Roo she had done, and she felt a sort of mist around her. She couldn't be like one of those women. She refused. It was too terrible a fate to consider. Imagine letting go of your body like that? Totally giving in to the ravages of time and age and fatness and not caring at all. What did their husbands think? Did they dutifully roll on top of them on Sunday morning and grope at their slack squashy breasts until they came, purely to be polite? Just to pretend that they still thought they were attractive.

Roo should be grateful. She'd made sure that that would never happen to her. She weighed herself every day. He got all angry with her when she got drunk at parties or there wasn't any food in the house, but he'd be furious if she gained weight. After Inigo was born, Roo had pushed his finger into her lower stomach and asked how long it would take to go away. It wasn't like there was even a question. Not 'if' it would go away. When.

She had considered eating again, eating properly, to punish him, to show him what it would be like to be with one of those mummies, the real ones. The ones he seemed to admire when he told her she should do more activities with Inigo and join in more and enjoy him more. But he would hate her if she did that, and when Roo was angry he was horrible. He had a skill for knowing what to say, the exact thing that would reduce her to absolute nothingness. He had come home one evening, when she was still trying to breastfeed because she had read how many calories it burned and because everyone kept telling her it was what real mothers did, and found her lying on the sofa in nothing but her knickers. Her nipple was bleeding, Inigo was screaming and she hadn't been able to bring herself to wear clothes. The flat smelt like the ready meal she had burned earlier, forgetting to peel back some plastic. Roo had poured himself a large whisky, looked her up and down and said, 'Sometimes I wish you had a mother to tell you what to do. Then you wouldn't be such a mess.'

Lila had sobbed, which had only made him angrier. He'd stormed out and weeks later she'd seen a night in a hotel in central London on their credit-card bill.

'Nancy said we should go inside,' said Lila, trying again. She pointed towards the door, though she wasn't sure why. It wasn't like Roo wouldn't know where inside was.

'I don't give a fuck what Nancy said.'

'I'm fine! It's a party, Rupert, people are drinking, that's what happens.'

'No one in that room is drunk, Camilla. Other people know when to stop.'

'Brett doesn't. He's an alcoholic. That's why he isn't drinking. Did you know that? Nancy told me.'

'He's not the only one,' Rupert muttered under his breath. Was she supposed to have heard that?

'What did you say?'

'Nothing,' he retorted.

'Yes, you did. Say it again. Say it.'

'I said he's not the only one. OK? He's not the only one who has a drinking problem.'

Stupid Rupert. Always so dramatic. So obsessed. So controlling. He wanted to be in charge of everything she did and that wasn't healthy or normal. She knew that for a fact, the magazines and websites all said so.

'I do not have a drinking problem,' she replied, trying

to enunciate every syllable so he couldn't accuse her of slurring her words. 'I am trying to have fun. Remember when we used to have fun?'

Even as she said it she questioned whether or not it was true. Had they had fun? They'd done fun things sometimes. Restaurants at the top of various very tall towers. Trips to obscure cities where Rupert would plan every single day from church visits to cocktail bars. But did they have fun? Was there laughing? It was hard to remember.

'Are you having fun tonight?' His voice was a bit softer now. He sounded less cross. Was he less cross, or was it because he'd remembered what Therapist Clarice had said at their last session about 'modulating their tone' when they talked?

Her head felt tight, like someone had wrapped a belt around it and pulled hard. She burped and felt bile burning the fleshy bit at the back of her throat. No. She was not having fun. Because this wasn't fun. There was nothing fun about shoving their husbands, who didn't really like each other, around Georgia's fancy hand-sanded kitchen table and trying to pretend that they still had stuff to talk about.

'Are you?'

She shook her head.

'We can go home, if you like.'

That would be worse. The babysitter would be cross that they'd come home early and Rupert would insist on paying her in full even though he'd started to get this tight look on his face every time he paid for something, like he was worried, or his money might run out. Maybe financially things weren't going well. She should look at the account. It was hers too, that's what he had said. But all those numbers seemed frightening, and what could she actually do if there was no money in there? She couldn't put any in.

'We can't.'

'Why not?'

'They'll all talk about me if we go.'

'They're probably talking about you now.'

'I know.'

'They worry about you.'

Lila laughed. 'Have you met them?'

'You three are so confusing.'

Lila pulled a cigarette out of the damp packet that lay on the bench next to her and held her hand out for a lighter. He didn't look pleased.

'Please?'

'I hate it when you smoke.'

'*You* smoke!'

'You know it's different.'

'It's not why. You know that. They said that's not why.'

Rupert didn't reply. 'If you don't like them, why are we here? Why do you spend time with them?'

'They're my best friends,' she replied, affronted.

'But you don't like each other.'

'You wouldn't understand.'

'Girls are so bloody complicated,' he sighed, sitting down next to her on the bench. 'Christ, that's damp. Aren't you cold?'

Lila shook her head, staring straight ahead into the

kitchen. The lights inside broadcasted the scene around the table. When Charlie and Georgia had bought the house, they had cheerfully knocked through the walls, or at least they'd paid some man with gold teeth to do it. Lila could imagine them, smug and newly married, holding hands as he swung the sledgehammer through walls that were older than America. She'd once suggested that she and Roo should do it at their house, to let more light in – Roo was always saying what great taste Georgia had. He'd told Lila not to be stupid. They couldn't afford it.

It was an enormous room now. Long and white and astonishingly clean. Every white tile gleamed. How much help did she have, Lila wondered. The smell of their kitchen was so familiar to her that she could conjure it instantly. Fresh flowers. Organic cleaning products. Garlic. Onions. Artificial sweet smells fighting with real, food ones. At the end of the room closest to the windows there was the dining table. The six of them, when they all sat around it, didn't fill it. There were twelve chairs. Georgia told a story about the saleswoman telling her she needed a smaller table because she was too young to need one that big. She did an impression of the woman, putting on a high-pitched nasal voice, and then smugly explaining how actually they'd had twelve people to supper at least once a month for their entire marriage. Lila had watched her lovingly massage wood polish into the auburn surface of the table time after time. She probably rubbed that table more often than she rubbed Charlie's cock. Poor Charlie.

Lila's parents had known Charlie's parents when they

were young. They'd all lived in Hong Kong at the same time, when living in Hong Kong meant money and champagne and success. They were friends. There were photos in an album somewhere. Charlie's mother and father with Lila's parents, laughing together in double-breasted suits and taffeta dresses. Charlie's mother had come up to her at Charlie and Georgia's wedding, while the bride and groom were having their fifteen thousandth picture taken. Charlie's mother had asked her how she was, and then said, without a hint of embarrassment, 'It should have been you, you know.' Lila had laughed and got away from Charlie's mother as quickly as she could. But looking into the kitchen, at how everything gleamed with cleanliness, she wondered if maybe Charlie's mother had been right.

THEN

Lila

Lila threw her school bag down on her bed and then collapsed next to it, lying on her back with her feet up on the wall. How was it only Wednesday? Two more hideous days of school, and then an entire weekend trapped here with sweet fuck-all to do. Last weekend she and Nancy and Georgia had spent three hours in the gym, then ruined it all by bingeing on snacks bought at the tuck shop because they were so bored. How did the boarders who were stuck here all the time cope with it?

Across the room, sitting on the bed Lila had always planned to have when she shared this room with Nancy and Georgia, was Jenny McGuckin, chewing on the wire from her headphones and staring up at the ceiling. Jenny sat up and pulled one earbud out of her ear. The tinny music spilled into the room.

'There's a note for you,' she said, not meeting Lila's eye.
'What?'

Jenny had barely spoken a word to her since they'd been forced into sharing a room. She pointed a stubby finger at a note on Lila's desk. The writing was turquoise and curved.

Lila – the cleaners have complained that it's impossible to hoover the floor because your clothes are everywhere, and it's not much fun for your room-mates either. I know you're busy, but please take half an hour this week to clean up. Miss Brandon

Lila rolled her eyes. 'She is such a colossal bitch.'

Jenny said nothing. Nancy would have launched into a whole discussion about what Miss Brandon's worst quality was, but Jenny just sat there with her bug eyes empty, saying nothing.

'How can the cleaners complain about cleaning? That's their job,' she said, grabbing at piles of clothes from the floor and shoving them into her wardrobe. Again, Jenny said nothing.

'Did you complain?' Lila turned to look at Jenny. 'This note says that you've got a problem with how I have my stuff. Is that true?'

Jenny shook her head.

'It must have been Heidi then.' Jenny didn't reply, and picked up her other earbud as if she was about to put it back in.

'Where is Heidi anyway?' asked Lila. 'We all have to be back here by ten.'

'Therapy,' said Jenny impassively. 'She comes in late because of it.'

'Therapy?' asked Lila.

Jenny nodded. 'In town.'

Since when was Heidi in therapy? What the fuck did she have to be that upset about? Why did she get some special dispensation to go into town and talk about her stupid life to someone and get back late? In what world was that fair?

'Why is she in therapy?' she asked Jenny.

Jenny shrugged. 'I don't know.'

'You must know something. You're her friend.'

Jenny's face was unchanged.

'You're telling me you've been sharing a room with her for however many years and you don't know what's going on with her? It's fine, you can tell me. I live with you guys now. I should know.'

'She's never said anything,' said Jenny, who had picked up her book and seemed increasingly less interested in talking about this.

'What does she say when you ask?' demanded Lila. If Heidi was in therapy it might be because she was telling tales about Lila, talking about how they used to be friends, about how Lila had ditched her. Lila had a right to know. Lila went to sit on the end of Jenny's bed, leaning in towards her. She caught a faint whiff of body spray and body odour. Lila realized Jenny hadn't changed out of her games kit since they'd had hockey that afternoon.

'I don't ask,' said Jenny. 'If you're so bothered about it then why don't you talk to her. That's why you're in this dorm, right?'

'I'm sorry?' Lila blinked at Jenny. 'What?'

'Forget it,' said Jenny, picking up her book.

'What about why I'm in this dorm?'

Jenny sighed, putting the book back down. 'I don't

want to get into this, I really don't want anything to do with you and your friends, OK?'

'It's no big deal,' Lila reassured her. 'I just don't understand what you mean.' That wasn't entirely true. Lila had a sneaking suspicion that she did know what it meant, that she knew exactly what Heidi had done, but she needed to hear it from Jenny to be sure.

'Heidi told me that she told her therapist she wanted to share a room with you.'

'What? Why?' Lila tried to repress Nancy's words, which were filling her head, the words about how Heidi fancied her, how she wanted to be more than friends.

'She said you were her friend. That you'd be there for her if things got bad again.'

'Bad?' asked Lila, trying to process it. 'Again?'

Jenny looked surprised. 'She tried to overdose in the holidays?'

Lila caught herself before the surprise could show on her face. 'Yeah, I know about that,' she said. 'I thought you meant things had got worse since then.'

Jenny looked confused. 'Look, this is between you and her. But I don't think she went to Miss Brandon about your stuff being on the floor. So don't have a go at her, OK?'

'OK,' said Lila, retreating to her side of the room. She shoved a wodge of clothing under her bed, finding one of her Ugg boots in the process. She'd been looking for it for days.

Heidi had taken an overdose. Lila desperately wanted to pump Jenny for information, to find out what she'd taken and how many – to assess how seriously she'd tried, whether it was an attention-seeking stunt or whether she'd really tried to die. But that would mean admitting that she didn't know about Heidi, that Heidi hadn't called her. Why hadn't she called?

They didn't speak often, it was true. And Heidi knew the rules. When they were at school they didn't speak, they didn't interact. Lila would deny all knowledge of their occasional phone calls at weekends, of the fact that they met up sometimes in the holidays when their mothers wanted to have lunch together. And in return for Heidi's silence, Lila kept Georgia and Nancy off her back.

And yet this had happened, and Heidi had said nothing. Instead she'd just ruined Lila's plan to share a room with her best friends. If Nancy ever found out – Lila stopped herself. Nancy could never find out.

As if she could hear Lila's thoughts, Jenny spoke across the void of carpet that lay between them. 'Lila?' she said.

'Yes?'

'Don't tell your friends about Heidi, OK?'

'I won't,' said Lila. 'Promise.'

NOW

Georgia

What was Roo thinking, taking Lila outside? As if that much wine could be dissolved by some cold air. But of course it wasn't about sobering her up. It was about shutting her up. Classic Roo, always treading on the end of their sentences and replying 'Well, actually . . .' to anything they said. Once they'd cleared the plates away – Lila's food left untouched – she knew what he'd do. He would clap his arm around Charlie and persuade him to go outside for a cigar. They'd make noises about 'leaving the girls to it' and stand out in the garden for most of the rest of the night, leaving her to clear up. Charlie would stink of that wet hay cigar smell all night.

Even in spite of Brett's idea to cover the meat with the sauce before it reached the table, it had still been dry. Why had she decided to do pork? It was the easiest meat to overcook, the hardest to get right, and no one even wanted it. She and Charlie had been to a dinner party weeks ago where a friend of theirs had served this exact dish and it had been effortlessly perfect. She'd carved it easily and the herby stuffing had sat in a neat ring in the middle of the joint. Georgia's version had not worked.

Dragging the knife through the flesh had been an enormous effort, and the stuffing had leaked, burning a sticky black crust on to the bottom of the pan. It sat soaking in her porcelain double sink, ready for the cleaner to deal with tomorrow morning. Charlie always liked them to have Larissa, who had cleaned for them for years, to come in the morning after a party. That way when he emerged from his shower around midday, he could make a bacon sandwich in a gleaming kitchen. Larissa charged them double to come at the weekend, and Georgia didn't blame her.

Pudding, at least, had worked properly. It was a huge wide ring of meringue topped with whipped cream and passion fruit. She pulled her phone out and snapped a picture, she'd post it in the morning.

'Can I help, darling?' asked Charlie. He'd left Nancy and Brett sitting at the table, laughing at something one of them had said. She'd been cooking all day without his help and he'd waited until now, seconds before they were about to eat dessert, to offer assistance. Why did people always do that?

'You can waiter for me, when those two come inside.'

'Might be a while,' said Charlie.

'What?'

'Outside. I reckon it'll be a while.'

'Why?'

Charlie looked embarrassed. 'No reason. But maybe we should start without them.'

Something was up. Charlie looked like a little boy who had been caught with contraband in his first term at prep school.

'We can't do that. What's up?'

Charlie stepped closer to her and threw a glance across the room to Nancy and Brett. They were still tied in conversation. She hoped Nancy would look up, see them obviously exchanging secrets and press her later to find out what had been said.

'I don't think I'm supposed to say anything.'

Georgia had learned years ago that the worst way to make someone tell you a secret was to push for it. If she showed Charlie how much she wanted to know, he would start to think what he had was valuable. If she treated it lightly, like she didn't care much, he wouldn't think it was anything to spill. She took the packet of strawberries out of the fridge and picked up a knife.

'Oh?'

'I mean, he didn't exactly say that I shouldn't.'

'Right.' Charlie was close to spilling. His tight forehead was so sweet. She allowed herself a second's vision. A little boy with Charlie's thatch of strawberry blond hair and serious face, scuffing his toe on the floor as he worked up the courage to tell her something. The picture brought her a warm happy feeling, a second rush of love towards Charlie that evening.

'I saw Roo at the Harbour Club last week. When I went for physio.'

Georgia knew immediately what was coming next. But she mustn't crowd it. The more she asked, the less detail she would get from him. Her therapist had a habit of leaving silence between them, which was supposed to push the patient to talk more. It didn't work in Georgia's case. She didn't like to be manipulated. But it was a sensible trick.

'He wasn't alone,' Charlie whispered to the floor, following Georgia close behind as she moved around the counter, plating up portions of pavlova.

'He wasn't?'

'He was with someone.'

'A friend?'

'A girl. A woman.'

She stopped, setting the plate down on the side. 'A friend?' she asked tentatively.

Charlie shook his head. 'He had his arm around her waist. They'd been playing tennis. He was all over her.'

She hadn't expected to feel sad. That was a surprise. An unwelcome one. There was no room for sadness. It was a shame. The whole big mess was a shame. But it couldn't be helped, and it would do no good to dwell on it. Another picture filled her mind: Lila, in her wedding dress – a see-through lace thing – her hair heavy with flowers, laughing and looking at Roo like he was her saviour.

'Don't tell anyone,' said Charlie, his face suddenly pinched again. 'He caught up with me in the changing room and started giving me all the guff about how she was an old friend from work, that Lila would be jealous if she found out, that she'd get the wrong end of the stick. He looked pretty spooked. I said I'd keep schtum, but she's not in a good way, is she? Do you think that's why they haven't come in? Do you think they're talking about it? On top of the miscarriage, it isn't good, is it?'

Georgia smoothed her hands over his temples and stroked his hair. 'I don't know. I won't tell anyone. I promise. I love you.'

He looked happier now. Would their sons be like him? Easily hurt, but easily healed. All his emotions swimming at the surface. She hoped so.

'You're sure they're sleeping together?'

He nodded. 'He had his tongue down her throat when I walked past him. Stupid cock.'

'In public?'

Another nod. 'Must have been going on for a while if he's got that lazy. I probably shouldn't have said anything—'

'Don't be silly. Anyway, you did the right thing. I can give Lila better advice this way.'

Charlie's face clouded. Georgia spoke before he could: 'I won't say a word. But if she's thinking about calling it a day, I would have told her to stick it out before. I won't now. OK?'

'You're sure?'

She nodded. 'Positive.'

THEN

Nancy

'Nance, your mum's on the phone,' yelled Katie. Nancy stood up, rolling her eyes. 'Can you tell her I'm busy, please?'

The common room was full of girls in pyjamas, splayed over sofas and floor cushions, playing with their phones or half watching the TV, just as it always was on weeknights.

'I tried,' said Katie. 'She said you'd say that, and she said that you can come and talk to her or she'll stop your allowance,' she laughed.

'Classic Allegra,' said Nancy, relishing her audience. The fact that she called her parents by their first names was something that the rest of the year never seemed to get bored of. As if it were some big deal, it seemed endlessly exotic. Not like their families. They were all so typically, tediously middle class. Most of them didn't even live in London. The girls only boarded because their parents liked the cachet of it, or because they couldn't be bothered to take the Land Rover across Hampshire in traffic to pick them up by five thirty.

'Yep?' she said, picking up the phone. There were

three phone booths in the downstairs hall at Reynolds House, and one on each floor. They each had an ancient armchair and a box of tissues, separated by thin plastic walls. She heard a flurry of Spanish from the cubicle next to her. It was clearly an emotional conversation; the girl would be glad of the tissues.

'Darling, it's me,' came a voice. 'Listen, I need you to do something for me.'

'I'm very well, thank you. No, I didn't flunk my exam this morning and yes, I am looking forward to seeing you when I'm eventually unbarred from this place,' said Nancy deliberately. She sat down on the floor of the cubicle, the phone cord stretching as far as it could. She scraped her knuckles over the carpet. It had to be thirty years old. God this place was shabby. Boys' schools probably had proper modern phone booths with nice, new carpets.

Her mother was laughing. 'Sorry, sorry, I know. I'm the worst mother in the world.'

It was an old joke. If you could call it a joke.

Her mother had written a column for a broadsheet until Nancy was seven. It was called 'the worst mother in the world' and it largely consisted of a series of anecdotes about how Nancy had been unplanned, how Allegra hadn't been prepared to be a mother. The picture that accompanied it each week showed her, beautiful and aggressively thin, at a desk, with a cigarette in one hand. She looked the picture of a writer, only Nancy was sitting on the desk, clutching a fountain pen in her fist. She was covered in ink. Allegra still told people the story of that day – how the photographer had come along and found Allegra in nothing but T-shirt and knickers, trying to clean up four-year-old Nancy, who had tried to suck on the end of the pen.

It was a complete lie, of course. The whole thing had been set up. Nancy could still half remember the photographer dabbing her skin with the ink, while her mother stood around chatting with him. Did Allegra believe her own story by now, Nancy wondered. How often do you have to repeat a lie before it becomes true?

'What do you need?' she said, pulling herself back to the conversation.

'I've heard a rumour,' her mother said. 'And I think there's a feature in it.'

Whenever anything interesting happened in any of their lives, Allegra would cry 'That's a feature!' Her friends thought that Nancy's parents were amazingly, gloriously welcoming. They loved sleeping over, they were always invited to. But they didn't realize that they were paying rent with their stories. Allegra and Daniel didn't turn a blind eye to smoking and forgo curfews because they were nice. It was because they needed young people. They'd always bemoan their daughter's tendencies. 'She's just so bloody mature,' her father would say at dinner parties. 'I know it sounds like a dream but honestly, we were banking on her to keep us relevant!'

Clearly, it was a brag. He only cloaked it in an insult so no one would think that he was praising her.

'What rumour?' Nancy asked.

'One of the girls interning in the office has a friend

who's recently started working at a boarding school. Her name's—'

'Miss Brandon,' said Nancy flatly. 'She's the one who barred us.'

There was a pause.

'Ah. Does that mean you're not exactly simpatico?'

'You could say that,' replied Nancy. 'She's a cunt.'

Her mother sighed. 'Darling, cunt is a celebratory word for a beautiful organ.'

Nancy said nothing.

'Anyway,' her mother went on. 'I have gossip about what she's going to do.'

'Yes?' said Nancy.

'Well, if you're not interested, darling . . .' her mother trailed off. Nancy knew this game. Her mother wanted to tell her, but she was stubborn enough to withhold if she didn't feel suitably appreciated.

'I am,' she said quickly. 'What's going on?'

'Well,' her mother said slowly. 'That's why I'm calling. Have you heard anything about this social next month?'

'The one with Whitlowe School?'

'Yes. Apparently, it's not happening—'

'Not happening? But everyone's been planning outfits. Lila's decided she's finally going to get off with Jack Bull.'

'Well,' her mother sounded excited now, 'this girl at work says that Phoebe – Miss Brandon – thinks these socials are outdated and antiquated and sexist. So she's cancelling it.'

'I'm sorry?' Nancy's head was hot. She gripped the phone. 'What?'

'Yes, there's going to be an announcement. I mean, you can see her point. The way they get you all dressed up and then send you over to a boys' school and then let you flirt for a few hours and God knows what else, and then bring you home. It's like they're trying to get you all married off, isn't it?'

'Or like they're trying to make sure that we don't go an entire half-term without seeing a member of the male species,' Nancy ground out from between her teeth.

'Anyway,' her mother went on, 'the exciting bit is that, because it's called a "social" and she wanted to replace it with something, she's planning a different event.'

Nancy didn't want to ask. But she had to know. 'What kind of event?'

'Not sure yet. It sounds like it'll be all about you girls working together.'

Nancy considered smacking the phone against the wall of the phone booth, wondering if she could hit it hard enough to shatter the white plastic.

'Nancy?' echoed her mother's voice.

'Yes, I'm here,' she replied. 'They haven't told us about it yet.' She wanted to add that it was a fucking ridiculous plan and she felt sick at the idea that the school was trying to score attention and publicity instead of letting them see the guys they'd been friends with for years.

'I was wondering how you felt about it, darling?' Allegra said. Great. She wanted a quote.

'I think the social enterprise aspect is a wonderful idea,' said Nancy, tossing her hair back. 'However, I do feel there is some issue in attempting to break down the existing relationship between the Fairbridge Hall girls and the Whitlowe boys. Many of us have been friends for years,' she finished.

'You're a star,' her mother said. 'I might need to rough it up a bit though, to make you sound more like a normal teenager.'

I'm not a normal teenager, Nancy wanted to reply. You pay thousands of pounds a term for me not to be a normal teenager.

'No problem. You'll skewer her, right?'

Her mother laughed. 'Obviously not. Think how Fairbridge would react! Imagine if they kicked you out and you had to move back home with me and your father.'

'Imagine,' replied Nancy flatly.

'One other thing – if any of your friends try to talk to the press, remind them it's against the code of conduct for the school, and they can get suspended,' Allegra giggled. 'That way I've got an exclusive.'

'Sure thing,' said Nancy as she tangled her finger in the cord of the phone.

'Fairbridge are going to love it. They'll probably give me a discount on your school fees.'

If there was one thing her mother liked more than a scoop, it was getting something for free that other people had to pay for. The idea of it revolted Nancy.

'What are you up to tonight?' she asked her mother.

'Tonight? We've got people over for supper, and we've got to make some wall space because we've got that painting being delivered tomorrow. How about you?'

'Nothing much,' said Nancy quietly. She could see her

mother standing in the kitchen, leaning against the counter, doodling as Nancy spoke, drawing trees and flowers on the notepad where her quote was written. She could almost smell the toast and laundry aroma that filled it. To her shame, she felt a huge wave of homesickness swallow her. It had been years since she'd felt that. Homesickness was permissible during the first weeks of school when you were eleven, not when you were about to turn seventeen.

She started to ask, 'It wouldn't be so bad if I lived at home, would it?' but at the same time her mother said, 'Well, I'd better go, darling. Chin up.'

Nancy didn't say anything. Tears were spilling on to her cheeks. Ridiculous, inexcusable tears.

'Nancy?'

'Yes. Have a good evening,' she managed to force out, before reaching up and clapping the handset back into the cradle. She sat still for a moment, pressing her hands tightly into her eyes to stop the crying. She told herself that she was waiting for the flush in her face to recede before she could walk out of the booth. But she knew that she was waiting to see if her mother had caught the break in her voice, whether she would call back.

Nancy gave herself until the count of forty. If by forty her mother hadn't rung back, she would go.

At twenty-seven, the phone rang. She snatched up the handset. The voice on the other end was thick with an accent. 'Is Rocio able to speak on the phone?' it asked.

'Sure,' she sighed. 'I'll go and find her.'

Nancy stepped from the phone booth, intending to make a half-hearted attempt at finding Rocio before telling the person on the phone that they'd have to call back. But as she looked down the corridor, she was confronted with a sea of backs clad in floral pyjama bottoms and hoodies, the default uniform in winter.

'What's going on?' she asked as everyone continued to file past her.

'No idea,' replied Carmen, a tall Spanish girl whom Nancy had a begrudging respect for on the basis of her toned upper arms and impressive academic record.

'Nance!' called Lila from behind her. She ran up, wrapping her arms around Nancy's shoulders.

'There's a house meeting,' said Georgia, pulling her jumper down over her hands. 'God knows why.'

Nancy doubled back and hung up the phone, not bothering to tell whoever was on the other end that Rocio wasn't around.

'I think I know,' said Nancy darkly. The sofas in the common room were already full so they grabbed a couple of the floor cushions from the pile in the corner and collapsed, cross-legged, in a heap.

'What?' asked Lila.

'She's cancelling the social.'

'Social?' asked Georgia. 'Why?'

'Cancelling the social?' asked someone from behind them.

'I wasn't talking to you, Harriet,' Nancy snapped.

'They're cancelling the social?' Nancy heard the words moving around the room. Perfect. It would have been utterly infuriating to have known first and done nothing with it. Admittedly, it would have been more fun to have done something – organized some kind of protest or petition – before Brandon even announced it, but still. Better than nothing.

'Guys, can I have your attention?' a voice came from the back of the room. Brandon was standing in front of the TV. This long room, high-ceilinged and lined with books, was where they did everything. Prep was here, house meetings, movie nights. All of it happened here. House meetings were usually only once a term, a bollocking about their rooms not being tidy enough and an announcement that because it was the end of the term they'd be subjected to double chapel before they were allowed to go home.

Miss Brandon pulled a chair out and sat on it, cross-legged. What an affectation.

'So, I want to talk to you all about the social next week.'

Silence. Brandon ran her hands through her hair and pulled it up into a messy bun. She'd clearly changed into her 'house' clothes after teaching all day. As if wearing the same Abercrombie tracksuit bottoms that the rest of them wore was somehow going to make them like her more. 'I wanted to have a word with you about the upcoming social. I wanted to discuss whether we feel like this type of thing is what we really want to be doing with our time.'

The room erupted with whispers. 'Guys!' she said over the noise. 'We need to all have our say, we can't just whisper to each other.'

'She's pretending that we get a say in it,' Nancy whispered to Lila.

'I fucking hate her,' Lila whispered back. Georgia's face was in profile, looking resolutely at Brandon. She wouldn't join in, of course. Nancy wasn't unsympathetic to the whole scholarship thing, but Georgia could be a bit precious about it when she wanted to. No one got their scholarship taken away for getting one detention.

'I'm going to tell you my thoughts about the whole thing and then we'll talk about it. OK?'

A murmur of assent.

'So, I didn't go to a school like this, I never had one of these socials, but to be honest they seem really, really weird to me.' She paused. God, she was such a drama queen. 'You guys are amazing. You're smart and bright and charming and you've got these incredible futures ahead of you.'

Get on with it, thought Nancy.

'So the idea that on a weekend we just let you, encourage you really, to put a load of make-up on and then stick you on a bus and drive you to a boys' school, like you're some kind of delivery, and then leave you to pretend to have a normal social life for like three hours, before bringing you home, it's not something that I feel comfortable with. You guys are better than that. Right?'

Nancy tried not to smile. This woman had no authority, she didn't even try to speak like a grown-up around them. Who did she think she was? Any minute now she was going to open the floor and the rest of the girls were going to show the silly bitch exactly how little she knew about them, and it was going to be great.

'I'm not saying that you shouldn't spend time with boys – obviously you should. I'm saying that we should be bringing boys to you! We should be organizing more normal ways for you to hang out – like activities. I mean, how many of you actually want to start making out with a guy in front of your teachers? That's weird! If we revamp the system, you'll probably end up seeing *more* boys!'

There was another murmur, but to Nancy's horror, it didn't sound like anger. It sounded like she was winning them over. Heidi was sitting at the front of the group, nodding along with everything Miss Brandon said as if her neck was in spasm.

'So,' Miss Brandon looked around the room. 'We're going to take a vote. If the majority want to cancel the social, we'll cancel it. But if you don't think it's outdated or sexist and you still want it, we'll go ahead.'

Nancy pushed her hand into the air. 'Can't we just go to the social if we approve of it, and not go if we don't?'

'Please wait to be asked to speak, Nancy,' she replied.

Jesus Christ, it was like being back at nursery.

'Can't we though?' asked Lila.

'I understand why you're asking,' Miss Brandon replied, smiling at Lila, 'but no, we can't, and I'll explain why after we take the vote. So, is everyone ready? Good. If you'd like to change the way that we do socials, put your hand up now.'

Unadulterated horror filled every cavity of Nancy's body as she watched the hands go up. All of the loser group, who would have stood around the sides of the social looking tragic. Half the Chinese girls. A chunk of the horsey group. Miss Brandon was looking smug as she counted. 'Thirty-five votes for change! That's more than half of you, so I guess it's motion carried.'

Nancy got to her feet.

'Where are you going, Nancy?' asked Miss Brandon, who was clearly trying to sound relaxed.

'Sorry, is the meeting not over?' she snapped.

'No,' smirked Brandon. 'It's not.'

Nancy sat back down, her heart thudding. It was about to get worse, though she wasn't sure how.

'I've been wanting to put together a house team-building activity for you all, but it's been difficult because so many of you are weekly boarders who go home at the weekend.'

It was true. But that was how it was supposed to be. All the losers with no friends and the foreign girls would stay at the weekends. They'd be forced to do pathetic activities like going to see some embarrassing musical in London or taking a nature walk. Anyone who wasn't completely tragic would get picked up on Saturday morning after lessons, to be driven home or to stay with friends, and would spend the weekend doing stuff that was actually fun.

'But, all of the weeklies who'd usually be going home have signed up to stay in for the weekend because of the social. So . . . I've put together a plan. We're all going away for a girls' weekend!'

Half the room started to chatter with excitement. The other half remained painfully silent.

'I'm getting in touch with all of your parents tomorrow,

but basically we'll be heading up to a mystery location, doing a trek in teams and then camping out overnight. We'll do songs, make s'mores, all the camping classics!'

What was this, a bad American film? Didn't she realize that no one in this room had any idea about the 'camping classics'? Holidays for them meant Mauritius, Val d'Isère, Tuscany, the South of France, the Hamptons. Holidays were not backpacks and walking. And certainly never, ever, camping.

'Permission slips go out tomorrow! Thank you all for being such game young women! I'm so excited to see what a difference we can make together.'

Brandon got up and threw her arms out, as if she was trying to hug the room. The losers filed out, excitedly chattering, leaving a group of girls sitting ashen-faced and furious.

'What the fuck was that?' said someone behind Nancy.

'Is she on crack?' asked someone else.

Georgia draped her arms over Nancy, resting her head on her shoulder. 'Well, that's some good news, at least.'

'Why?' Nancy asked.

'Now other people hate her as much as you do,' she said. 'I don't think we'll have to put up with her for long.'

NOW

Lila

Looking through the French windows into the kitchen was like watching a play. Nancy was talking, while Brett and Charlie watched her. Georgia stood at the other end of the kitchen, holding a knife, slicing something. Her face was pink and some of her hair had stuck to her face. It must be hot in there. It would be nice to be hot.

'Roo, let's go away.'

'What?'

'Tomorrow. Let's go to the airport and catch a flight to somewhere and go. Just us.'

He chuckled. 'It's a nice idea.'

'So, let's do it.' She turned to put her hands on his legs. 'Please?'

Roo almost never wanted to be spontaneous. Holidays had to be booked and planned. The only time he'd ever given in to her whim, he'd called in sick and they'd fled to Devon. Rented a cottage on the beach. It's where they had conceived Inigo. Roo had grumbled all the way there in the car. He said it was a waste of time to go away in England, that he'd probably be fired for turning his phone off. It wasn't a proper break because it didn't involve a plane, if they were going to the south-west, why couldn't they go to Polzeath at Easter like everyone else did. Lila had said nothing, but watched the greyness give way to greenness out of the window of the car. Roo had driven, naturally. He didn't like it when she drove. His mood had worsened, but when they finally arrived, he had understood. The river was dark green, and the water was cold. He'd smiled as he watched her peel off her clothes and throw herself into the water. She'd told him how she liked this water, with its green-brown tint, far more than a swimming pool which looked so temptingly blue but was impossible to hold in your hands. They'd jumped and splashed and played in the water like children, Roo's bad mood forgotten, left behind in London along with everything else.

She hadn't told him, though, that she had been there once before, decades ago. Her mother had bundled her and her brothers into the car and driven them to Devon in the middle of the night. She must have known she was ill then, Lila realized. It had been a perfect day. They had played in the same river, throwing themselves off the bank and into the water, fighting and jumping and laughing until their tummies hurt. The mud had seeped between their toes and under their nails. When they got home, her mother had put her in a bath, the water stingingly hot, and she marvelled at how the water turned brown, at the grit left in the bottom of the bath. She wasn't sure why she didn't tell Roo then. Or why she'd never found the words to tell him since.

'You know we can't.'

'Why not?'

'We have a child? I have a job? It would cost a fucking bomb?'

The buoyancy in her chest deflated. She should have known he would say no. If he had said yes that would have meant he loved her. He had to know how much she clung to the idea of escaping, and yet he wouldn't let her have it. She said nothing, slumping back in her seat and staring into the house. Brett looked bored. Nancy was boring him. She'd want to talk about books and exhibitions and things like that, not real stuff. Brett would want to talk about real stuff, surely.

'Why don't you care?' she asked, pricking the silence.

'I do care,' Rupert replied, leaning forward and putting his hands through his hair. 'I really do.'

'It was our child.'

'We have a child.'

'We had two.'

'No, Cam, we didn't. We have one healthy, wonderful little boy who loves you. And we had a miscarriage. A miscarriage is not a baby.'

'It was to me,' she replied quietly.

Rupert stood up. 'I don't know what to say, Cam. We've tried the therapy twice, we've seen the doctors. You won't stop drinking, so those pills are sod all use. Is this it? Is this all I get? Because it's been two months and I can't do this for much longer. I want my wife back.'

'I'm right here,' she said, because it seemed like the right thing to say.

Roo looked sad. He wasn't a sad person. It wasn't a face she was used to him making.

'I miss you,' he said. 'I don't understand you. What's going on in there? I wish you'd be honest with me and tell me what you're thinking, what's going on in there.' He reached forward and tapped his finger against her head.

'I wish I could,' she said. It was true. She dreamed about saying the words out loud and feeling them weaken with every person she told. But she knew the rules. Never say it, never think it, never even think about telling anyone. 'There isn't anything to tell,' she said. 'We should go inside.'

'Are you sure?'

'Are you going to talk to me if we stay out here?'

He didn't meet her eye. 'I don't know what else there is to say.'

'Say that you're sorry. Say that you give a shit that our baby died.'

'It wasn't a baby, Camilla. Inigo is a baby, our baby. And he's at home with a babysitter and you haven't touched him in weeks.'

The sky was moving up and down, pressing into her and pulling away. There was laughing inside. Probably about her and Rupert. About how they couldn't get through one dinner without her passing out, about how she drank too much and didn't have a proper job or any other friends because she was boring and a shit mother.

How dare they? She might have expected it from Nancy, but Georgia? Anyway, she didn't need them to tell her any of those things. As if she didn't already know.

Her teeth felt numb. She stood up, this time managing to control her sway as she walked towards the house. She ground the half-smoked cigarette into the patio floor, she knew it would piss Georgia off.

'Cammy – please.' She turned; Rupert hadn't moved from his spot at the end of the garden. 'We can go home now – make an excuse. We can be with Inigo.'

It would be easy to say yes. His stupid soft face would light up and he'd be happy. But he shouldn't be happy. He should be sorry. He should be sad, sad like she was. He probably just wanted to save money on the babysitter.

'Lighten up, Roo. It's a party. Go inside, OK? I'm having one more cig and then I'll be in. Just stop being such a killjoy, OK?'

He walked straight past her, pulled open the glass door and slammed it behind him. He didn't even look at her.

NOW

Georgia

Georgia glanced up at the clock on the wall, a huge copper thing that she'd chosen for her thirty-second birthday. She had dropped dozens of hints to Charlie about it, but still acted surprised when it arrived. Roo and Lila had been outside for too long. 'Nancy,' Georgia called across the kitchen. 'Shall we go out and check on Lila?'

'Sure,' Nancy replied with a smile.

Lowering her voice, Georgia turned to Charlie, 'Will you go and keep Brett company? He's probably feeling a bit lost with all this drama.'

'What's going on?' Nancy asked, sotto voce, as Georgia opened the French windows.

'Roo's sleeping with another woman.'

The smile on Nancy's lips wouldn't have been called a smile by anyone else, anyone who hadn't watched her win arguments for the better part of a decade.

'Perfect,' she purred.

Trying to shake the sense of disquiet that had settled at the pit of her stomach, Georgia watched the way her shiny hair caught the light from the kitchen. Nancy was moving through the open door as Roo marched past, hitting shoulder to shoulder with Nancy, striding into the kitchen and picking up a glass of wine that probably wasn't his. Nancy stumbled slightly, knocked off the edge of the heel of her ankle boots.

'Hey,' said Brett, getting up. 'Watch it.'

Lila was standing outside, swaying, a cigarette hanging from between her chapped lips. Georgia leaned out. 'Come inside, Lila. It's freezing.'

To her surprise, Lila listened. She dropped the cigarette on the ground and came to the door. 'What did Roo do?' she asked.

Georgia followed her eyeline as she closed the door. Roo was sitting at the far side of the table, refilling his glass, and Brett was standing squarely above him. 'Calm down, mate,' Georgia heard Roo say.

'I'm calm,' Brett replied. 'But you pushed my fiancée. You owe her an apology.'

Roo smirked. 'I didn't realize you needed protecting, Nance? How does this fit with your feminist ideology?'

'Shut up, Roo,' said Nancy, taking her seat at the table. 'It's fine, Brett.'

'It's not fine. He smacked into you, he should apologize.'

'Just say you're sorry, mate,' said Charlie lightly.

'It's fine,' replied Nancy, her voice tight. 'It's not a big deal.'

'See?' said Roo. 'She's a big girl.'

Brett's hands were clenched. Georgia tried not to look at them. 'Does anyone want more water?' she called out. It was a stupid thing to say. Pointless. No one even bothered to reply.

'Fine,' said Brett. 'But if you'd done that in a bar I'd have kicked your ass.'

Roo laughed. 'You need a drink, mate, relax. I can smell the testosterone coming off you.'

Georgia watched as Brett pulled himself up to full height, towering over Roo, who was slumped smugly in his chair, smiling. The red wine had stained the insides of his lips. How could Lila go to bed with him every night, Georgia wondered. Was there a moment at some point in their marriage where Lila had suddenly realized that her husband was a total arse? Or did she not see that people's faces dropped when they realized they were going to be obliged to sit next to Roo at a dinner party? Did Lila notice how people switched off the moment that Roo started lecturing the room about politics?

'I don't want to fight you, bro,' said Brett in an even voice. 'I just want you to say you're sorry to Nancy.'

Roo looked up. From where he was sitting, Brett must have looked angry and huge because Roo cocked his head to the side, looked at Nancy and smiled. 'Sorry, Nance. Didn't mean to bump into you. Are you OK?'

Two dark-red patches had appeared on Nancy's cheeks. 'I'm fine.'

'Please can you come live with us and make Roo apologize when he's horrible?' said Lila. Every head in the room turned to look at her. She was eerie by the door, white top, white skin, blonde, almost white hair standing in contrast to the blackness of the night outside. She giggled. 'I was joking!'

Georgia forced herself to laugh. Nancy sniggered. Roo guffawed ostentatiously. The stone in the air broke and Georgia allowed herself a little sigh of relief. 'Are we ready for pudding?'

NOW

Nancy

Nancy waited until everyone was distracted, and then she made her move. 'Can I borrow you for a sec?' she whispered in Brett's ear, smiling.

'What do you need, baby?'

'Just follow me.'

She could feel his eyes on her as she walked out of the kitchen, up the stairs and slipped into the bathroom on the first floor. It was ridiculously big. Georgia had probably ripped out a perfectly good bedroom to make way for this enormous copper free-standing bath which probably took about half an hour to fill. Heavy robes hung on the back of the door and she was pretty sure she could see a basket of hotel slippers. Nancy tried not to scream.

The door knob twisted and Brett stepped into the room. She slid the heavy bolt across the door and ran the tap.

'What's going on, baby?' He looked confused, taking in the locked door and the running tap.

'What the fuck was that?' she ground out through her lips.

'What?'

'Why did you do that?'

'Do what?'

Nancy slammed her open palm against the pale blue wall. 'That display. Just now. Downstairs.'

Brett's face was a picture of hurt and confusion. 'What do you mean? Nancy, I don't understand, what did I do?'

'That whole "apologize" stunt you pulled. What was that about? What the hell did you think you were doing?'

'He bumped you?'

'And?'

'He should have apologized.'

'Of course he didn't apologize. He's a cunt, Brett. He's spoiled and selfish and he doesn't apologize, that's who he is. That's his thing. He's a nasty little man.'

'Why are you mad at *me*?'

Nancy sat on the edge of the bath, trying to calm her thudding heartbeat. 'You humiliated me.'

'Humiliated you? I was protecting you.'

'I don't need protecting.' Her voice was louder than she had anticipated. Not by much, but the lapse in control frightened her. She lifted her chin, slowing her breathing.

It was OK. The evening was affecting her more than she had realized. She had let it get to her. It was time to stop. There was nothing to be gained by starting a fight with Brett – Brett who didn't matter in the slightest. He wouldn't understand. She was only doing this because she was angry she'd lost her chance to get Lila alone with Georgia, because she was worried that Georgia might actually have been right, that things were as bad with Lila as she had feared. But none of that was on Brett.

Brett had nothing to do with any of it. She shouldn't have brought him here. She shouldn't have made him part of this whole hideous spider's web.

'I'm sorry,' she said slowly. 'I didn't mean to raise my voice.'

Brett smiled, so easily won over. 'It's OK.'

'No,' she said. 'It's not. Really. I am sorry.' Some people, she knew, found it difficult to apologize when they didn't feel that they had done anything wrong. Even at work she saw full-grown adults refusing to say things because they didn't 'believe' them, even when it would have made things easier and neater. She'd never understood that. Even at school, when other girls were wrongly accused and refused to take the blame. She had known that a good apology got you miles further than shouting and scream-ing that it wasn't you and that it wasn't fair.

'Don't be,' he said. 'I'm kinda glad that you did, if I'm honest.'

'What?'

'I'm kind of glad you yelled.'

'Stop it,' she replied.

'No – really. It's good that you're letting go a bit,' he said. 'I feel like I'm getting to see the real you when you do stuff like that.'

She dipped her head, letting her hair hang around her, buying herself some valuable privacy. She was suddenly very aware of his eyes on her skin. His gaze was heavy on her. This wasn't how it was supposed to be. He wasn't that smart. He wasn't supposed to see through her arti-fice. Even if she had become lazy, even if she'd allowed a tiny chink in her armour, she had chosen him because he was average enough not to be able to tell.

'I do,' he went on. 'Really.'

'You want me to shout at you?' She reached for his neck, smiling suggestively. Perhaps she should go down on him? Anything to distract from this hideous situation, from his desire to claw her open and understand things that didn't need to be understood, that were better left alone.

Brett laughed. 'OK, so I don't want you to yell at me exactly, but I want you to know that when you're really mad you can yell. We're going to be married a really, really long time. You have to be able to be real with me.'

No we're not and no I don't, thought Nancy.

'You're right, baby,' she smiled.

She had known that she couldn't marry him, of course not, he would be scared of her parents and the idea of co-hosting dinners with him made her feel nauseous. But she had become fond of him. She had occasionally pondered the idea of keeping him on as a bit on the side. She knew now that that could not be allowed to happen. She couldn't keep the puppy. She needed to take the puppy back to the pound, where it belonged.

But not yet. Not until this evening was finished and she had done what needed to be done with Georgia and Lila, and they were safely back in Boston where Brett couldn't touch the world that existed here.

THEN

Lila

There was a knock at the door of Nancy and Georgia's dormitory, and just as Lila was opening her mouth to form the words 'piss off' it opened. Not waiting until someone said to come in was up there among the worst sins imaginable at Fairbridge Hall. Probably because they all woke up together, had lessons together, ate lunch together, lay around the common room together and spent the entire evening hanging out. Privacy, at least a tiny film of it, was the only thing that made life bearable. Without it, you had pretty much nothing.

Lila was conscious that all three of their heads spun towards the door at the exact same time, like they were puppets on the same strings.

From behind the door stepped Miss Brandon. Lila's heart thudded in her chest. Nothing good would come of this visit. She'd already ruined the dorms and the social. What was she going to do now?

'Phones please, ladies,' she said brightly. In her hand was a wide flat box full of padded envelopes.

None of the girls said anything.

'Ladies?' said Miss Brandon. She was putting on a fake

cheerful voice. She clearly wanted them to think that she was fine, that this was no big deal. But Lila could see the way that her fingers were digging into the box. It was piss-easy for her to be brave and up herself when they were in class, or there were other teachers around. But she was on their turf in the dorms. She hadn't done her trick of changing into 'house' clothes this evening. Some-one clearly wanted to retain their armour. Lila looked her up and down, slowly drinking in everything from the shoes (pink ballet pumps, shamefully similar to a pair that Nancy owned) to the navy trousers and cream blouse. She had a body underneath it – her tits were pretty perky and while her blouse wasn't giving much away, she clearly had a waist. She was young. That was what was so weird about her.

How could anyone be twenty-six and such a knob? And how could anyone be twenty-six and want to be stuck at Fairbridge Hall? Twenty-six was for living in London and having friends and going to parties. Twenty-six was about sleeping with guys who bought you nice stuff. Twenty-six was not supposed to be tragically loafing around a girls' school pretending to be some kind of inspiration and all the while torturing teenagers because you didn't grow up with the same privileges they had.

'Sixth form don't hand their phones in,' said Nancy. They all knew what was coming. But they needed to hear it from her. They needed the actual words to leave her actual mouth so that they could believe that it was happening.

'We've had a re-think on the technology rule,' Miss

Brandon said, again with this hideous happy voice. 'When it was originally implemented, phones only made calls and texts. Now you girls are getting all sorts of new hi-tech phones, there's so much pressure on you all, with guys texting you and this new social media. We thought it best if we take them away at night to make sure that you get a good night's sleep – we're only trying to protect you.'

The girls said nothing. 'There's a lot of research about how the blue light can stop you from achieving restful sleep,' she added.

Lila stared at Georgia, who was fiddling with the fringe of the blanket on her bed, seemingly intent on not looking up.

'Cookie always said we'd be old enough to make sensible decisions by the time we were in sixth form,' said Lila. 'It's supposed to be one of the perks.'

Miss Brandon leaned against the wall, lowering the box of phones, her smile fixed in place. It was like she was in some bad amateur dramatics production.

'Getting to the top of the school isn't about perks,' she said, 'it's about responsibility.'

'Surely it can be about both?' said Nancy, who had pulled up to her full five foot ten. 'Responsibilities are supposed to be tempered with benefits, no?'

Brandon looked perturbed. 'It's probably not a debate for tonight.'

'Is it a debate we can have another evening?' Nancy asked. 'I think a policy change like the removal of our phones would probably merit some kind of year-wide discussion?'

Lila could see that Georgia was worried. She had that expression like she was going to cry and be sick at the same time. Obviously she was in a complete panic that this discussion would somehow result in their barring being extended, meaning she'd have to go even longer without a weekend at home. Much as Georgia hated missing out, she'd bail on weekends at Nancy's place in London to hang out with her mum. Georgia was soppy about her family. Even when her brother wasn't going away. Why she should feel that way was a mystery to Lila. Georgia's house was sort of depressing, what with the carpets and the crockery and her younger brothers sharing a bedroom, and everyone using the same bathroom every morning. When they stayed at Georgia's house her parents were so parenty, always asking them how things were going and how their results had been. It had taken, like, a year before they'd told Nancy and Lila not to call them Mr and Mrs Green. Nancy said it was because they were common.

'The phone policy isn't up for discussion,' said Miss Brandon. 'But if you've got any other suggestions about how we could run the house better, you know where the suggestions box is.'

'So it's a dictatorship now?' said Lila.

'No, Lila, it's a school. And schools have rules.'

Lila opened her mouth to tell Miss Brandon that they'd looked her up and they knew she hadn't been to a real school, or a proper university, so what would she know about rules? But Georgia interrupted.

'Here's my phone, Miss Brandon,' she said sullenly. She held out a Nokia 3310. Lila tried to suppress a laugh. How could she have possibly forgotten? In the years when handing your phone in was standard, when they were younger, everyone had had a dummy phone. You'd swipe an old phone from home, and hand that in. Cookie had been too ancient to know the difference. Once Georgia had handed in a calculator and no one had noticed. They'd nearly wet themselves laughing.

Nancy went into her bedside drawer and retrieved a similar brick. 'And mine,' she said, pouting.

Miss Brandon put the phones into separate envelopes labelled with their names. Lila tried not to grin. What an idiot. Maybe where she came from people still used ancient mobile phones.

'I'd also like your real phones,' said Miss Brandon.

'I'm sorry?' said Nancy.

'I realize that we're still getting to know each other, but I'm not stupid, girls. I've seen you on your phones for the last four weeks. I'd like you to hand them in, now.'

Georgia went first. She said nothing as she handed over her Razr phone. Nancy followed, putting her iPhone into an envelope. 'It's fragile,' she said, as she placed it in the box. 'And you're liable for it now.'

Lila couldn't bring herself to say a word, she merely dropped her phone into the box.

'I presume they'll be available for collection at breakfast?' asked Nancy, 'like when we were thirteen?'

'Usually, yes,' said Miss Brandon. 'But obviously, in light of your decision to lie, I'll be confiscating them for twenty-four hours.'

Georgia made a noise a bit like a whimper and Nancy's neck stained red. Lila watched them both, hoping desperately that one of them would know what to do. How could they make this bitch back off?

'Oh, and Lila?' Miss Brandon's voice cut through her thoughts.

'Yes?' snapped Lila.

'Shouldn't you be making your way upstairs for quiet time?'

Lila looked at the clock on the wall. 'I've got another four minutes until quiet time.'

Miss Brandon gave her a beaming smile. 'Well then, you'll be a bit early. Come on. We can walk up together.'

Miss Brandon picked up the envelope with Georgia's name on it. 'I can add another week to the confiscation, if you'd like?'

Georgia made a dramatic whimper at this. Lila stood up and wordlessly moved towards the door. She heard Miss Brandon's voice from behind her as they both tramped up the stairs. Lila focused on the banister in front of her, looking down the swirl of floors. How high was it? She'd read somewhere that it was almost impossible to survive a fall of more than one floor.

'Camilla, I think I'd rather you were in your own dormitory before phone collection in future. Your roommates want to spend time with you, you know.'

Lila said nothing.

'I know Heidi is very appreciative of your support,' said Miss Brandon, quieter this time. 'She needs her friends at the moment.'

Lila took the stairs faster, two at a time. When she reached the triple dorm she shoved through the door, grabbed her pyjamas from underneath her pillow and turned back to the door. 'I'm changing in the bathroom. Stop talking to that bitch about me behind my back. Got it?'

She fled to the bathroom before Heidi, who was sitting on her bed drawing, her mouth slack with surprise, had a chance to answer.

'Lila?'

She ignored Heidi's pathetic little voice.

'Lila?'

She pulled the sheets off from over her head and sat up. The metal bed gave a whine, the mesh which held the mattress up rasping.

'What?'

'I was going to turn the light out early. Is that OK? I thought you could keep listening to music with it off.'

Heidi was still wearing her uniform. Was she seriously going to change in the pitch-dark?

'Don't you want to change first?'

Heidi retreated to her own bed. What was she trying to hide?

'Are you worried about Jenny perving on you?' she sneered. Jenny was lying on her bed at the other end of the long room, with her headphones in.

'Shut up!' replied Heidi. 'She's not like that. And she'll know you're talking about her.'

'I'm fine with that. Everyone knows what she's like. She'll be rubbing one out to the idea of us getting naked as soon as you turn that light off.'

Heidi said nothing but she sort of half smiled. Lila felt a sense of triumph. Heidi still liked her better than Jenny, then.

'You can't change in the dark all term. You have to get over it.'

Heidi rummaged in the wardrobe that stood at the end of her bed. The wardrobes were nowhere near big enough to fit a proper amount of clothes. Hideous pine wood, tiny mirror – everyone said the mirrors were small on purpose so that they couldn't obsess over their image. The real crime, they all agreed, was the lack of shoe space.

Lila pretended to focus on the screen of her iPod, but allowed her eyes to creep over to Heidi. She had turned her back to the room and was doing some deeply complicated changing routine to try and hide her body. It didn't work. The livid red scar, raised and angry against her pallid skin, was impossible to ignore. With something that ugly on her body, Heidi never stood a chance.

Minutes later, Heidi flicked the switch.

What would Georgia and Nancy be doing downstairs, she wondered. Moving between floors was forbidden in the fifteen minutes before lights out, and they turned a blind eye to talking for forty-five minutes after the lights went off. So they'd have had a whole hour together.

Last year, when they'd all been on the same floor, they'd taken to doing half an hour of yoga before bed, to tone their arms for holidays. Then they'd go to the bathroom together and brush their teeth over the triple sink. Sometimes they'd take over one of the attic bathrooms, which still had a huge chipped white bath. They'd fill it up with so much hot water that it was practically a sauna, and sit around, topless, talking about how chic it was to be topless. This term would have its own tricks and games. Tricks and games that she'd miss.

'Cammy?'

She and Heidi hadn't exchanged a single word after lights out since the beginning of term, since Lila had thrown her stuff on to the best bed in the room, shoved some clothes in the wardrobe and studiously ignored the other two. Lila suspected Heidi knew Jenny had told her about the arrangement, about how she'd been put in this dorm at Heidi's request.

'What?'

'I'm sorry.'

'What?'

'About the first day. The fight.'

'What are you talking about?' Lila couldn't remember having spoken to Heidi on the first day of term, let alone fighting with her.

'With Nancy and Georgia. The sign-up sheet – Miss Brandon. I didn't mean to get you in trouble.'

'I'm not in trouble. Don't be stupid.'

A pause hung between them in the darkness. There was a strip of orange light which fell from the gap between the ancient curtains and illuminated the carpet. There was something so resolutely schoolish about the carpet. Tough and unforgiving. She'd fallen on it once, in first year, and taken the top layer of skin off her knee. When she went home each half-term she would wait until she was alone in her bedroom and sink her feet into the carpet, revelling in the feeling of something designed for comfort rather than longevity. It was funny to think that some people – normal teenagers who went to normal schools – went home to that kind of comfort every single night.

'Sorry,' came Heidi's voice again.

'I'm not in trouble,' she repeated. 'They're my friends. You don't get in trouble with your friends.' That wasn't true. Of course you got into trouble with your friends. Your friends were supposed to tell you if you were being a bad friend or pissing them off.

'I didn't mean it in a bad way. Just, I know they don't like me and they seemed pissed off with you, and if you ever want someone to talk to . . .' she paused, swallowing loudly. 'I mean, we are sharing a room now and we did used to be friends after your mum and everything – we used to—'

'Thanks,' Lila replied flatly. 'But it's fine.'

There was a sniff. Heidi wasn't crying, was she? For fuck's sake. She swung her legs out of bed and crossed the room to stand next to Heidi's.

'Are you crying?'

Heidi said nothing, but her breathing was uneven.

'Please don't.'

Nothing. Lila sat down on the very edge of the bed and put her hand on the bulk of her body, on top of her duvet. 'I'm going back to bed now. Don't cry, OK? Goodnight.'

'Goodnight,' came a small voice from underneath the covers.

NOW

Lila

Someone had suggested that they have a break before pudding. Probably Nancy. Clearly, they didn't think that Lila had noticed the way that she and Georgia had sniped at each other all evening. But she had. She'd watched as Georgia gave Nancy a tiny slither of food, trying to force her to ask for a second helping. She'd seen Nancy leave half of it on her plate in response.

They weren't like that with her. Was it because they liked her better? Or, more likely, because they didn't think she was competition? She wasn't, really. Never had been. Georgia and Nancy had had all the same lessons, they'd gone to Oxford together. They'd spent their whole lives trying to pull in front of each other and pretending not to care who was in front. Lila had never posed a threat.

She had gone to stay with them at Oxford in their first year. Georgia had invited her to stay on her floor and she'd said yes, but then Nancy bought an air mattress so Lila stayed there. Georgia had said it was fine but Lila had known it wasn't. They'd gone to some pub full of boys in round-neck jumpers and old-fashioned glasses

193

and girls in bootleg jeans and Lila had felt, for the first time in her life, like a fish out of water. Her art school friends weren't like this. The pubs they went to had sticky floors and music and offers on drinks. Here, everyone sat around the tables having debates.

'It's not like this usually,' Nancy had claimed defensively when Lila asked how they coped without any clubs or bars or anything to do. 'There's loads of good places, it's just that everyone's got exams coming up.'

They'd shared a bottle of wine and halfway through the evening she had realized that Georgia and Nancy were really listening to each other's answers when Lila asked questions. They clearly hadn't seen each other all term. 'We've been friends forever,' Nancy had said. 'We don't need to be on top of each other all the time.'

Georgia had admitted it the next day, as she walked Lila back to the station. She said they'd gone for drinks in the first week and it had been awkward, as if the weeks since the end of school had swelled up between them and shoved them apart. Nancy had cut her hair off and was ordering beer. Georgia had started doing a London accent and didn't eat meat. Lila hadn't said anything. As they'd waved at her as the train left for London, Lila had been drenched with relief. Freedom. She had wondered if Georgia had felt the same way.

You wouldn't think it now, though, thought Lila as she watched them across the room. Nancy was holding court, Charlie and Roo watching her, listening for her to make a mistake that they could jump on. Georgia was watching, not saying anything, but smiling. She liked it when people had debates at her house. It made her feel like a hostess.

Brett was standing by the door, smoking another cigarette. He smoked a lot. Maybe it was because he didn't drink. It must give you something to do with your hands. She looked down at the glass cupped between her fingers. He must be very brave, being able to talk to people without a warm coat of alcohol to hide behind. The idea of it scared her. Even seeing people she actually knew without a personality-boosting drink first was scary. He looked very sad standing there, she decided. Very young and very sad.

'Come with me,' Lila whispered into Brett's ear.

'What?' he asked.

'Come!' she giggled. 'It's good, I promise.'

The others were all caught in a conversation, a boring one. Lila had sat on the outside thinking about saying something, but every time a sentence felt right, every time she'd felt sure it wouldn't make her sound stupid, she'd realize that they had moved on and her point didn't make any sense any more. They didn't seem to notice her and Brett slipping away.

'What's going on?' asked Brett, behind her on the stairs. She turned. He really was perfect. Sort of famous-person-perfect, his hair all tousled and his skin all glowy.

'Are you scared you'll get into trouble?' she asked.

'No,' he replied as Lila trotted up the stairs and swung into one of the bedrooms. 'But you can see why Nancy might be pissed about this—'

'She's not the jealous type,' said Lila. 'She doesn't like that sort of thing.'

'What are we doing?' asked Brett, standing in the doorway, looking scared to come in. Lila pulled the tiny plastic bag out of her pocket and held it out. 'I thought you might want a line.'

Brett grinned. 'You're bad.'

Lila shook her head like a little girl. 'Not bad. Naughty. You want some?'

He nodded. 'You're a bad influence.'

Lila took the mirror down off the wall and sat cross-legged on the bed. 'You do it,' she said. She could feel herself doing the baby voice again, the one that Nancy hated so much. She watched Brett's long fingers as he tipped the powder out and pulled a card from his wallet. 'Only the one, yeah?' he said.

'Sure,' Lila agreed. She didn't want him to think that she did this a lot. Because she didn't. Not *a lot* a lot. Well. Not any more. Not since Roo had started being so tight about money.

'Have you got a note?' she asked.

Brett shook his head. 'Don't you?'

She dug in her jeans pockets but nothing. Looking up, she caught sight of the bookshelf in the corner. Georgia had arranged the books by the colour of their spines which kind of said everything about her. Lila pulled a book off the shelf at random and ripped a sheet from the middle. She heard Brett laugh a surprised kind of laugh. 'Hey! I'm a writer. That's sacrilege.'

'These aren't for reading.'

'They're books.'

'In this house, they're decorations.' Brett made a

wrinkled face and Lila felt triumphant. He liked her better than Georgia now. She rolled the page between her fingers.

'What is it?'

Lila looked at the top of the page where the title was written. *'Lord of the Flies.'*

'Have you read it?' Brett asked, pushing the white powder around on the mirror.

Lila shook her head and offered him the rolled-up page. His fingers brushed hers as he took it. She could smell him. He smelt clean. So incredibly clean. How could he smell like that when he'd been smoking all night?

Lila didn't usually think about smells much, not like other people did. Other people always went on about how powerful they were and how they took them right back to their childhood. One of the other mummies at her Bump and Baby class had cried because she missed the smell of her newborn baby so much as he had grown up. Lila didn't care how Inigo used to smell. Like baby powder and washing powder, as far as she could remember. And more lately, like shit. She'd nodded along when all the other mums joined in, saying that when they caught a whiff of someone else's baby their ovaries twitched and they begged their husbands for another one.

Lila watched the muscles in Brett's back as he leaned over, bending his head to the mirror and taking one long, clean gasp. He tipped his head back and pinched his nose. 'I haven't done this for a long time. I feel like a kid again.'

'You are a kid. Don't you find it boring, hanging out with us?'

'You're not much older than me.'

'Six years. That's a lot, it's a whole life stage. You should be having fun with your own friends, people who are your age.'

'I've always liked the company of older people.'

Lila giggled. 'I'm telling Nancy that you called her "older".'

Brett's face clouded. 'Don't.'

'Of course not,' Lila replied, feeling guilty. 'I was joking. I wouldn't do that.'

They had a secret now.

The idea that she might make Brett sad, that he might feel anything that wasn't nice, frightened her. She wanted him to like her. If she was honest, if she let the feeling fizzing between her legs have a voice, she would say that she wanted more than that from him. But she would have to settle. She had a picture in her head of Nancy and Brett getting into bed that night, when the party was finished, and whispering even though Charlie and Georgia were a floor above. Brett would say something nice about Lila, and Nancy would pretend that she didn't care but she'd be jealous.

'Lila?' Brett's voice jolted her. He was holding out the roll of paper. She looked at the end, the end which had been put to his nose. It should be disgusting to her. It wasn't.

'Are you OK?' he asked. 'Are you sure you should have any more?'

How long had it been since someone had asked if she was OK? Roo had stopped asking months ago. He knew the answer, she supposed. Georgia didn't ask either. Nancy skirted around it. She wondered what would happen if she answered the question honestly, if she told him that she wasn't OK and that all she wanted in the world was someone to hold her very, very tight while she sobbed. Would he wrap her up in his arms and let her soak his navy-blue T-shirt with her tears?

Probably not.

He'd go and get Roo. He'd think that Roo would care, that he would be kind. She yanked the corners of her mouth into a smile. 'I'm fine.' She twisted her hair up into a knot, keeping it out of the way, and bent her head, watching her face reflected in the mirror, pinching one nostril shut and waiting for the lovely bitter rush.

'What are you doing?'

Lila dropped the piece of paper and jerked her head up, her chest contracting. For one terrible moment she thought that it was going to be Roo standing in the doorway. But it wasn't. It was Georgia. Thank fuck, it was Georgia.

Brett looked worried. 'Hey – sorry, we're so rude. We'll be down in a moment.'

'It's fine,' Lila said. 'Gee, I'm sorry. It's my fault. I asked Brett if he wanted a line,' she said guiltily. 'Please don't tell Roo.'

Georgia was hard to understand sometimes. Lila stared at her, all lit from behind. Was she angry?

'Only if you don't tell Charlie,' Georgia said. Her voice

was funny. Flat. Lila watched with surprise as she crossed the room, twisted her hair out of the way, rerolled the piece of paper and deftly snorted.

'Gee!' Lila exclaimed. Brett looked shocked.

'I'm not that boring,' said Georgia. Lila could tell that she felt quite cool, that she was glad she had surprised them. 'I used to be fun.'

'You're still fun,' lied Lila. 'The funnest.' She leaned over the mirror and finished the line.

Brett was looking properly uncomfortable. Georgia must have noticed too because as she was running her finger over the surface of the mirror and swiping it over her gums, she paused, telling Brett, 'Don't worry – Nance is in a row with Roo and Charlie about the welfare state. The three of us could have an orgy up here and they wouldn't notice.'

Lila laughed.

The others looked at her.

'What?' she asked. 'That was funny!'

Georgia hung the mirror back on the wall, gave it a final wipe and rearranged her hair. 'Seriously though, don't tell Charlie,' she said to them both.

'Or Roo,' Lila added.

'Or Nancy,' smiled Brett.

THEN

Georgia

The concert hall was a huge stone building in the middle of the school, used for special assemblies, school plays and prize days. Underneath it, like an artery, ran a tunnel which opened out into a dressing room. Tradition stated that on the first night of their first year at Fairbridge Hall, each new girl had to walk from one end of the tunnel to the other, in complete darkness, while the older girls waited in the dressing room. It would have happened a few weeks ago, when term had started. A load of terrified tweens in brand new pyjamas shivering and terrified. Even the teachers turned a blind eye to it, it had been going on so long. Once you managed it – the seemingly endless walk through the suffocating darkness – you officially belonged to the school.

Georgia had noticed Nancy immediately. She had refused to look at all scared, clearly attempting to deny the older girls the satisfaction of it. Georgia had whimpered and legged it down the entire corridor, arriving at the end flustered and frightened, begging to be let out. But Nancy had been different, even then. 'This is much less dangerous than walking home on your own from

201

the night bus,' she'd declared, prompting the other girls to ask whether she had really been taking the night bus on her own at thirteen years old. By the end of the night, they had all been in awe of her.

The older girls hadn't liked her. They had said she was 'up herself' and when she made it from one end of the tunnel to the other and tried to open the door out into the dressing rooms, they had held it shut. It had only been a few minutes but Georgia had listened to them laughing and felt a wretched sympathy for the girl behind it. Eventually the girls opened the door and there, with a cheerful expression, was Nancy. Georgia would never forget how she'd given an affected yawn and strode out into the light saying, 'I think your door's a bit sticky.'

They were older now than those girls had been then, much older, which seemed strange. They still seemed so grown-up in her memory.

The tunnel no longer held any fear for them. The lights were on, the doors unlocked and they finally had their phones back, to act as torches if necessary. It was weird, Georgia thought, how all those years ago this had seemed the most frightening place in the world but now it felt like a shelter. It was one of the few private places in the school and their only opportunity to exchange secrets – whenever Miss Brandon, who managed to be everywhere, saw them huddled together, she tried to break up their private conversation or, even worse, join in.

They sat, their backs against the stone walls, legs splayed out. Georgia was conscious of the scuffs on the toes of her ballet pumps. Now that her feet had stopped growing her mum didn't think she needed new school shoes every year.

'It's fine. Look, we'll come up with something, and we'll sort it out. It's one weekend. It's hardly the worst thing that's ever happened to anyone,' Georgia said.

She could hear her dad's voice coming out of her mouth. Why did she always have to be the sensible one? It wasn't fair. And it wasn't like anyone was going to listen to her.

'It's not just about the weekend though, is it?' said Lila. Nancy nodded.

'She barred us, remember? She made you miss seeing your brother for the last time this year. She's deliberately trying to change things, because she doesn't like us.'

'So what do we do?' asked Lila, as if they were in a film and formulating a plan would somehow help.

'Let's just suck it up, do this stupid weekend trip, make her think we've learned whatever lesson she's trying to teach us and wait for her to back off. She's not going to be like this forever,' Georgia reasoned. 'She's only doing that teacher thing that they all do where she tries to come over all strict and stuff at the beginning so we'll think she's tough. I guarantee you, by the end of this term she'll have chilled out.' As she spoke, Georgia watched both of their faces fall.

'What?' she asked. 'What's wrong with that idea? The fact that it's not going to give you two the chance to go up against her? That's exactly what got us into this situation. Anyone remember that?'

It was as if Nancy hadn't heard a single word Georgia

had said. 'I've got an idea,' she announced, getting to her feet. There was no way that this idea would be better than keeping their heads down and letting this whole thing blow over. But it was, inevitably, what they would end up doing. Georgia leaned back against the wall as Lila sat forward, eager to hear a new approach.

'We play nice on the way there. Act like we're having a good time, then, once she's gone, we get lost.'

'Lost?' asked Lila.

'Not like, trying to work out who to eat first lost, just a bit lost. Overnight or something. Enough that they'll have to call someone out to look for us. She'll look totally incompetent,' Nancy's eyes lit up. 'Endangering our lives . . . She'll get the sack. It's perfect.'

Georgia opened her mouth to tell Nancy that this was really not a great idea, but before she had found the words, Lila spoke up. 'Genius,' she breathed. 'There's no way Brandon can punish us for getting lost. Everyone will think it's her fault.'

There was no point in fighting it. It wasn't a terrible plan, at least not as Nancy's plans went. Lila looked delighted by the prospect. Georgia considered telling Nancy that it was a bad idea, that actually Brandon might punish them for getting lost because she might see straight through them. She might never believe that it had been an accident. But there was no point. Lila and Nancy didn't understand, or rather they chose to ignore the fact, that it was different for her. It must be nice for them, knowing that however much trouble they got into there was always a net underneath them. A new sports wing for their parents to donate to, to keep the peace. Even if they completely fucked up, girls like Nancy and Lila didn't get expelled, they got 'asked to leave' – and then they started at another even more expensive school.

Georgia had been given detention once, in her third year, after the three of them had been caught out of bounds in the local village. Her father had taken her for a walk the following weekend and explained how she couldn't get detention. The girls who were paying to attend Fairbridge Hall could get away with that, but she was different. Georgia was there on someone else's goodwill, and if she gave them cause to think she wasn't grateful, they might take it away. There was no way that her parents would be able to afford the fees to keep her there. If she lost the scholarship, it would all be over. 'If you lose your scholarship, you'll have to come home, and you'll have to go to Barnards,' her father had warned her.

There was nothing wrong with Barnards. Her brothers had gone there. Her parents had gone there. But people from Barnards didn't go to Oxford.

'Can you imagine how popular you'd be there now?' her father had asked her, as they'd rounded a corner for home. 'With that accent?'

'So we're agreed?' said Nancy. It sounded like a question, but it wasn't. Georgia nodded. Somewhere in the distance, a bell rang. All three of them jumped to their feet, well trained after so many years of having their every move commanded by a bell.

'It's going to work,' said Nancy, as they walked through the tunnel, back up to the twisted steps and emerged into the daylight. 'I know it is.'

No it won't, thought Georgia, saying nothing. She had an undeniable, uneasy feeling that something about this plan was going to go spectacularly wrong.

NOW

Georgia

'What's going on with you?' asked Charlie, giving Georgia a sideways look.

'Nothing,' she said. 'I'm just happy. That does happen sometimes, you know.' She shouldn't have sat next to Charlie, but the others had reached the kitchen before her and it was the only chair left. He was staring at her. It was irritating. Was it so unusual that she had fun? That she wasn't in a miserable slump of a mood? Maybe it was, but then she'd been pumped full of hormones and headaches and false hope for the last six months. Surely he'd understood why she had been unhappy? Lila was chatting away, a hundred words a minute. Roo was looking at his phone, while Nancy quoted statistics about the pay gap at him. Condensation had settled on the windows and the music was low and gentle in the background.

Charlie reached out and caught her chin between his fingers. To anyone else it might have looked like a loving gesture, but she knew what he was doing. She knew what was coming.

'Your nose is running.'

'No, it's not,' she replied, putting her index finger to

her nostril. Lila was still rambling, talking about a shoot she'd done years ago where the model had been on her period and leaked on all the borrowed clothes. Brett seemed to find the story hilarious, and his laughter spurred Lila on. She was too loud and exaggerating like mad. But at least it was a distraction.

'Did you do coke?' His voice was rich with horror. Hypocritical horror.

Georgia picked up a bottle of wine. 'I'm going to top everyone up.'

He caught her arm and yanked on it. 'Come back.'

'Drop it, Charlie,' she ground out, her neck tight and her gaze fixed. 'This is not a conversation I'm going to have with you right now.'

'I want to talk about this. Let's go.'

'Go where?'

'The drawing room. The hall. Our bedroom. I don't care.'

She looked across to the table. Roo and Nancy were still going at it. Georgia caught the words 'scroungers' from Roo and realized that, yet again, they were arguing about benefits. Roo's favourite topic. Lila was listening to Brett now, her eyes half closed, a smile on her face, dipping her fingers in the candles.

'Can you ask Lila to stop playing with the wax? It'll go all over the table. Last time it took me a day to get it off. She might listen to you.'

'I am only going to ask you to come next door with me once more and then I'm going to have this conversation in front of your friends.'

Georgia tipped wine into her glass. He knew he had her over a barrel. She followed him into the corridor, feeling like a child who was about to be told off.

The light in the hall was much brighter, it made her eyes hurt. She switched on the soft yellow lamp, turning the overhead light off. That was better.

'What do you think you're playing at?' Charlie asked.

Georgia leaned against the wall, feeling the coolness of it on her back. 'It was one line, Charlie.'

'So you admit it?'

'Yes, I admit it,' she said. 'Who are you – the police? My fucking parents? Get over it.'

Georgia saw his hand twitch at his side – would he hit her? She screwed up her face.

'Don't flinch,' he snapped. 'I didn't do anything – I would never do anything – I wouldn't – I would never do that.'

Georgia dropped her gaze, staring at the floorboards. 'I'm sorry. I didn't mean to. I know you wouldn't.'

It was true: he wouldn't. He couldn't risk the whispers. If anyone ever suspected that he'd hit her, it would end his career. She considered telling him that, but thought better of it. He had never laid a finger on her. He wasn't like that. She was letting her suspicions about his father colour her thinking. That wasn't fair. People didn't have to become their parents. God knows she was aware of that.

'Do you understand why I'm upset?' he asked.

'Yes,' Georgia said, thinking of the ovulation sticks upstairs.

'So why did you do it?'

There was no answer to that question. Not when she'd spent their entire relationship hiding it from him. It wasn't possible to give him a single strand. If she plucked one out, the entire thing would unravel. She allowed herself a moment – one tiny one – to think what it would be like to tell him everything that had happened at school. They'd go for a long country walk and she'd tell him the story and he would hold her and tell her that it didn't matter, that she deserved to be happy, that she was safe.

'If anyone found out that someone had been doing drugs in this house, it could end my career.' His voice punctured her thoughts, dragging her away from her honesty fantasy.

'How could anyone find out?' she heard herself retort.

'One picture, one stupid comment, it happens all the time. You have no idea how many people I've seen lose their careers over this stuff, over stupid little mistakes.'

'You used to do it all the time!'

'Used to,' he snapped. 'We're adults, Georgia. We're having a fucking dinner party. You shouldn't need to put that stuff up your nose at a dinner party. I expect that kind of behaviour from Lila, and Christ knows what Nancy gets up to, but not from you. You're not like that.'

'Maybe I am like that,' she replied. She should stop. She should apologize and promise never to do it again. She should tell him that she hadn't done it for ages, she didn't need it. She was just tired and nervous and looking for something to take the edge off. And if she'd tried to stop Lila, she might have left, or caused a scene. But she couldn't force her lips to make conciliatory words.

Georgia never fought with Charlie. Never. She let him have literally anything he wanted. Sex when she was tired and aching and they weren't supposed to on the IVF cycle. Late nights. Parties. People over to dinner who patronized or ignored her. Making him happy was her life's work. She was the scaffolding around his edifice. She was his mother and PA and courtesan. She looked up at him through her eyelashes and saw his hurt, confused face. Her entire existence had been about supporting him for as long as they had been together and now here she was, acting as if she didn't care. He must be so confused. So worried. She reached her arm out and ran her fingers over his chest. It wasn't huge and broad like Brett's but it was nice. And it was hers.

'I'm sorry,' she whispered. 'Really.'

'It's OK,' he replied. Georgia's chest untightened. He was going to forgive her. It was going to be OK.

'I just don't understand why you would do it. How do you ever expect to get pregnant if you go around doing stupid things like that?'

Georgia's head snapped up. The kitchen door had clicked shut. Someone had been there. Nancy or Lila? Which would be worse?

'Who was that?' she asked.

'What?'

'There was someone by the door – someone was listening to us.'

Charlie sighed. 'Stop it.'

'There was, Charlie, I saw them,' she replied, her voice rising.

He shook his head, taking a step away from her. 'I think it's the drugs, the hormones,' he clarified. 'They make you paranoid.'

'I'm not paranoid,' she replied, louder and higher than she'd intended.

He looked worried again. 'Look, even if there was someone, it doesn't matter. It's not a big deal.'

'Of course it's a big deal,' she snapped. She had forgotten to modulate her tone. Charlie looked like she'd hit him.

'Why do you care?' he asked. 'Why does it matter?'

Georgia sighed. There was no way to explain.

'Even if someone was there, they might not have heard anything,' Charlie ventured.

Georgia nodded. 'You're right. Sorry.' She stepped on to her tiptoes to kiss his lips. He didn't turn away, but he hardly returned the kiss either. 'I'll make it up to you. I promise.' Steadying herself she ran her hand over his crotch. 'You remember what coke does to me?'

That part, at least, was true. When they were younger, when partying had been part of their lives, Charlie had loved it when she got high. He'd never tell her that she was boring, that he didn't like the way she lay quietly and enjoyed gentle waves of pleasure when they had sex. But she knew. Maybe it was the lack of inhibitions or maybe it was the chemicals, but inevitably if she did drugs they'd end up having clumsy, urgent sex in a loo or against a wall.

Not any more, obviously. The idea of having sex right now with her dry throat and feeling of creeping horror that it might have been Nancy, that she might have heard, that she might know about the IVF, made her feel ashen inside. But Charlie was so simple and it was easy, blissfully easy to distract him and to defuse his anger.

Charlie smiled. He pushed a strand of hair away from her face and dropped a kiss on her forehead.

'Sorry, baby,' she simpered. The words burned her tongue. She didn't usually mind this game – letting Charlie feel like the big man, letting him think she was sorry for whatever she might have done to irk him – but today, with everything so fragile and breakable and teetering on the edge of smashing, it was almost impossible to push the words through her lips.

'But I love you anyway,' he said.

'I love you too.'

THEN

Lila

Miss Brandon, Lila decided, was even more irritating outside of school. She had announced that they would be sitting in their assigned groups on the bus in order to promote 'team bonding' from the outset. When she'd noticed Sophie and Lauren sharing a set of iPod headphones at the back of the bus, she had confiscated the iPod. Lauren had rolled her eyes and Lila had been able to feel Nancy's excitement at the prospect of another ally until music burst out of the speakers of the coach. 'Now we can all listen,' said Miss Brandon, turning the volume up. Everyone, apart from Nancy, Lila and Georgia joined in, screaming Britney at the top of their lungs. How could anyone be that happy after seven hours on a bus and the prospect of sleeping outdoors in a rainstorm?

To make things even worse, Heidi had plonked herself next to Lila on the bus that morning, looking cheerful. Lila had spent most of the journey resting her forehead on the cool window, watching the roads sprint past her and wishing she were anywhere else in the world. Georgia and Nancy had ended up across the coach aisle from each other. She wondered what they were talking about, as Heidi sang the wrong words to the final chorus of 'American Pie'. How was anyone supposed to survive this? It was literal, honest to God torture. She thought longingly of her phone, hidden in a pair of socks in her rucksack. Last time they'd stopped for a loo break she should have rung Clarissa and forced her to fake an emergency. She could be halfway to London by now, where her dad had just got Sky Plus.

'Here we are,' came Brandon's husky voice. The bus pulled into a lay-by at the side of the road. Great. Absolutely fucking great. The sky was grey. The landscape was grey. Everyone's skin looked grey under the bus's fluorescent lighting. There was no point in any of this. It wasn't even going to look good on her art school application. If anything, she was sure they'd take one look and ask what kind of tragic loser went walking in Scotland for a weekend and then acted like it was an achievement.

'Come on!' said Heidi, who was already standing up and pulling her enormous rucksack down from the overhead locker. 'Hurry up!'

Miss Brandon had insisted that they wear their games kit, despite the fact that there was absolutely no reason for it. This entire thing would be about fifteen per cent less agonizing if she were at least able to do it in her own clothes. Standing in a line at the side of the road, Lila tried to quash the embarrassment of it all. To add insult to injury, Brandon had performed a spot check on their packing before they'd left. The sheer venom from Nancy's eyes when Brandon had made her surrender a tube of Eight Hour Cream and a silk eye mask would have melted a lesser woman. At least they were well rehearsed in hiding real contraband. The booze, cigarettes and the coke that Nancy had scored from some guy in the village were all safely hidden and distributed between their bags. Thank God. There would be no getting through this hell without that.

The excitement on Heidi's face was disgusting. 'Look at it, Cammy!' she said, spinning around. 'It's like being in a film!'

It was not like being in a film. It was like being in a field. A field full of cow shit.

'Right, guys,' came Miss Brandon's voice. 'Can you all gather round for a moment?'

The girls, almost fifty of them, shuffled into a semi-circle around the three teachers.

'You know the plan,' said Miss Brandon, flashing her bright white teeth. 'But just in case anyone was texting their boyfriend rather than listening to me – I'm looking at you, Katie,' she was doing an enormous smile and everyone was giggling.

Why was Miss Brandon like this? Why did she so badly want to be everyone's friend? And why was anyone buying it? Couldn't they tell that behind all the jokes about boyfriends and decent clothes she was a massive bitch?

Miss Brandon went on, her bouncy red ponytail swinging. 'We've got the green team, the red team and the blue team, and each of those teams is divided into three groups: A, B and C. Green team, I'll be following your route.' She held up a map. 'Blue side, you'll be followed by Miss Bush.' She gestured at dumpy Miss Bush, who clearly signed up to assist because she had no other weekend plans. 'And Mrs West will follow the red team. We'll give you your space, but we'll be nearby if anything goes wrong.

'You've each got a slightly different route on the map, but you'll all end up at the mountain.' Miss Brandon pointed across the expanse of land at an ugly chunk of brown, poking out of the ground.

'The idea is that you climb to the first base – it's really clear when you get there – plant a flag and come back down. Then make your way back to your team campsite. Obviously, I don't need to tell you not to go any higher than first base, because you haven't got climbing equipment and none of you are stupid. Whichever side gets all of their groups back to their campsite first is the winner. Everyone got it?'

There was a murmur of assent. Lila looked up. The sky was a weird yellow colour, like a bruise. 'Oh,' Miss Brandon called out, 'phone signal can be a bit patchy out here, so the nearest payphone is also marked on your maps.'

The expanse of land lay rudely open in front of them. Lila realized for the first time how it was possible for a person to be afraid of open spaces. It was too big. There was too much sky and too much horizon. Something about the whole landscape was weirdly foreboding. She wanted to go home.

'You'll need these,' said Miss Brandon as she handed

Nancy's group their maps. Lila wondered whether Brandon had put Nancy with her group out of spite. She was at least a head taller than every other girl she'd been teamed with – Laura Sullivan, Katie Leyland and Sophie Speck. Usually the longness and slimness made her look like a model, but next to those girls she looked freakish. Like Gulliver. On the upside, Laura, Katie and Sophie were as beige as a person could be. Talking them into the plan would be easy.

Georgia's job would be a piece of piss too. She had two of the Chinese girls, Mengwen and Ju, who had joined for sixth form, and the Spanish girl Carmen. They were probably minor royalty or something back home, but here the foreign students sat right at the bottom of the social hierarchy. It would be easy for Georgia to ditch them when the time came.

If anyone was going to cock this up, it was going to be her. Lila's group was a complete blister of an arrangement. She had Heidi, of course, since the school seemed to have appointed her Heidi's keeper. And Heidi's wet little friends Jenny and Maddie. Maddie wore retainers which made her breath smell like dead people. Her neck was spotty and her hair lank. One year they'd found out that Maddie's dad was about seventy and her mum, who wasn't even forty yet, had once presented the weather on the regional news. What must it be like to be less sexy than your mum? If Maddie ever got a boyfriend she'd never be able to take him home to meet her parents. Even Lila had struggled. When she brought boys home – less to meet her father, more to have somewhere to have sex – they always salivated over Clarissa. 'Your mum is so fit. That means you're going to be fit when you're old too.' She couldn't find the energy to tell them the truth. But at least she could compete.

'Cammy? Are you coming?' Heidi was looking back at her, calling out, 'It's time to go! Hurry up – we want to be first to the meeting point.' The three of them began to sing one of the songs from the bus, at the top of their lungs.

Lila sloped off after them. The only thing making any of this bearable was the plan. It had to work. She wasn't going to be able to survive forty-eight hours of this without killing someone.

NOW

Lila

'Shall we all come back to the table?' boomed Charlie. 'Pudding looks delicious.'

It might have looked delicious when Georgia had put the finishing touches to it, but now, with everyone running in and out of the kitchen, it had started to melt. Lila had styled a cookery shoot once, when she had still thought that her career was going to happen. She'd watched as they did weird stuff to the food. Covered everything in olive oil to make it shiny. Used scoops of mashed potato to look like vanilla ice cream because it didn't melt. If Georgia could have got away with it, Lila smiled to herself, she'd probably have done the same thing.

'What are you smirking about?' Roo shouted at her from across the kitchen. He had been talking to Georgia and looking down her top. That was what he did at dinner parties. One woman, a friend of his from university, had even rung her up to tell her that he wouldn't be invited to things any more because he kept putting his hand on the hostess's arse as she took something out of the oven. Lila had laughed in her face. People were so judgemental these days.

'None of your business,' she shouted back to her husband. 'Anywayyyy – Charlie wants you to come and sit down, so you should all come and sit down.'

'Quite right,' agreed Charlie.

'Only if you're hungry!' added Georgia in that tinkly voice she did when she wanted people to think that she didn't care about something that she cared about a lot.

Lila slumped into Nancy's seat. 'I want to sit next to Brett,' she said. 'I want to hear all about America.'

He laughed. 'We're going to need a long time if I'm going to tell you everything about it!'

'I have ages,' she cooed.

'Lila, this is for you.' Lila looked up. Standing above her was Georgia, holding a wide coffee cup with a twisty blue pattern and a gold rim. She placed it down on the table in front of her. Lila picked it up. She knew she should show willing. Last time Roo took her home early he'd screamed at her the entire time she was in the taxi and then, when they finally got home, things got even worse.

She took the cup and tipped a huge gulp into her mouth, where it burnt the soft flesh of her tongue. Unable to stop herself, she spat it back into her cup. Some of the coffee missed the cup, dribbling over the white tablecloth.

'Sorry,' she whimpered. 'It's too hot.'

'What the fuck, Lila?' said Roo.

'I'm sorry,' she said, looking down at the tablecloth. 'It was too hot.'

Roo shook his head. 'Georgia,' he called across the room. 'I'm sorry. Send me the bill for the tablecloth.'

'Don't be silly,' said Georgia, smiling her pretend smile. 'Poor Lila. Are you OK, babe?'

Georgia fussed with a napkin, brought her a fresh cup and a glass of ice water, and then, finally, sat down. Lila held the coffee cup between her hands, forcing herself to take tiny sips of it even though the heat of it scalded her mouth every time.

They were talking about politics again. Nancy was half shouting at Roo, saying things like 'with the best will in the world' and 'with all due respect' while he talked over her. Lila caught Roo's eye. 'I'm sorry,' she mouthed. He gave her a sort of smile. No teeth, just his mouth pulled sideways. He was still cross, then. He would still be cross when they got home, and for the rest of the week, and next time they were invited to something – if they were invited, which seemed to happen less and less – he would say that she shouldn't come, that he should go on his own because remember how she had behaved at Georgia's? Then it would be another night all on her own at home, staring at her toddler and willing herself to love him.

The new baby was supposed to be a fresh start. It had been different with her. Inigo had made her horribly, horribly sick for almost the entire nine months. But with her baby girl she had felt fine. She hadn't wanted to drink or smoke from the day she'd found out, she'd sort of glowed from the inside, it was like having the best-ever secret. Everything about her was exactly as it should be. It had been Bonfire Night and they'd wrapped up in lots of layers and gone to see the fireworks at the Hurlingham Club, the one place Roo had kept his membership, even with all the nasty bills that kept arriving. They'd laughed and posed for pictures and drunk mulled wine, and when they'd got home he'd been nice to her, and they'd made a baby.

She knew that it had been a girl, the baby. It was more than some vague feeling. Roo had said that it was a waste of money, but Lila had dragged him to Harley Street for an early scan where they'd confirmed that there was a heartbeat and taken her blood. Then the blood had been whizzed away to some lab somewhere and they'd done all sorts of tests and rang her back to say congratulations Mrs Brear, you're having a little girl.

After the miscarriage, Roo had told her she shouldn't have had the scan. 'Next time,' he'd said, ruffling her hair, 'We won't get your hopes up. That's why the NHS don't let you find out what flavour it is until three months, to avoid stuff like this. Cheer up.'

But she hadn't cheered up. And Roo had found it harder and harder to understand why. The first day or two he'd been sweet while she lay on the sofa and watched *Breakfast at Tiffany's*. Then he'd been tough, trying to make her come for a long walk with him, telling her that if she didn't start getting out of bed he'd cancel the nanny so that she'd have to get up and look after Inigo herself. And then, when he realized that this was what she was like now, that she was a sad person – for a while at least – he simply stopped bothering. He took to coming home late. He didn't ask about her day. Some nights they didn't even talk at all. He'd walk in, kiss Inigo's sleeping forehead and then head straight for the spare room to watch the huge television. Lila would lie on the green sofa in their living room – the sofa they'd chosen together when they'd bought the house, the sofa they used to get merrily pissed on and order takeaways or lazily fuck on, on Sunday afternoons – and think about how much happier they would probably all be if she just disappeared like her daughter had done.

NOW

Nancy

The passion fruit on Nancy's plate shone, slick and yellow. She closed her eyes and turned it to frogspawn, quashing the ache in her stomach. Nancy knew that Georgia had a clever trick when it came to dinner parties. She always served tiny portions. That way everyone had to ask for seconds or finish their plates at the absolute least. God knows where she'd learned it, Nancy couldn't imagine Georgia's parents had been much for entertaining.

'Brett, I want to hear all about America,' slurred Lila.

'What do you want to know?'

It was tempting to ask Lila quite what she was going to learn about an entire country while undressing Brett with her eyes. But there was no point. Lila was no threat. There would be no chance that Brett would be even the slightest bit tempted by Lila. Her head kept tipping forward showing a long stripe of dark at the roots. Someone clearly hadn't bothered to have their hair done for a while. The coffee she had managed to spit everywhere had stained her blouse. Her fingernails were uneven scraps, bitten down, ugly and raw on the stubs of her fingers. Looking at Lila was depressing. Everything about her screamed 'help me'. It was so sad. She had been stiff competition once – the default second choice for anyone who wasn't brave enough to try it on with Georgia. Nancy had been considered the least desirable of the three back then. Dark-haired, opinionated. Not Barbie enough for the kinds of boys that they spent time with. That was why she felt pleased with Lila's state. It was perfectly natural. Not nice, perhaps, but natural.

She had seen a therapist when she first moved to Boston. Everyone else did it, and she was curious to learn more about herself, to see what someone who studied the human mind might make of her. Nancy had made an appointment to see a middle-aged man with an office in a skyscraper.

It hadn't gone well. Everything about him from his bow tie to his little round glasses was contrived. He was trying to force her into feeling safe and comfortable when everything about this situation was artificial and wrong.

For every three true things she told him she would also tell him one lie, and would watch to see whether he noticed that she was lying. He never questioned her, but after a few weeks his PA had rung Nancy to say that he was having to reduce his client list and would no longer be able to see her. He could recommend several colleagues who were extremely talented.

Nancy had won.

'Everyone start,' said Georgia, lifting her spoon. 'I

hope it's OK,' she said, prompting them all to respond. Predictably, her comment was met with a wash of compliments.

'It's divine,' said Roo, his eyes on Lila. 'I can't remember the last time I had a proper pudding.'

'Probably the last time you cooked one,' said Lila, still looking at Brett.

'Pudding,' said Brett, doing a British accent. 'I love the way you guys say that.'

'Pudding,' repeated Lila in an exaggerated accent, laughing. Surely she wasn't drunk enough to think that this was legitimately funny?

'How's work?' Nancy asked Charlie, fixing him with her eyes. 'Last time I saw you it was the election.'

'He won,' said Georgia, smiling as she put her spoon to her lips.

Charlie blushed. 'Well, it's a bloody safe seat and the other candidate wasn't much cop.'

'You did brilliantly,' said Georgia.

'Hear hear!' said Roo, sloshing more wine into his glass. 'To Charlie.'

'It was months ago,' he protested, his hands over his face, as the others raised their glasses. 'But thank you.'

'You showed that fat bitch who was boss!' laughed Roo. Nancy turned her torso, watching him. There was a smudge of cream above his top lip and his hairline was receding. How was he still managing to fuck these women, these mistresses of his?

'I'm sorry?' she asked.

Roo laughed. 'Uh-oh, now I'm in trouble.'

Nancy folded her napkin in her lap. 'Not at all.'

'You're not going to tell me off?' said Roo, making a face. 'That makes a change.'

'I'm not sure you're interested in a discussion,' she replied evenly. Winding her up was Roo's hobby. She wasn't going to rise to it.

'Oh come on, she was a fat bint, aren't I allowed to say that? Aren't we allowed to say anything any more?'

'You're arguing with yourself,' she said, taking a tiny dip into the passion fruit. 'I haven't said anything.'

'You didn't need to,' said Roo. 'Look at your face.'

'Perhaps you should start judging women on what they say rather than what they look like,' she replied, the words escaping her before she could stop them. She heard Brett laughing from the other side of the table. Roo looked up.

'You think that's funny, mate?'

Brett stopped laughing. 'Sorry.'

'Don't apologize,' said Nancy.

'Does anyone want more pudding?' asked Georgia brightly.

'Me!' shouted Lila.

'How can you want more when you haven't even finished your first portion?' asked Georgia. Nancy looked up to see how full Lila's plate was, and noticed Brett put his fingers to his lips and pull something from his mouth.

'What was that?' she asked.

'Nothing.'

'You just took something out of your mouth.'

'It's only a seed or something.' Brett looked guilty.

'Are you sure?' she asked, leaning over and taking it off his plate. It wasn't a seed. It was a piece of blue plastic.

'Everyone should stop eating,' Nancy announced, trying to keep the satisfaction out of her voice. She watched as they each put down their spoons, apart from Charlie, who resolutely ignored her.

'What?' asked Georgia.

'This was in Brett's food.' She held the chip up. 'And it's sharp.'

'Let me see,' said Georgia, rushing around the table and staring at it. 'Oh fuck, it's a bit of the spoon I was using to mix the cream. Don't worry, it's only tiny. Honestly I wouldn't let it put you off.'

Nancy watched the redness spread up Georgia's neck and across her face. She adopted an expression of regret. 'I hate to be that person,' she said, her voice quiet. 'But I read this thing about someone who severed an artery from swallowing a tiny piece of glass and I'm probably being paranoid but I don't think that we should take any risks.'

It was true. She had read that. And she didn't want anyone to cut themselves. Of course, the chances of anyone actually having anything in their food was tiny, and most of them had already eaten most of their pudding. But still, Nancy couldn't quite persuade herself to drop it.

'That was glass,' said Charlie. 'It's not glass in the food.'

'It's not "the food",' yelped Georgia. 'It's only in one tiny bit.'

Lila's spoon clattered to the plate. 'I was done anyway.'

'You just said you wanted more?' Georgia said, her voice steely.

'I changed my mind.'

'I'm sure it's fine,' said Brett, picking his fork back up. 'Really.'

'Please don't,' said Nancy. 'I know it's silly but I hate the idea of anything happening to you.' Brett flashed her his smile and yet again she marvelled at the perfection of his features.

'OK, if you're so sure.' He looked around the table. 'She's such an adult!'

Everyone had put their cutlery down. Even Roo. Nancy tried not to look triumphant.

'I guess I'll clear the table then,' said Georgia. She sounded like she might be about to cry. 'There's cheese. I'll bring that out.'

'As long as you haven't accidentally sprinkled it with cyanide or something!' Roo called as Georgia whisked the pudding away from the table and set it down heavily on the marble side.

'Shame, it was delish,' Nancy said as she passed her plate to Charlie, who didn't return her smile. 'Sorry for being paranoid, you know what I'm like.'

Charlie didn't know what she was like, actually. He hadn't ever shown any interest in finding out. He and Nancy didn't like each other, there was no secret about that. Charlie was typical of his breed. Men like him thought that women were for relationships. Men were friends. If girls weren't soft and pretty and on offer, he didn't know what to do with them. He enjoyed Lila. Liked her, even. He understood her. She was for parties. For fun. For making stupid comments like, 'Wait, I thought unicorns were extinct?' which made them all howl with laughter. And even now, when Lila had become the antithesis of fun, they had enough memories left over from mad weekends in the country that could always fill a silence. 'Remember when we did lines off the back of that stuffed rhino in Jonty's dad's study?' one of them would say, and they'd laugh. To people like Charlie, that was enough to hang a friendship on.

Nancy had met Charlie before Georgia had. At some party in the second year of college. He'd been holding court, giving a speech about how anyone who wanted to could make a million in a decade if they tried hard enough. Nancy had intended to ignore him, but he had knocked into her and spilled her drink. It hadn't been difficult. She'd grown up at the knees of politicians and writers after all. All she'd done was ask him a few questions, use some long words and cite a couple of economists she'd barely heard of herself. It was a happy memory for Nancy, the vision of a teenage Charlie grappling for words and stammering to answer her questions while his friends looked on in stunned silence. Eventually she had asked him what he was reading and he had told her it was History and Politics. 'Thank fuck it's not economics,' she had said, and left the group laughing as she walked away. He hadn't ever forgiven her.

Georgia didn't know about their first meeting. At least, Nancy hadn't ever told her, and she assumed that Charlie wouldn't have done. They'd turned up together at a party in their last year. Charlie had pretended not to remember and Nancy had returned the favour. Strange really, to think that they had their own secret from Georgia, despite the fact that Charlie would never have wanted to share anything with her. She liked it.

'If everyone's finished, I'm going outside for a cig,' said Lila, standing up. She wobbled as she got up and slammed her hands down on the table to catch herself. The glasses rang with vibration and the candles in their glass storm lanterns wobbled. But nothing fell. Lila didn't seem concerned.

Georgia caught Nancy's eye within a second of Lila's words. It might have been decades since they were at school, but that kind of telepathy never went away.

Roo took Lila's arm and tugged her back into sitting position. 'You've spent half the night out there, Lila. Stay put.'

Roo was not going to ruin this. Lila was finally drunk enough to be honest with them, but not so drunk she was about to pass out. Georgia needed her and Nancy alone. Now.

'She can keep me company,' said Georgia, standing up.

'You're smoking?' said Charlie, sounding shocked. 'Seriously?'

Georgia nodded. 'One won't hurt.'

'Me too,' said Nancy, standing. Georgia watched Brett's expression with interest. He raised his eyebrows but said nothing. Clearly he knew better than to question Nancy.

'Girl time,' slurred Lila, kicking her chair out of the way.

'Exactly,' said Nancy. 'Girl time.'

THEN

Nancy

The rain was a relief, to start with. Cool and fresh on her sweaty skin. Nancy knew it was short-sighted to be glad of it – it would make everything more difficult. The tent would be damp, their food would get sodden. They'd have to spend the entire evening cramped into the wet tent rather than sitting outside and watching the sky. But in the moment, as the drizzle pricked coolness into her skin, it felt nice.

The mountain, huge and brown and rudely protruding from the earth, was slippery and unforgiving, and as they climbed higher she felt sweat at the back of her neck. She hated sweating – unless she was in the gym, watching the calorie count on the treadmill creep up. How anyone could actively want to do this, she couldn't understand. The path they were following had started wide and tarmacked, but eventually it had shrunk away, replaced by a dirt track only a metre or so wide, flanked by aggressively sloping ground.

Nancy tried not to look down, the severity of the drop making her pulse even quicker. The other girls were dancing along it, linking arms and jumping around, as if the steepness of the ground either side of them meant nothing. It must be nice, Nancy thought, to be so utterly unaware of everything around you.

'We're nearly there!' said Sophie.

Sophie, Laura and Katie had barely stopped talking since they'd started off. Nancy now knew the intimate details of how Laura lost her virginity to her boyfriend (he scattered rose petals on her bed, which was apparently something Laura thought was impressive). She had also been treated to a long meditation on whether or not Katie should get a fringe, and a genuine debate about whether skinny jeans would ever go out of fashion. Occasionally Nancy had wondered whether she, Georgia and Lila cloistered themselves too much, whether they should be friendlier with the rest of the girls in their year. Today had been enough to convince her that wasn't a good idea. At least Lila and Georgia discussed people, events and theories. Was it possible to lose IQ points by proximity to vapidity?

'Let's run the last bit!' said Katie, starting to gain pace. 'Bikini body prep!'

Nancy shuddered, thinking that Katie was the exact reason that women's magazines should be burned to the ground, but fixed her eyes on the ground in front of her and followed suit. Her rucksack was dragging on her shoulders and the walking boots she had begrudgingly bought for the occasion were inordinately heavy. The sooner they got there, the sooner this would all be over.

A blue flag was waving at the top, and next to it a red one. She smiled to herself. Georgia and Lila had managed it, they'd dragged their teams here as fast as they could so that they had a chance with their plan. It rankled that she was the last of the three, but it was no wonder, with the other three girls expending so much energy talking. She looked up. The sky was a deep bruise purple with a sickly yellow tinge. The clouds looked fat and angry. Another raindrop fell on the parting of her hair, slipping down on to her cheek. Would they get back to the camp-site before the real downpour started, she wondered. The pathway that had wound its way upwards had given out to a small clearing, sort of flat and sheltered by gorse plants. It was dotted with girls, mostly sitting on their rucksacks, in various states of exhaustion.

'Nancy!' She whipped around, seeing Georgia running towards her. 'Thank fuck!'

She wrapped her arms around Georgia's narrow waist, feeling her chest pressing into her, thinking not for the first time what a ridiculous body she had been blessed with. As if she had been drawn by a teenage boy.

'I've never been so bored,' Georgia whispered. 'I had Carmen and two of the Chinese girls.'

Nancy took a step back. 'Mine did nearly an hour on whether or not Katie should get a fringe. I win.'

As if on cue, the three blondes from her group sidled up. 'Hey, Georgia,' said Katie. 'How's your brother?'

They all giggled. Jesus, they were like children. It was hard to believe that in a year's time these young women were supposed to head out into the world and start university.

Georgia looked bored.

'He's fine.'

'Is he . . . single?'

'Yes,' Georgia said. 'And he's on a submarine for the next three months.'

Nancy couldn't take it any more. The reaction to Georgia's brother, who was painfully average, annoyed her. The fact Georgia was enjoying it so much was tragic. It wasn't her fault – God knows her background gave her fuck all else to feel proud of, but it was beyond irritating. It was as if none of the girls had ever even met a boy before. 'Where's Lila?' Nancy asked, interrupting the giggles.

'Trying to get a phone signal so she can see if Jack texted her back.'

'I'm going to find her. Coming?'

She watched Georgia smile at the blondes before following her.

'Which way did Lila go?'

Georgia pointed upwards. Nancy followed her finger and saw Lila standing on a rock, perilously close to the edge, waving her phone around.

'Lila,' she shouted. 'Come on.'

Lila looked up. 'I'm trying to make my phone work,' she shouted back.

'I'm not retarded. No shit. Come down, we need to go.'

Scowling, Lila made her way towards them, sliding down a section of the hill. Nancy's stomach twisted as she watched Lila, apparently oblivious to how high up she was.

Hearing Georgia whimper, 'Be careful,' Lila laughed.

'You mean, don't do stuff like this?' She stepped closer

to the edge, tiptoeing along a piece of rock that jutted out. Behind her there was only purple-yellow sky. Georgia gasped and turned away.

'That's not funny,' said Nancy. Lila was wasting time, and showing off. 'I mean it.'

'I mean it,' mimicked Lila, doing the stupid clipped voice she always used when she was doing an impersonation of Nancy.

'Come on, Georgia. Let's go.' Nancy knew that the only way to deal with Lila was to treat her like a child. She began to walk away, heading back to the clearing. Georgia kept pace with her and, as if by magic, a moment or two later Lila ran up behind them.

'Hey, guys,' shouted Georgia, standing in the middle of the clearing. 'Nancy and Lila and I are going to go up a bit further and explore. We'll meet you at the camp, OK?'

'What?' said Heidi.

Inevitably, Heidi was going to be the problem. She probably thought an overnight camping trip where she got to sleep next to Lila was the greatest thing that had ever happened to a human.

'We're only going to explore a bit higher up,' said Lila. 'It's no big deal.'

'Aren't we supposed to stay in our assigned groups?' asked Carmen.

'I don't think it matters,' said Georgia. 'Honestly, it's fine. We've all finished the task, right?'

Carmen didn't look impressed.

'Miss Brandon said we weren't supposed to go any further than the first base,' said Heidi resolutely.

'I doubt you've ever been to first base,' laughed Nancy. The other girls joined in, giggling at the joke. Heidi stuck her bottom lip out. 'Miss Brandon told us not to,' she repeated.

'It's starting to rain,' said Katie, looking at Georgia. 'Mind if we just meet you at the campsite?'

'Good plan,' said Georgia sweetly. Nancy decided to forgive her for the inane chat about her brother.

'We'll be right behind you,' Nancy added. They wouldn't be coming down, obviously. They were going to get 'lost' for long enough that Brandon had to call for back-up. But the others didn't need to know that.

'Are you sure?' called Heidi. 'We're supposed to stay in our groups.'

All three of them rolled their eyes. 'Want to take this one, Li?' said Nancy, under her breath. It was about time Lila did something about Heidi.

'Just go,' Lila called down. 'We'll be down in like ten minutes.'

'It's dangerous,' whined Heidi.

Nancy felt her frustration building. 'Tell her to fuck off, Lila,' she said. 'She'll listen to you.'

'Fuck off,' Lila shouted across to Heidi, who stood unmoving at the top of the path. Her face twisted with hurt and shock. Nancy realized that in all the years Heidi had been a complete pain in the arse, she'd never heard Lila say a bad word to her. Heidi turned on her heel and fled down the path.

'Thank fuck for that,' said Georgia as she watched Heidi's navy-blue anorak get smaller and smaller. Nancy heard the click of a lighter and her nostrils filled with the comforting smell of smoke. She reached over and took Lila's cigarette, pinching it between her thumb and finger and dragging on it.

Nancy sat down, back against the steep grassy ground, legs dangling over the side of the path. 'We can have a little break, but then we need to start walking. We'll go down the other side of the mountain, and then start walking that way,' she pointed. 'It'll be totally plausible. We only need to get far enough away that it takes them a while to find us. Did you check the map?'

Georgia smiled as she settled on the ground next to Nancy. 'Yep. She so didn't want us finding any pubs. It's got basically nothing on it.'

Lila stepped forward, leaning out over the path, looking at the sharp drop down.

'Stop it, Lila,' said Georgia. 'It's too high, you're making me feel sick.'

'Do you really think she'll get in trouble for losing us?' said Lila, sitting down.

'One hundred per cent,' said Nancy. 'You know how anal they are about their reputation. Even if it only makes the shitty local news, it still makes them look stupid. They'll be furious.'

Lila sighed loudly and threw her head back. 'Guys, look at the sky. It's amazing.'

'You're so gay,' replied Georgia.

'She's right,' said Nancy. 'When was the last time you were this far away from everything?'

'It feels like a whole different world,' said Lila, lying

down on the ground, her rucksack a pillow. 'I wish we could stay here forever.'

'How long d'you reckon we'd last?' asked Georgia.

'Depends,' Nancy replied. 'How many cigarettes have you got?'

Lila laughed. 'Two packs. Had to keep space for the vodka.'

'George?'

'One pack. Don't forget the coke, Nance.'

'I still cannot believe that you brought coke on a school trip,' Lila laughed. 'You're my actual hero. I love you.'

A silence settled between them as they sat, watching the sky. Nancy knew they should move. They needed to get going, the sky was angry and it was getting darker. But there was something so raw about sitting here, so completely free of everything that had felt oppressive back at school, that it was hard to make herself move. The others felt it too, she knew they did. So they sat. They sat and watched the clouds change and the sun taint the sky, and they spoke without saying anything, because that was what it meant to have spent every waking moment together for the last five years.

NOW

Nancy

'Hey, sweetie,' said Nancy, sitting down on the bench next to Lila. The bench was cold on the back of her legs, dampness seeping through her tight trousers. Great. Now she'd get to enjoy a wet arse for the rest of the evening. Georgia hovered in front of them, looking nervous and goose-pimpled. Georgia never had been able to handle the cold. She had still worn vests underneath her school uniform until she was embarrassingly old, and spent most of the winter term swaddled in cardigans that her mother had knitted for her. At least she'd had the foresight to bring a bottle of wine outside with her. She caught Georgia's eyes and looked pointedly at Lila's hand. Nancy leaned over, topping the half-empty glass up, almost to the top. It was what they used to call a 'Lila measure', back in the days when getting blackout drunk was still acceptable. Nancy could sense Georgia's disapproval at the top-up, but now that they had Lila alone, Nancy wasn't going to give Lila a hint of an excuse to go back inside, not until they'd talked to her. Not until Nancy had got the truth out of her.

Lila brought the glass up to her lips and slurped noisily

on it. It left a red ring around her mouth. God, she was a mess. There was something seedy about her that hadn't ever been there before.

'What's going on with you, Li?' said Georgia.

'Nothing,' she slurred. 'I'm fine.'

'You don't seem fine,' said Nancy. 'Georgia says you haven't for a while.' She leaned forward and looked into Lila's face.

'Is that why she's here?' said Lila, talking to Georgia.

'No,' Georgia replied, too quickly. She hadn't expected Lila to clock anything suspicious about Nancy's visit. Couldn't she take a holiday and visit her friends without an ulterior motive?

'I'm here because I wanted to see you both. And I wanted you to meet Brett,' said Nancy.

Lila snorted. 'Sure.'

'It's true.'

'You're here because she told you she didn't like the way I was acting. She couldn't deal with it so she told tales.' Lila looked up at Georgia. 'Right?'

Georgia looked embarrassed. 'I told Nancy I was worried about you, yes. You've been so low. It's because I care, Li. It's not like I told tales on you.'

'We're a team, remember?' said Nancy, copying the voice Georgia was using, low and gentle. It wouldn't do for Lila to spook and run inside, or even worse, leave. She needed this over and done with so that she could go back to Boston with Brett and get on with her life. 'We've always been a team, ever since school. If you're down, we're down. That's how it works.'

Lila was drinking greedily from her glass again. 'We're thirty-three, Nancy; this isn't like a sleepover.' She hesitated before adding: 'And you can't do anything anyway.'

'You've been through something incredibly hard,' Nancy went on. This wasn't going the way she wanted. Not at all. 'We understand.'

'No you don't.'

'I do, actually,' came Georgia. 'I've been there.'

Lila looked up. Her face was nasty. 'You can't get pregnant. That's not the same.'

Nancy tried not to let the surprise show on her face. It wasn't like Lila to talk to Georgia like that. Or to anyone like that.

Georgia looked like Lila had thrown a drink in her face. She was young and healthy and fit. Her hips were designed for childbearing and she'd been talking about baby names since she was twelve. And Georgia didn't fail at anything.

'I know it's not exactly the same, but I'm just saying, I get it. Whenever a cycle doesn't take, it's like a loss every time—'

Georgia had said 'whenever' – which meant there had been multiple cycles. Which explained the hidden pregnancy tests and ovulation sticks under the bed and the sad, secret box of baby clothes in the wardrobe.

'It's not the same,' shouted Lila. Her voice was wrong in the soft quietness of the late-night garden.

Nancy studied Georgia. The increase around her waistline and the slight puff to her face made more sense now. How many times had she tried? And why hadn't she said anything? Nancy knew doctors. Experts. She could have given Georgia advice. Set her up with the best people in the world. She could have helped.

'You know why you can't have one, right?' said Lila, quiet again. 'You know why I lost mine?'

Neither of them said anything. 'It's because of what we did.'

Nancy felt a sensation akin to falling.

So Georgia was right. Things were that bad.

Without needing to hear another word she knew exactly what Lila had done. The story that she had concocted in her mind. A fairy tale. A children's story. Stupid, childish Lila had written herself a myth and now she had convinced herself it was true.

Georgia had been right. Right about all of it. Now everything that Nancy had tried to squash down inside herself was spilling out, into her bloodstream, pumping around her body. For the last few weeks, ever since she had read Georgia's email, she had repeated the same thing over and over inside her head. 'It's ridiculous, she's overreacting,' had become a kind of mantra. She said it in the cab in the morning, in the bathrooms at work, in the dark kitchen of Brett's apartment at three in the morning.

But it wasn't ridiculous. Georgia wasn't overreacting. It was true.

Lila wanted to talk.

'It's because of what we did. That's why. And sometimes . . .' she paused. Nancy held her breath, willing herself not to say anything. 'Sometimes,' Lila went on, 'I think we should tell someone.'

'About Miss Brandon?' asked Georgia, her voice almost too quiet to catch.

Lila's head slopped from side to side. 'We're being punished.'

A sharp noise caught Nancy's attention. She and Lila simultaneously looked up. Standing in front of them, looking horrified, was Georgia. She had dropped her glass.

'Sorry,' she stammered. 'Sorry.'

Nancy watched as she crouched down, hurriedly picking up shards of glass and casting glances back behind her to the kitchen, like she was worried someone would come out.

'Shit,' Georgia winced. She'd stood on a shard, bright in the orange lights of next door's upstairs windows. Nancy looked at Lila's bare feet. She'd always wondered if the shoeless thing was natural or whether it was an affectation. It had been so long that it might be both by now.

'I'll help,' swayed Lila, stumbling towards the pile of broken glass.

'No,' yelped Georgia, holding an arm out, protecting her little pile of treasure. 'You'll hurt yourself.'

'You've hurt yourself,' said Lila. 'I'm not as shit as you think I am,' she slurred.

'I don't think you're shit.'

'You're acting like I'm a baby.'

'If the shoe fits,' Georgia said. She lowered her voice but no one was stupid enough to think that she was trying to stop Lila from hearing her.

'What?' asked Lila, resolutely picking up shards of glass with her bare hands.

Nancy knew she should intervene. She should interrupt their stand-off.

The jagged stem of the wine glass had rolled underneath the bench. Lila crawled forward and picked it up, getting unsteadily to her feet. Nancy contemplated confiscating it and was reminded, for the hundredth time, why she didn't want children.

'Give me that,' said Georgia, but her voice was empty of authority.

'I'm going to put it in the bin,' said Lila, holding the sharp end in her hand.

'You'll cut yourself,' said Georgia.

'No I won't.'

'You will,' retorted Georgia, her voice rising. She reached forward, trying to snatch the stem from Lila's hand. 'Look at you – you're a mess.'

Lila looked shocked. Nancy registered the surprise on her face and realized that perhaps Lila didn't know, maybe she had no idea what a mess she had become. But how was that possible? Didn't she see how they all looked at her? Georgia said that Lila and Roo couldn't get a social invitation to save their lives, after all the drama and mess they'd caused at dinner party after dinner party.

'You always act like I'm so shit,' said Lila, her voice rising. 'And I'm not. I'm not.'

Nancy should step in. Take the lead. Be the grown-up. That was what she'd been summoned for, after all. But after years of making their decisions for them, she wasn't sure they deserved any more help.

'Just give me the glass,' Georgia was insisting. She seemed to be trying to sound like a grown-up but Lila's coldness about the IVF had clearly rattled her.

'Fuck off,' Lila shouted.

'You've cut yourself,' said Nancy. A trail of blood was leaking out of Lila's closed fist. The stem clattered to the ground. Both Georgia and Nancy were inspecting her hand in seconds.

'It's not deep,' said Georgia, the relief dripping from her voice. The last thing they needed was for Lila to bleed out on the patio.

'I'm sorry,' said Lila, tears running down her cheeks.

'It's fine,' said Nancy. She tried to inject as much sympathy into her voice as she could as she pulled a tissue from her pocket and pressed it to the tear in Lila's skin.

'Georgia's right,' said Lila, looking from one friend to the other. 'I'm a fucking mess.'

'I didn't say that,' Georgia replied.

'Why aren't you two like me?' asked Lila, swaying. 'Why don't you care? Why don't you feel guilty about it? Why don't you feel anything?' She shouted the last word and Nancy felt her patience fraying. A window slammed shut somewhere above them and Nancy watched as Georgia, predictable Georgia, searched for which one it had been, which one of her neighbours might now think that she was less than perfect.

'It wasn't our fault,' Georgia said. 'We were kids, and we didn't do anything wrong. Remember?'

Jesus. If that was the most convincing line Georgia could think of, if that was all she had to silence Lila with, then it was very lucky that Nancy was here.

'Let's sit back down, Li,' said Nancy conspiratorially. 'Come sit next to me, OK? We want to talk to you, we want to sort this out. We love you. And we want to make things better. But you've got to work with us if you want us to help you. OK?'

Lila looked from Georgia to Nancy, her eyes wide and her lip wobbling. It was the face of a child, a child who desperately wanted to believe what she was being told.

'OK,' she whispered.

THEN

Nancy

It was a bit like getting out of bed. They all knew that it had to happen eventually, that they had to get back on to their blistered feet and trail up the narrow path, up the mountain, to get 'lost'. It was the plan. It was how Miss Brandon was finally going to get what was coming to her. But every stolen moment, every moment they put it off, felt like a treat. Nancy wasn't sure how long they had been there, but something inside her shifted. She stood up.

'Come on. It's almost dark. We'd be stupid not to.'

Georgia sighed a long sigh, the kind which usually irritated Nancy. For some reason, today it didn't. 'I wish we didn't have to go. I wish we could just stay here.'

'Me too,' said Lila. As if on cue, a bead of rain landed on the bridge of Nancy's nose.

'I know,' she said. 'But we need to stick to the plan. Back on the path, and up we go.'

Georgia looked around them. 'You're sure about that, Nance? It's not that light any more. You don't think it's too dangerous?'

Nancy quashed the voice in her head which agreed with Georgia, the voice that said they should go back down, put their safety above point-scoring over Miss Brandon. 'It'll be fine,' said Nancy, trying to sound sure. 'We don't need to get very far to get lost anyway.'

'OK,' said Georgia. It was gratifying how easily Georgia seemed to believe her.

'I hate this rucksack,' whined Lila as she dragged it on to her back.

'Just a moment, girls,' came another voice. Nancy didn't need to look up. She knew who it was. Standing in the middle of the path was Miss Brandon. Next to her was Heidi.

'What are you doing here?' Nancy asked Heidi. Lila and Georgia stood either side of her. Together they filled the path. Nancy felt a passing sense of gratitude that she wasn't standing on the outside, with nothing but raw empty space next to her.

'I'm supervising this trip, Nancy, and Heidi was worried about you,' said Miss Brandon. 'What were you three thinking?'

'I wasn't talking to you,' Nancy said. They were already in trouble. There was no point in sugar-coating it or sucking up to Miss Brandon. 'Heidi, what is your problem?' Heidi seemed to shrivel. She didn't answer.

Nancy swivelled her eyes, working out her options. They could turn and go up the path, putting more distance between them. But it was impossible to ignore the distant rumbling noise that sounded suspiciously like thunder, and the rapidly increasing darkness. And Heidi had seen them. She would defend Miss Brandon – tell tales on them.

'Any chance you girls would like to explain to me where you were going?' asked Miss Brandon.

'We were taking a break,' replied Lila, her voice sweet.

'Don't lie to me,' said Miss Brandon. 'Heidi told me what you girls were planning to do.'

'Planning?' asked Georgia, making her blue eyes even wider than usual. 'We don't have a "plan".' She made air quotes with her fingers as she said the word. Nancy smirked. It was a nice touch, it implied that Heidi was lying and Miss Brandon was paranoid. Miss Brandon's eyes narrowed. She looked confused. Like she wasn't quite sure who to believe.

'I have no idea what you're talking about, Miss Brandon,' replied Nancy. This was fun. It wasn't as good as staring up at the sky with a cigarette between your lips. It wasn't even as good as Brandon getting bollocked for losing students on her disaster weekend trip. But they'd got to her – made her doubt Heidi, doubt herself. Miss Brandon was standing so close to them that Nancy could see the faint lines on her forehead. Not so perfect now. The new job was taking a toll, clearly.

'Like Lila said, we were resting for a while. Nancy was feeling faint. We were planning to re-join the girls and carry on with the trip. You can ask the rest of the groups, if you like?' Georgia smiled. 'They'll tell you.'

Nancy rewarded Georgia with a wide smile. She was good when she tried.

'If you don't mind, Miss Brandon,' said Lila, 'we're keen to get down to the bottom before it gets any wetter.' She picked up her rucksack. 'Are you coming, girls?'

As if on cue, the wind picked up, screaming through the long grass and filling their clothes with freezing air.

Sad though she was to take her eyes off Miss Brandon, Nancy stooped to pick up her rucksack. The dirt path under her feet was starting to soak with rainwater and Nancy wanted her feet back on flat ground. Immediately. But Miss Brandon and Heidi stood stock still in the middle of the path.

'You were told to complete the trip in your assigned groups, and you were told to come down once you reached the first level on the mountain. Heidi told me that you pushed the other girls into leaving you up here, and that you were going to go further up on purpose, because you wanted to get lost.'

Nancy turned to Lila, seconds from opening her mouth to berate her for telling Heidi the plan, but she stopped herself.

'If that's what Heidi told you then you need to ask Heidi why she's making up stories about her friends,' came Georgia's voice. Her tone was husky, raised over the noise of the wind. The rain was beating down now, harder and harder. Nancy's legs were sodden, rainwater was creeping into her shoes.

'Miss Brandon,' said Nancy, 'it's getting dark, we're getting wet. Don't you think it would be best if we made our way back down to the bottom of the mountain? You wouldn't want to put us in any kind of danger, now, would you?' It was meant to be a threat, but the words came out like pleading. Nancy didn't care, though. The wind was pushing her sideways, throwing her off balance.

She was frightened. Her fear must have been contagious because Heidi piped up in a little voice, 'Maybe we could talk about this when we get down to the bottom?'

'Yes,' shouted Lila, having to raise her voice so the words weren't lost to the wind. 'Let's do that.' Lila took a step forward, bringing herself even closer to Miss Brandon and Heidi. The lack of space between them looked wrong. Why wouldn't Miss Brandon just step backwards?

'Come on, let's go,' said Nancy, at the same time that Georgia shouted, 'We need to start walking.'

They were all talking over each other, all saying the same thing but with different words.

'Stop it,' shouted Miss Brandon. 'All of you, stop talking – I need to think.' Her voice was different, higher pitched than Nancy had ever heard it. She ran her hands through her hair and wiped the rain away from her face, smearing her mascara. She looked so young. Anyone who saw them would think they were a group of friends, not a teacher and her pupils.

'This is ridiculous,' shouted Nancy. 'We need to go.'

If Miss Brandon wouldn't move, she would push past her. Focusing on the ground below her feet she steered her eyes away from the sheer drop below them. She tried to walk around Miss Brandon, stepping off the path and on to the sloping bank at the side. Her foot slipped on the sodden earth. She yelped and grabbed Georgia, who caught her arm.

'See?' shouted Georgia. 'Please, Miss Brandon.'

Miss Brandon had stopped replying. She was completely silent, looking into the distance.

'What's wrong with her?' asked Lila. Nancy shook her head. 'I don't know.'

Things had gone too far. It was too high and too dark and too frightening to keep playing this game. The rain was coming from every angle, the wind was driving it into their faces. Nancy could hardly hear her friends speak.

'Miss Brandon, seriously, we'll go back to our groups,' Georgia was saying. 'Let's go back. Please. It's slippery.'

Georgia's voice seemed to revive Miss Brandon, who pulled herself up to full height. Heidi was frozen next to her, her face ashen. Nancy wondered if Heidi understood what she had done. If she realized that this would be the final nail in the coffin of her sad little 'friendship' with Lila.

Miss Brandon took another faltering step forward, closing the last inches of distance between them. She was so close to Georgia now, their noses were almost touching. Nancy watched Georgia, trying to catch her eye, willing her to step backwards, to give Miss Brandon more space. But Georgia wasn't moving. It was like she didn't want to lose face.

'Miss Brandon,' said Heidi, reaching her arm out, 'Miss Brandon, I think we should—'

Miss Brandon's voice was thick with anger as she spoke over Heidi: 'You three will do exactly as I tell you – all three of you are going to listen to me, right now. I have had enough. Am I making myself clear? I am—'

Miss Brandon turned, seemingly determined to address all three of them at the same time. Nancy watched as Miss Brandon's walking boot found the edge of the path, as the loose gravel moved underneath her foot.

A rip of thunder.

A scream.

Nancy looked over to Georgia. When she looked back, Miss Brandon was gone.

NOW

Lila

Lila's hand hadn't stopped bleeding. She shoved it between her legs, hiding it. It couldn't bleed for much longer, not if she squeezed it really hard. If she told Georgia and Nancy about it they'd start doing those faces again and Nancy would say that Georgia was right, Lila was a mess. Georgia already thought she was drunk and stupid, and she'd love another excuse to tell her off. She was picking up the last bits of glass and putting them in a pile on the garden table. She was such a drama queen.

At least Nancy was being nice. Georgia always talked about Nancy like she was evil, like she hated them, and Lila had started to believe it. But Nancy was being way nicer than Georgia tonight. Maybe it was all backwards, maybe Georgia was the mean one and Nancy was the nice one.

'I like your boots, Nance,' she said, trying to change the subject. It was true. They were nice boots. Theory, maybe. Or Zadig & Voltaire. Expensive boots. She couldn't have boots like that because when she bought stuff Roo asked her what value she thought she was bringing to the home. No value at home. No value to her friends. Not after this, anyway.

Georgia picked up a watering can and started washing away the broken glass on the floor. Lila couldn't help laughing. The watering can was clean and cream and probably cost, like, a hundred pounds from an interior design shop. Stupid Georgia, spending all her money on tacky watering cans. All Charlie's money. Lovely Charlie.

Nancy was doing that voice again, like she was trying to calm down a frightened animal. It was annoying.

'It's OK,' was what she kept saying. 'You don't need to feel guilty.'

'But I do,' she slurred. Words were all sticky. They weren't behaving themselves. 'I feel so guilty, all the time.'

'You know what happened wasn't our fault. The school told us that afterwards. They apologized.'

She did remember. But she remembered the other thing too, and it was too loud in her head to turn down.

Brandon had asked her to come to the study before lights out. It had been tuck shop that day, when the desk was covered with boxes and boxes of pick-and-mix sweets and the whole room smelled of sweet, sharp sugar. They were allowed to spend seventy-five pence each. You were allowed to count your own sweets. Everyone cheated.

Lila had been nervous. Every time she'd seen Miss Brandon she'd got in trouble. But she'd offered her tea and sat on the sofa. Lila had tucked her legs underneath herself in her armchair, feeling weird about the fact that she was wearing pyjamas in front of someone who was fully dressed.

'I wanted to talk to you about Heidi,' she had said. Fucking great, she remembered thinking. I bet that bitch has complained.

'You're a very important support system to her,' she had said. Lila hadn't been able to hide her surprise, but Brandon had gone on to explain that Heidi's doctors thought she had made a huge improvement since the beginning of term. 'They think that's because of you,' she said. 'You should be very proud.'

Lila hadn't felt proud. She had felt a bit sick.

'Does this mean I have to keep sharing with her?' she had burst out, forgetting to sound sympathetic. Brandon's face had clouded. 'No, that's not what I'm saying. I'm trying to say that you've done a good thing by being so kind to Heidi. You've made her feel happier and safer, and it looks like she's on the mend. All I wanted to ask was that you keep an eye on her. If you see that the scratching or the sleepwalking is starting again, I need you to let us know. And just keep doing what you're doing – being kind and supportive. That's all we need from you. OK?'

'Lila?' Nancy's voice pulled her back.

'What?'

'You've gone quiet. What's going on?'

She stood up. Maybe it was cold out here. Her glass looked empty-ish. Too close to empty to be good. She wanted more. It was nice red wine, soft and fuzzy and it made her head feel quieter. Her throat felt acidic and her teeth were numb. Roo would want her to stop. He would make that angry face at her across the table and tap his own glass and people would pretend not to notice, but they'd talk about it later.

'Let's go inside.'

Neither of them spoke. God, they were being annoying this evening. Their eyes were wide and serious and they were all panicky. Like kittens. They scattered every time you reached out towards them.

'I want to go inside.' She stepped forward, feeling wetness under her toes. She'd forgotten to put any shoes on, and now she couldn't feel her toes properly. Were they wet or cold? She staggered forward. It was hard to walk with her toes all funny and numb. She stumbled.

'I want to get another drink and I want to see the boys.'

They probably thought they were being really clever and discreet, the way that they were giving each other surreptitious looks. 'I can see you doing that,' she said.

'Doing what?' asked Georgia. God, that voice was annoying. 'We're not doing anything.'

'Christ, Lila, why aren't you wearing any shoes?' Nancy demanded.

'You'll cut yourself,' said Georgia. She was doing a shocked face now too.

As if she cared.

'It's fine. I don't need them. It's not cold.'

Lila turned to face Georgia. 'She's gone all American. They don't like it when it's really hot or really cold. They're wet,' she spun back to Nancy. 'You're wet. Wet and American.'

Nancy's face was so cross that it was funny, so she laughed, casting her eye towards the kitchen. The boys were still sitting around the table, they weren't laughing. They looked quiet. They wouldn't have anything to talk about. Roo wasn't having fun. She could see from the way his jaw and his neck were, even from outside. It would be time to go home soon. He would want them to go home. Whenever they had an invite to Georgia and Charlie's house, he got pissed off. Maybe it was because Charlie and Georgia lived in Notting Hill and they couldn't afford a proper house there. That was the sort of thing Roo minded about. He would tell her off on the way home for being embarrassing. That's what happened last time, when she was sick down the side of the taxi and they had to go to the petrol station and buy bottles of water to wash it off because the driver wanted them to pay fifty quid for cleaning, which they didn't have to spare. Tomorrow, when he wasn't cross about the drinking any more, he would complain that Charlie talked about work all evening and Brett was boring and it was obvious why Nancy was seeing him (and then he'd do a wink just in case it wasn't obvious to her, even though it was).

'Let's go back inside,' she said. She should go and save Roo. 'Come on.' The words had come out much louder than she intended. They sounded a bit like shouting. The boys had turned to look at her, so it must have been quite loud. She waved. Why were they staring?

She followed Georgia and Nancy back into the kitchen, aware of the black smudges her feet were leaving on

Georgia's pristine stone floor. She'd probably wait until they'd all gone home and then get on her knees and start scrubbing.

'Lila, why don't you go and sit with Brett?' said Nancy. 'He'd love to chat to you.'

Lila knew they were trying to get rid of her. The second she sat down they'd be off together, talking about her, about how she was a mess and her hair looked shit and wasn't Roo a saint for putting up with her. But it was fine. It didn't matter. She'd just go and sit and talk to Brett, lovely Brett who didn't judge her and hate her and make her feel guilty because she was the only person who actually wanted to have fun at a party.

NOW

Georgia

Nancy's grip on Georgia's arm was tight, painful even. God, she was strong. Georgia followed as Nancy steered her into the downstairs bathroom and spun the porcelain tap, filling the sink with a rush of water to cover the sound of whatever she was about to say, and then sat down on the loo seat. Georgia watched the tap flow. It would be so nice to be in water. She slid her finger under the stream, back and forth, enjoying the feeling of droplets splashing on her skin. It would be good to have it on her face, too. But that would ruin her make-up.

'What the fuck is wrong with her? She can't seriously think she's being punished?'

Nancy's panic was frightening. It was like seeing your parent lose control, a sudden rush of fear underpinned by a realization that the person you trust to have their shit together was, in fact, human. If Nancy started losing it then they were all fucked. Lila would just have to pretend to be calm. Act like it didn't matter.

Georgia shrugged. 'I don't know.'

'Well think. We can't leave her out there on her own with the boys for long. Fuck knows what she might say.'

Georgia allowed herself a split second of triumph. Nancy had seen it. Nancy understood.

'Why is this happening now? Why is she suddenly so obsessed with the Miss Brandon thing?' asked Nancy impatiently.

Georgia felt she could have reached out and taken handfuls of the air that stood between them. They did not talk about this. Ever. There was nothing to be gained from it.

She tried to calm herself. The thudding in her chest was making her skin fizz. 'I don't think it's the Miss Brandon thing.' She steadied herself, one hand on the basin. It had to be said: 'I think it's the Heidi thing.'

She would never be able to erase the expression on Nancy's face from her mind. It was twisted. Ugly. It transformed her perfectly symmetrical, probably surgically altered beauty into something truly grim.

Panic didn't suit Nancy.

It went against her character. It was the kind of character that only someone with money could have. The kind of character which came from knowing that she could buy her way out of anything, that there would always be someone who could make a problem go away.

That was what had always made them different.

'We can't let her tell anyone,' said Nancy, stating the obvious.

Georgia nodded. 'She won't. Not if you talk to her. She'll listen to you, she always does.'

'Did you hear her out there? That "joke" at dinner

earlier? She's lost it. She thinks she's fucking cursed, Georgia. Cursed.'

'I heard her. I've been here for the last few weeks, trying to stop her from doing anything, OK? You're the one who's been living on the other side of the world. You didn't even tell me about the miscarriage, which is clearly what's caused all of this.'

'It's not my fault!' Nancy's pitch rose.

'I'm not blaming anyone. I'm saying that I get it. We can't go on like this. OK? We have to fix this. We have to do something. We need a plan.'

Nancy turned the tap off and looked into the mirror. She smoothed her hair down and took a long, deep breath. 'We can't let her leave tonight. OK? Whatever happens, don't let Roo take her home. We can't risk her saying something to him, not while she's all fired up.'

Georgia nodded. 'She sleeps over all the time.'

'Fine. Good. That's something.' Nancy reassured herself. She ran her fingers under her eyes and smiled, then she turned the gold key in the lock and opened the door. Georgia didn't know what else to do, so she gave herself a glance in the mirror, putting her fingers through her hair and pushing at the roots, trying to recapture some volume. The bun Lila had put it in earlier had given her a headache, so she had let it down. Charlie had watched her doing it, a look in his eye that she couldn't remember seeing for months.

Nancy was right. They needed a plan. But as she watched Nancy extend her hand to open the bathroom door, words slipped from her lips.

'What if she's right?' Her voice sounded thin and stupid. But even so, she needed to ask.

'What?'

'About the babies.'

'I'm sorry?'

'What if it's why I can't get pregnant. What if it's why she had the miscarriage? You don't exactly have dozens of tiny tots running around.'

Nancy gave her an incredulous look. Georgia knew how it sounded. They were adults. Sensible, educated adults. They didn't believe in curses and magic spells. Yet Lila's words had made her skin tingle and she didn't know how to shake them off.

'Lila has a baby, Georgia. Did you forget that part?'

She didn't meet her eye.

'How can we be "cursed" if she's got a kid?'

Georgia stared at the floor. She couldn't meet Nancy's eyes, but she knew what she needed to ask. A question that didn't belong at a dinner party.

'Have you ever been pregnant?'

THEN

Georgia

It was hard to say how long the four girls stood on the path on the side of the mountain, waiting, not sure what they were waiting for. Sirens, Georgia supposed. It was an emergency, and when emergencies happened, there were sirens. That was how it worked. But of course, none came.

She had smashed a glass during the summer holidays. It had slipped between her fingers while she was washing up, her brothers splayed out in the telly room, watching football. It had tumbled to the floor and shattered into fragments. Georgia had stood, watching the sea of glass around her bare feet and waiting for an adult to come, someone who would know what to do. This was just like that.

It was Nancy who spoke first. Shouted, really, her voice weak against the wind.

'We need to get down to the bottom.'

Georgia felt grateful that Nancy had decided to be in charge. Carefully she moved her foot across the path, testing it. It was slippery.

'We should keep going. The rain is only going to get worse.'

'Are you joking?' came Heidi's voice. 'We need to call an ambulance.'

Nancy shook her head, throwing her hands up to gesture at the rain, as if it was possible Heidi hadn't noticed. 'We need to get back down to the bottom, then we can talk about this.'

Heidi's face was twisted. Her complexion was always red, marred by acne, but it was even ruddier as she drew closer to Nancy, her eyes little slices in her face. Her hair was sodden, dark with the rain and matted against her forehead. 'You know this is an emergency. Call an ambulance.'

'I don't have any signal,' Georgia yelled, taken aback by Heidi's distress. She pulled her phone out. It had been her brother's, but she'd managed to convince him to lend it to her while he was away, so she'd finally have the same as everyone else. She wrenched it open and held it up to Heidi's face. 'See? Nothing! We can't call anyone.'

'We should go and find her then,' called Heidi.

'Don't be stupid,' Nancy retorted. 'Come on, let's go.' The rain was sideways now, slapping her skin, her ears. She cupped her hands over her eyes, trying to shield them from the onslaught.

'What is wrong with you?' Heidi shouted. 'What the hell is wrong with you all? Lila? You're not going to go along with this, are you?'

Georgia turned to look at Lila. Of course she was. She knew what was good for her. 'Go along with what?'

'We need to go down there and find her. You know we do.'

'We can't,' said Lila.

Heidi was almost screaming now. 'She fell off the side of a fucking mountain, you stupid bitches. She could be injured down there.'

Georgia watched Nancy step forward. She was so long, so elegant in her composure, it was as if the force of the wind and the water wasn't touching her like it was touching the rest of them. It was like watching a ballet. 'No one has signal, Heidi. Now calm down. You're putting all of us in danger.'

The other girls stared at her dumbly.

'There's nothing we can do right now, Heidi,' Nancy went on, taking another step forward. 'What were you trying to do, bringing her up here? To be honest, it seems like, on some level, you wanted this to happen.'

Heidi's mouth opened and closed, as if she couldn't find words. 'We have to go and find her,' she repeated.

'Sure,' said Nancy. 'If you want to take that risk because you feel guilty, that's fine. But it's dangerous, and if you fall you'll probably smash your head open, and that won't be any use to anyone, will it?'

'Please don't, Heidi,' Lila whimpered. Very good, thought Georgia. A perfect touch.

'We need to get down to the bottom of the mountain to be safe, we have to look after ourselves here. We'll see if we can get signal at the campsite, and if not,' Nancy said, 'tomorrow morning, when it's light, we'll go and find Miss Brandon. She's probably going to be fine. She might even walk round and meet us at the campsite. But we can't put our own safety at risk,' Nancy concluded decisively.

'This is a load of shit. If we leave her there, she'll die. We need to go down and get her, or we need to walk to a road and find help.'

'What's this, Heidi? A guilty conscience?' asked Georgia.

Heidi's face filled with pain. Real, animal, wounded pain. She was definitely crying now. Looking at her swollen face made Georgia feel sick. It was like driving past a truck full of piglets and knowing they were on their way to be slaughtered. Part of her wanted to step forward and wrap Heidi in her arms and tell her that it was going to be OK. The other part wanted to give her a shove and watch her fall, too. Something about her was just completely revolting. Perhaps it was the weakness of her shuddering sobs.

'Stop crying,' said Nancy, her voice flat. Heidi ignored her, and kept sobbing.

'Stop crying,' Nancy repeated. 'We don't have time for this. If we don't get our shit together and get down the mountain before the path gets flooded, we'll be stuck here all night, and I don't know about you lot but I really don't feel like trying to pitch a tent up here.' Nancy was practically screaming to get her voice heard over the wind.

Heidi took a deep shuddering breath.

'Heidi, we can talk about it later,' Georgia said. 'But we need to get down.' She stooped to pick up her backpack. 'Come on. Let's go.'

Heidi's feet stayed static. Georgia watched Lila cross back to her, hold out her arm and say something, something Georgia couldn't make out. Heidi's face softened slightly. She took Lila's hand and, finally, began to walk.

★

The journey down to the bottom had been fraught. They moved slowly, clutching at each other, torches held between fingers which were solid with cold. But they had made it, and it was warmer now among the trees. Looking straight ahead, Nancy could see that the other girls had found a clearing at the base of the mountain and pitched their tents. A little part of Nancy had been frightened of what they might find when they got there. As the path had twisted she had lost her bearings. Would they find the ground splattered with Miss Brandon's blood? Nancy tried to wipe away the image in her mind, the picture of Miss Brandon with her limbs splayed at odd angles, whimpering for help. They had seen nothing, and Nancy was grateful for it.

'What are you going to tell them?' Georgia hissed. Nancy kept walking in a straight line.

'That she fell.'

Nancy slowed slightly, allowing Georgia to catch up with her. 'Where's Heidi?'

'Behind us, clinging to Lila.'

'I don't trust her.'

'Of course not,' replied Georgia. 'We need to do something about the phones.'

'What?'

'The phones. Everyone will have smuggled a phone in – apart from Heidi, because she loves rules. If she gets her hands on a phone, calls someone, an ambulance, they'll go out and find her. She might still be—'

Nancy nodded.

'What if she is?' Georgia said.

Nancy shrugged, the shoulders of her waterproof jacket wrinkling. Her hair, which she had tied into a bun that morning, had come loose from its tie and was sticking in wet tendrils to her neck. She walked fast, she knew she should slow down, to give Georgia, who was five inches shorter, an easier time keeping up, but it felt important to get as far away from the base of the mountain as possible. Every metre was a tiny relief.

'I don't know,' she admitted. 'I don't know.'

'What would happen to us?' Georgia asked, her eyes firmly on the grey-green ground underneath her feet.

Nancy snorted. 'I'm not exactly an expert on this,' she replied. Why did Georgia seem to think she would have an encyclopaedic knowledge about everything – even this?

'OK, but what do you think would happen?' asked Georgia. Her voice was getting higher and higher with panic.

Nancy stopped and turned, looking at the figures of Lila and Heidi catching up with them. She nudged the ground with the toe of her boot. 'I think,' she replied, 'that we'd be kissing goodbye to going to Oxford. Or anywhere else. Probably to A levels too. Maybe the rest of our lives.'

Georgia ran her hands through the sodden tangle of her hair. 'You think?'

Nancy tried to smile, tried to turn her words into a joke, tried to find a tiny ounce of humour to make Georgia less afraid. 'I'm sure we could do Open University courses from prison.'

It didn't work.

They both knew the deal. Brandon was almost certainly dead, but if she wasn't, a night in the elements would do it. The noise of her scream was still locked in the hollows of Nancy's ears but it would be gone soon enough. And even if it wasn't, no good could come from their getting into trouble for this, ruining their lives over it. And anyway, it was true. They had no phone signal. Searching for her would be dangerous. What else could they do?

They were almost at the campsite, where they would find the rest of the green team and have to guard every word they said.

'That's the plan?' asked Georgia. She sounded like a lost child. Nancy's shoulders were tight and there was a pricking in the back of her eyes. Why was it always her who had to be in charge? It wasn't fair. But that was a stupid thing to think. It wasn't fair, but it was reality. If she didn't protect herself, and Georgia and Lila, no one would.

She gave Georgia a curt nod. 'That's the plan. Make sure Lila knows too.'

NOW

Nancy

'Have you ever been pregnant?'

Georgia's head was still bowed, she was pretending to fiddle with a loose thread on her dress but it was doing absolutely nothing to hide how embarrassed she was.

Telling the truth would make everything worse. Nancy knew that. It had nothing to do with any of this, of course. She'd been born like this. Nothing she could have done at any point would have made her able to have children. But Georgia was stumbling, she was going the way of Lila. Nancy wouldn't let her fall fully. She couldn't. There wasn't space for both of them to fall apart.

'Yes. Twice. I had an abortion both times.'

Something akin to relief seemed to wash over Georgia's face. Nancy shut the door on the vision of herself lying on a cold leather chair, legs in stirrups. The consultant's horrified face. The stupidly soft voice she had used in the consultation room afterwards.

'You didn't tell me,' said Georgia. 'I could have gone with you. When was this?'

'Once at Oxford and once in Boston. I went on my

own, it was easier that way. I don't want to talk about it, if you don't mind.'

She would have to note that down somewhere to make sure that she didn't forget. It wouldn't do for Georgia to realize later that it had been a lie and go back to her ridiculous notion that it meant something. Georgia still didn't look happy.

'Look, there's nothing wrong with you. Not everyone gets pregnant straight away. A lot of my friends in Boston had to have IVF, and then they got pregnant naturally the second time. The worst thing for you is stress. If you obsess over this, it will be self-fulfilling. You'll ruin your own chances. OK?'

Georgia nodded. 'You're right. They keep saying that stress is the worst. But it's hard not to be stressed when I'm thinking about it all the time, and Charlie's convinced that it's his fault, even though he's had all the tests and they're saying it's fine, which means it's my fault, but they can't find anything wrong with me either. There's a chance that we're just incompatible, and that would be so awful, and I know there are options like sperm donation but—'

The words coming out of Georgia were laced with pain and panic. It was unbearable. 'George?' Nancy said.

'Yes?'

'We should get back. If we're gone for ages it'll look strange. They'll notice.'

As if on cue, a roar of laughter came up from the kitchen.

Georgia nodded. 'Sorry. It's just been a while since I had anyone to talk to about this.'

A therapist, Nancy thought. That's who she should be talking to about this. Someone whose time she paid for. Someone who could be trusted to keep their mouth shut.

'Let's go. We'll serve coffee, and then we'll take Lila upstairs for a chat. OK?'

Georgia got up, ran her hands over her skirt and checked her reflection.

'Yes. OK. Let's go.'

'Why do you always insist on going to the loo together?' asked Roo, as Nancy bumped straight into him. She laughed. 'You know what we're like. We've got to make the most of every moment.'

Roo grinned and ran his hands over Nancy's torso, his fingers lingering on the narrowest part of her waist, drinking it in. Nancy stiffened. Usually she'd have stepped smartly away from him, making it perfectly clear that this kind of flirty banter was unacceptable. But tonight she chose to laugh. How often did Roo do this? Was it just the girl from tennis, or were there others? An intern at the office, the occasional call girl in a hotel room? Lila had confessed once, over a long night of tequila and secrets, back before they had stopped sharing, that Roo liked things she couldn't bring herself to do. He wanted her to hurt him, to force him to do things. Much as she tried, Lila had told Georgia, she couldn't. It had, she said, all seemed so utterly silly. Maybe that was why Roo went elsewhere. Perhaps he couldn't help falling into bed with women who were different from Lila, women who wanted to humiliate themselves to please him. The vision of notes being pressed into a woman's hand in a plasticky hotel, the idea of Roo tied up under cheap lighting, made Nancy feel slightly sick. She wondered if things were as bad for Georgia, if she dutifully dressed herself in La Perla lingerie, if she made a point around his birthday to ask if there was anything he wanted that she wasn't doing. Nancy could see Georgia fussing at the silly straps in her walk-in wardrobe, lighting hundreds of candles and practically throwing a parade just to give her husband a blow-job.

Nancy would never be like that. She would never allow sex to become a chore, or for it to be something she did exclusively to please her partner.

'Watch where you put those hands, Mr Brear,' she said to Roo, keeping the laugh in her voice.

Roo smirked. 'Move out of the way then, I'm dying for a whazz.'

He would leave drops of piss all over Georgia's loo seat and floor. There was no question about it. Nancy wrinkled her nose. He really was vile.

'Let's get a drink, Gee. See you in a moment, Roo.' Nancy paused for a moment to adjust the dimmer switch.

'What are you doing?' asked Georgia.

'It looks warmer like this,' she replied, then, realizing she might have irritated her friend, added, 'It's a great colour in here.'

Georgia smiled, mollified. As she did, Nancy heard an enormous uproar from the kitchen, the sound of shattering glass and a loud, pained scream.

THEN

Lila

'Guys,' shouted Georgia, 'can everyone come here please?' Lila watched the slow surge of movement as girls came out of their tents, damp and muddy, clearly exhausted. 'What's going on?' asked Katie.

'We'll explain in a moment,' said Nancy.

It still felt like a bad dream. People always said that, but it really did. It was like when she had nightmares that her dad was dead, or that she was alone somewhere dark and cold, and then woke up with her neck wet with sweat. Lila couldn't quite believe that she wasn't about to find herself in her dorm, flooded with relief that what had happened on that mountain hadn't been real. It was hard to believe she'd made such a fuss about sleeping there, about being separated from the others. She'd happily spend the rest of her life at Fairbridge Hall, sleeping in that same dorm, with Jenny snoring and Heidi crying, if it meant that all of this would go away.

Nancy was counting the girls, making sure that everyone was there. She was clever like that. She'd know that everyone needed to hear the exact same facts at the exact same time or there would be fifteen different stories going around by morning. Next to her, Georgia looked tired. There were violet smears underneath her eyes.

'Is everyone here?' asked Georgia. Her question was met by a general murmur of assent.

'There's been an accident,' she said. Nancy's eyes snapped to the side. Who had decided that Georgia was going to make the announcement? She was doing the 'strong but sad' face that she always used when she was in trouble. It was an expression she'd copied from celebrities in magazines who were on trial for a DUI.

'Miss Brandon fell,' said Nancy quickly.

Chatter broke out amongst the other girls. 'We need to stay calm,' said Georgia, raising her voice. 'And wait here for help.'

'What happened?' asked Katie.

'We were standing near the edge, working out our best route down, and Miss Brandon came towards us. Heidi had told her that we were trying to break away from the group,' said Georgia. Nancy watched as dozens of eyes looked for Heidi, finding her sitting down on a fallen tree.

'It's not her fault,' said Lila. 'It wasn't anyone's fault.' That was true, wasn't it?

'She was angry and out of control. She fell,' Georgia finished the story.

'Is she still alive?' asked Carmen.

No one answered.

'Shouldn't we call an ambulance?' said Laura.

The chatter started again, buzzing. 'We tried,' said

Lila. 'When we were up there. Our phones aren't working. Everyone should check their phone. See if you have signal.'

Lila watched as the girls fumbled in their jackets, scrambled back to their tents or searched their rucksacks. One by one they pinged open the screens of their phones.

'Anyone got a signal?' asked Nancy.

No one answered.

'It's like Miss Brandon told us,' Nancy said. 'There isn't any signal around here.'

'She also put the payphone on our map,' said Heidi. Lila felt the panic rise. She didn't like the idea of leaving Miss Brandon where she was. But she liked the idea of an ambulance coming, before she'd even had a chance to speak to Georgia and Nancy, even less.

'It's too dark to find it,' said Nancy. 'I wish we could, but we'll get lost, and we'll end up in even more danger.'

'We could go and find one of the other camps?' said a voice from the back of the group. It was Katie.

Georgia nodded, still wearing the strong-but-sad expression. 'I thought about that. But we don't know where they are. It's too dangerous to go for help now,' she went on in a small voice. 'It's terrible, what's happened. Everyone's in shock. But we can't put ourselves in danger. It's not what Miss Brandon would want,' she added.

Lila was surprised. She'd thought the other girls would fight harder for Miss Brandon, try to save her. Miss Brandon had done everything right, from her blow dry to her heels, and these girls had acted like they loved her. She'd even got them to vote against the social.

But when it came down to it, when it was dark and raining and there was even a hint of danger, not one of them was willing to put themselves at risk to look for her.

'What are we going to do now?' said Carmen, stepping forward. Nancy looked up. The girls had somehow ended up in a circle. It was getting darker, harder to see everyone clearly.

'What do you mean?' asked Nancy.

'What do we do next?' asked Mengwen.

'We should go and look,' said Heidi, her voice high and strange. 'For her.'

'Be my guest,' said Nancy. Lila shot her a sharp look. It was the kind of stupid thing Heidi might decide to go and do, and another missing girl was going to make things worse, not better.

'Heidi, it's too dangerous,' said Georgia. 'It's dark, and slippery, and we have no idea where she might be. We'll look in the morning.'

Thank God for Georgia. Heidi's shoulders slumped, all the fight had gone out of her.

'Promise?' asked Heidi.

'Yes,' said Lila. 'I'll help you look.'

'Are we going to get into trouble?' asked Katie.

Nancy sighed. 'No, we're not. It's going to be fine.'

'Are you sure?' asked Sophie. 'Really sure?'

Nancy took a breath. Lila could tell that she was considering her next move carefully.

'It was an accident. We've done everything we could.'

There was a murmur of approval. They wanted to

believe it. All of them. Lila didn't blame them. She wished she could join them in their blissful ignorance.

'Everyone, give me your phone,' Nancy said across the group.

'What?' asked Sophie. 'Why?'

'We need to put them all together in one place,' she said, a hint of a plea in her voice.

'Why?' asked Katie.

'It's a technology thing,' Georgia jumped in. Lila caught their plan almost instantly.

'If you put them all together, they're more likely to get a signal. Some kind of mass antennae thing,' she joined in.

'I think I've heard of that,' said Sophie, nodding. They were buying it. Thank fuck.

Lila stood up and held out her hands. Georgia handed over her phone. Nancy followed. Nancy looked into the dark, waiting to see if it was going to work. No one moved. Fuck. If they all kept their phones there was no way they'd get away with this, no telling how much shit would come down on them. Little pictures of iron bars and sobbing parents had been flickering behind Lila's eyes for the last two hours.

Then Carmen proffered her phone, a blue Pebble one. It had been the phone du jour last year, Nancy had had one herself until one of her parents was sent an iPhone for a press review and hadn't been able to make it work.

Katie and Sophie stood up, holding out their matching pink phones. Moments later, Lila held twelve shiny mobile phones in her hands.

'Put them in my rucksack,' said Nancy.

'What? Why your rucksack?' asked Katie.

Lila tried not to roll her eyes. This was delicate. If any-one got angry or upset they'd take their phone back. Until Nancy had the phones it was a tightrope. There was no signal now, but all it would take would be one person to get one bar, and they'd be in danger again.

'You're welcome to look after them, Katie,' she said. 'I mean, we weren't supposed to bring them on the trip, and fuck knows what's going to happen tomorrow when we call the ambulance. I was trying to do a nice thing for everyone and keep the phones out of the way so that we don't get in trouble when we get back to school on top of this whole mess, but if you'd rather look after them, that's fine. Really. Be my guest.'

Katie stared at the ground. 'It's cool. You can look after them.'

'I'm going to make a fire,' said Carmen. 'It's getting colder. Come and help me,' she said, looking at the two Chinese girls.

Lila opened Nancy's rucksack and slipped the phones in. The power she held in her hands wasn't lost on her. Any one of these phones would contain secrets, lies and blurry naked photos. She wondered for a moment whether she could keep them. Even just one. The joy of opening and slipping into the secrets would be gorgeous. But no. She scolded herself. That wouldn't be smart. She couldn't afford to make stupid mistakes. There were bigger things at play here. If just one girl got a hint that her phone had been looked at, everything would go to hell. They'd handed over the most precious things they owned. It would be suicidal to mess with that.

Next month they would all have new phones, of course. Mums would be glad to have something to do, something to make it better when they heard about this horrible, traumatic experience. Once they had checked if it entitled the girls to any extra exam credit, there would be shopping trips and spa sessions and money would wash away any residual unhappiness. And that was why no one would say anything. There was a story now. A story they could stick to.

NOW

Lila

Lila was lying on the cold floor of the kitchen, perfectly still. Her hair had fallen over her face and she felt numb. The scream from her lips turned into laughter and spilled out of her. Brett's face was twisted, Charlie had frozen, his glass halfway to his mouth. Even Roo seemed freaked out, his mouth open and slack. They all looked like they thought she was dead. She tried to sit up to stop them making those faces.

'I'm fine,' she said. Only when she sat up her head hurt. And actually her elbow. Her elbow really hurt. Maybe she had landed on it.

'Careful,' shouted Brett, as she went to put her hand down. 'There's a broken plate.'

The plate had smashed in half. It was white, with a blue and gold ring. It was all shiny. It was probably expensive. Georgia had a set of smart plates that she got out when people who mattered came over. She hadn't got them out for Lila for ages. Lila tried to remember how long it had been. Actually, how long had it been since she and Roo had been invited over with other people? They were only ever invited on weeknights, always just the four of them, and they could count on being home by eleven. Why? Was Georgia embarrassed? She was probably having Charlie's boring work friends over all the time. They were a million years old and only wanted to talk about work stuff. Lila was glad not to be invited to dinner with them.

When they were first married, Georgia and Charlie used to throw parties all the time. Proper ones. Then suddenly it was all dinner parties, which weren't fun. Maybe it was because doing all the cooking and setting the table took up a whole day. Probably more than a whole day. Knowing Georgia, how much she wanted people to think she was good and proper, it could probably take three days. And it wasn't like she did anything else. She would need something to do.

'What happened?' she heard Georgia's voice. She was standing in the doorway of the kitchen looking all annoyed. Georgia shouldn't have changed. The jumpsuit had looked amazing, it had made her body look good. The dress was boring, like something you'd wear to an office or a wedding, and she'd put those hideous nude heels on. She had kept the dark lipstick, which was probably because she was trying to be polite, but that lipstick didn't go with that dress. Why couldn't she see that? It was such a waste, Georgia having all that money. Well, Charlie having all that money. Was it because Georgia had grown up poor? She'd never learned how to do shopping?

Maybe, Lila wondered, she could sneak into Georgia's wardrobe and see what was at the bottom of her drawers or the back of the hanging rails – something that Georgia wouldn't miss. Roo had snipped up her credit card in front of her face and was giving her tiny bits of money in cash so she couldn't spend it on clothes.

'We were, er . . .' Oh. Brett looked embarrassed. 'We were bench-pressing Lila.'

Georgia looked cross. Probably jealous because no one wanted to bench-press her. She was too heavy now, surely. Double-digit dress size. DDD as Nancy called it when they were younger. She and Nancy had snuck off for cocktails a few years ago, when Georgia was on honeymoon. Nancy had said then that Georgia was naturally fat because her mother was big. Working-class women always got big after they had children, apparently. But Georgia didn't even have children and she was at least a size twelve. Did Charles still fancy her? Maybe he didn't mind. Her tits had got bigger, she still had a waist. Maybe he liked it. Maybe he liked grabbing at all of her body. Roo didn't like fatness. He made comments about women who walked past them on the street and frowned when their friends ordered pudding. They used to occasionally go to the pub with the couple who lived in the basement flat of their house, until Roo had told the girl that she shouldn't drink wine because it was liquid calories. He had pointed at Lila's vodka tonic and explained how much healthier it was. The girl had been upset. Lila had tried her hardest not to feel pleased.

Nancy was laughing. At least she had a sense of humour. 'Bench-pressing Lila?' she asked.

Lila got to her feet. 'And it's Brett's turn!'

'Oh, Brett didn't drop you?' asked Nancy.

'Course not,' laughed Lila. 'Charlie dropped me. On the table.'

'You were playing this game too?' said Georgia. She was flaring her nostrils, which meant she was cross. She wouldn't say anything because she wanted everyone to like her, but she was definitely cross.

'I'm afraid I was,' said Charlie, looking at his feet. God, Georgia was mean. This was the first fun part of the night and she was trying to ruin it. Lila turned to face Brett. 'Your go!'

Brett looked across the room to Nancy. Lila turned to follow his gaze. Nancy was leaning against the island, resting her glass of red wine against her chin. 'Please,' she said, 'don't let me stop you.'

Brett looked to Georgia, who shrugged. She couldn't bring herself to be the fun sponge. He stepped forward and put one arm behind Lila's knees and the other behind her waist and whipped her up into the air. Charlie had flopped around and grunted, he'd got her up a bit but then he had staggered and that's when he'd dropped her on to the table. This was different. It was smooth and easy, Brett made her feel weightless. The strength in his arms controlled her body. She felt something fizzing in her stomach and between her legs, something that she hadn't experienced for months. Years maybe. The ceiling came closer, and then further away. Suddenly she felt dizzy, dizzy and sick. The back of her throat burned and panic forced its way up her throat, hot sour panic. Not just panic.

'Fuck!' she heard Brett shout, and the floor came closer, closer.

Pain blossomed through her head, through her neck, into her arm, her elbow. The floor was cold. Solid and cold. Her mouth was sour. There was noise everywhere and people shouting and oh God, sick everywhere.

There was sick on Brett's face, his T-shirt, the table and the floor. She looked from Brett's horrified face to Nancy's grin, to Georgia's shock, listening to Roo and Charlie screaming with laughter, and ran, slamming the kitchen door, down the hall and into the bathroom where she threw herself on the floor, her head resting on the bowl of the loo, staring into the whiteness and waiting for it all to stop, like she had a thousand times before.

There was a knock at the door.

'Lila,' came a voice. It was Charlie. 'Lila, are you OK?'

'We reckon it was the pork,' came another voice, thick with laughter. Their cackles came through the door. She watched as her black tears dropped on to the pristine whiteness of the loo, trickling down the sides and into the water. Fuck them. Fuck them both. Fuck them and their laughter and their thinking it was funny and their stupid idea to see who could lift her up. They had done this to her. Probably on purpose. They probably wanted to make her look stupid in front of Brett. They had ruined the evening on purpose. That's what they had done. She listened as Charlie's footsteps receded. He had gone. He had left her here on her own. She retched again. It wasn't coming. Calmly she slid two fingers down her throat, felt for the sweet spot and wiggled them. A thick stream

of red wine, frothy and sour, came spurting up, splatter-
ing the whiteness. Good. That was better.

Lila choked a sob which echoed into the bowl of the
loo. None of it was supposed to be like this. If she were
here, would her mother know what to do? Would she
know how to fix things? They were supposed to, mothers.
Although Lila was a mother now and she didn't know
what to do. Everyone always acted like their parents
knew the answers to questions and they remembered to
buy toothpaste and they made everything fine. But other
people's mothers didn't just die.

Lila hadn't gone home the weekend that her mother
died. There was a match on. Her team were playing the
year above. Her father had gently suggested that she
should come, but the idea of an afternoon at the hospital,
trying to make cheerful conversation and pretend they
weren't all marinating in death, followed by her father's
attempt at cooking – soggy pasta drowned in sour red
sauce – was too grim to tolerate. So she had stayed at
school. It had been the best weekend ever. They had
slaughtered the year above's team, not least because each
time Lila batted she slung the ball way across the field,
leaving her time to saunter around all four posts, not
even raising a pinkness in her cheeks. Then there had
been a social that evening. Lila had worn a pink polo
shirt and a denim mini skirt with silk ballet pumps. She
had teased her hair into a cloud of blond. That night
she had kissed four boys. Nancy only managed three.
Georgia had got more of course, but as Nancy had told her
once, Georgia had sex appeal, and that meant that things

were different for her. Sometime that night, around the moment when 'Angels' by Robbie Williams was playing and a floppy-haired boy with braces and a pink polo shirt was putting his hand up her top while the chaperones turned a blind eye, Lila's mother had died.

Cookie had told her the following morning. They had excused her from chapel and taken her to the office. There had been a box of tissues on the table and the kettle was freshly boiled, as if Lila would want to sit around drinking tea with Cookie, weeping about how her mother had died. She heard the news, adopted the appropriate face and waited to be dismissed. Then she calmly asked if she could spend the afternoon with Nancy and Georgia. It was a prime opportunity to miss lessons together.

She wiped her fingers on some loo roll and flushed. There was still a ring of red sick around the bowl. She decided not to wipe it away. She'd leave it there for Georgia to find the next morning, a little punishment. She wasn't quite sure what for.

THEN

Nancy

'How did you manage that?' Nancy asked Carmen, who stood next to her, also watching the fire.

'The fire?'

'Yes. Wasn't everything wet?'

Carmen looked pleased. 'Only on the outside. This must be the first time it's rained for a while.'

'You've made fires before?'

Carmen nodded, but didn't say anything. Nancy considered asking how or why she had learned, but she realized she didn't care. And Carmen wasn't stupid. She didn't need to be manipulated into keeping her mouth shut. She had her eye on a US university. Anything legal or messy could ruin it. That was the wonderful thing about these girls, thought Nancy. Ambition. They all wanted things. People who wanted things were much easier.

On the other side of the fire Nancy could see Georgia holding court, Sophie, Katie and Laura hanging on to her every word. She watched as Georgia dipped a key into a little bag of white powder and offered it to one of the girls, who sniffed it ineptly, knocking half the powder on to the ground. The girls screamed with laughter and Nancy forced a smile. Idiots. Clearly they'd never snorted anything before. Lila and Heidi sat further back from the crowd, their faces orange in the firelight. Lila clutched her knees to her chest but Heidi's bulk prevented her from copying the position. She sat with her legs stuck out at angles, like a broken doll. Nancy felt a moment of affection towards Lila for taking one for the team, for utilizing Heidi's obsessive crush to stop her from doing anything stupid.

'Vodka?' asked Carmen, after a few moments of silence. Nancy smiled. There was more to this girl than she had thought. She watched as Carmen drank thirstily. The three blondes were getting gigglier and gigglier. One of them had produced a speaker from her rucksack and plugged a green iPod into it, spilling out bad, tinny pop. Before long, all four of them were on their feet, spinning and dancing. Nancy caught Georgia's eye across the flames.

'George!' she shouted. 'Heads up!' She threw the hip flask clear across the fire. Georgia caught it, unscrewed the lid and drank deeply. The other girls cheered and laughed, holding their hands out and clamouring to share.

Nancy stepped back, watching as they all spun and twisted around the flames. Georgia had grabbed hands with the other girls and they were circling the fire, all screaming the lyrics of a stupid song. The enormity of where they were struck Nancy, the fact that they could make so much light and noise, so much disruption, and yet no one was aware of them. No one in the world knew what they were doing or where they were. It was the first time any of them had truly been free. The girls were jumping now, opening their mouths to catch the light raindrops that had persistently drizzled for the last six hours, making their tents and clothes and skin wet.

Nancy lit a cigarette, more for the excuse of it than anything else, leaning against the rock. It was warm on her back, absorbing the heat from the fire. It felt nice. Solid, reassuring.

She didn't want to dance, or laugh. Too much energy today had already been spent on pretending. There would be even more pretending when they got back. Not for the rest of them – it would be easy for them to say they didn't know and they weren't sure. But for her, it would be work, at least to start with, at least until she was sure that Georgia and Lila could stick to a story.

'Nance,' called Georgia, 'come on!'

Nancy said nothing. Lila jumped to her feet and joined Georgia, taking her hands and spinning around, then stopping to peel off her jumper, left in only a thin white T-shirt. Lila never wore a bra. She enjoyed the power of confusing male teachers with her stiff nipples underneath her semi-sheer school shirt far too much for that. Nancy watched with a scientific interest as raindrops landed on her friend's skin, her nipples puckering under the damp cotton. Georgia, never one to be outdone, had pulled her T-shirt off, laughing in her pink lace bra. Her breasts were bigger than Lila's and her hips had a more aggressive angle to them. It was Georgia's body which got them served in pubs and bars and clubs. Not because anyone really thought Georgia was eighteen, but because they felt less guilty pretending that they did.

'Come on!' the girls shrieked. Nancy faked a smile and raised her top above her head. Then, because she never simply followed suit, she peeled off her jumper, her top, her sodden tracksuit bottoms, and her bra, leaving just her black knickers. She paused to let the other girls stare at her. A moment of stillness. A pretty note of confusion. And then, predictably, each of the other girls reached for their own T-shirt. Pastel-coloured cotton flew through the air, landing on the ground, in the fire, on the rocks, and around the fire danced a tribe of girl-women. Some high, some drunk, some simply swollen with their first real taste of freedom, or the illusion of belonging.

The only figure still fully clothed, sitting on the ground and watching the scene unfold, her face a picture of misery, was Heidi.

NOW

Nancy

Georgia was clearly heartbroken about the sick situation. She had ineffectually tried to get rid of the smell with a variety of organic, hypoallergenic, not-tested-on-animals, probably gluten-free cleaning products before eventually disappearing into the cellar and coming back up with a dusty bottle of bleach, which she was now splashing liberally over everything that Lila's vomit had touched. Nancy took a breath, letting herself enjoy the comforting, familiar scent. There was something so lovely about the smell of bleach.

'I'll pay for anything that's ruined,' said Roo, who had reclaimed his position at the door, smoking yet another cigarette.

'It's fine,' called Georgia, her voice icily cheerful. 'Nothing is ruined. I only hope Lila is OK.'

'She'll be fine,' said Charlie. 'She's a trooper.'

'Has anyone actually checked on her?' asked Brett, who was stacking plates at the other end of the kitchen. Nancy scolded herself inwardly. She had half forgotten that he was there. 'Should I take her some water?'

'No,' said Nancy, without thinking. Where had that come from? It wasn't like her to feel defensive of Brett.

She shouldn't have brought him here. What was this feeling? Acrid. Something which felt a bit like jealousy, but jealousy wasn't a feeling that Nancy allowed herself. Her mother had said, from childhood, that a person couldn't own another person and to try to do so was fruitless. Trying to prevent your partner from wanting another woman (or man) was a fool's game. It was about as petty as being annoyed at someone for going to the cinema with another person. Besides, becoming over-wrought about it just made you less appealing. The only thing you could do to keep someone, she had told Nancy, was to stay beautiful and interesting and to make a world with yourself in it much more appealing than one without. So that's what she had done.

Her lack of jealousy had proved useful. She didn't compete with anyone in the office, preferring to calmly plug away at her own ambitions. It had always worked. And boyfriends had liked it too. No temper tantrums about female friends or passive-aggressive messages about flirty waitresses in restaurants. Providing a threesome for a major birthday present was her signature move. She had lost track of how many times she had celebrated a beau's thirtieth, thirty-fifth or fortieth birthday by booking a woman from an escort agency (always the same reputable agency where the girls were clean, and never anyone equal to, let alone more attractive than she was). Sometime around the moment when she was kissing her flavour of the month while he pounded into a twenty-two-year-old Russian, he would look up at her and know what a joy it was to date a woman who wasn't capable of feeling envy.

At least, not until now.

'She's fine,' she replied. 'I'll go and check on her in a moment.'

'I think she should probably go to bed,' said Georgia. 'It's fine, Roo,' she followed, seeing that Roo was rolling his eyes. 'You don't need to take her home. She can fall asleep here and you can get an Uber later, or she can stay the night. Does Inigo need her tonight?'

He snorted.

'What?' asked Nancy.

'Inigo barely even knows who she is at this point.'

'What?' asked Charlie. Nancy registered surprise. She hadn't thought of Charlie as having any interest in anything other than work and, when they were younger, Georgia's chest.

'What do you mean?' added Georgia. Idiots. They were pushing him too hard. They had overreacted to his statement, which was going to make him think what he was saying was important. Now he would hold back and they would get far less information.

'Nothing,' said Roo. 'I didn't mean it.'

'Is she struggling?' asked Georgia.

This was interesting. And if Georgia wanted the dirt on Lila's mothering – or lack thereof – she was going about it entirely the wrong way.

'Lila's fine!' Nancy said purposefully, refilling her wine glass. 'Absolutely fine.'

Roo rounded on her. There was nothing Roo liked

more than disagreeing with someone, especially Nancy. He would seek out topics which he thought would inflame her and then needle her with them all evening. At the dinner party for Georgia's thirtieth birthday he had asked her whether she thought feminism was a waste of time before they had even cut the cake. At Georgia's engagement drinks he'd questioned her about whether she felt panicked that she would never get engaged, or that being so 'masculine' was the reason she could never keep a boyfriend. Announcing that Lila was fine was the quickest and easiest way of getting Roo to tell her what was going on.

'Actually, Nancy, she's not,' he said. She tried not to smile. How could anyone be so easy to play? She raised her eyebrows, pretending to be surprised at his reaction.

'It's none of my business, Roo, but I feel like she's doing a great job for a new mother, especially considering what she's been through.'

'She gets drunk every single night. Did you know that? She gets the teenagers next door to look after him while she goes to the pub and hangs out with a load of twenty-two-year-olds who she met there. They only like her because she used to buy them drinks. I had to take her credit cards away because her spending addiction was so out of control, and three weeks ago she dropped Inigo. She dropped him. What kind of a mother drops her own child? He barely knows who she is any more. All I asked was that she do some childcare, spend some time at home, act like a fucking mother for a few years, but of course she can't do that. And now she's pulling stunts like this every single time we go out.'

Roo's words bounced around the kitchen, highlighting Georgia's apparent objection to soft furnishings. When he finished, a silence floated between them. Nancy thought about telling him that it was his fault. She could explain how his lack of interest in his wife's career or feelings or life had left her isolated and miserable, which had clearly turned into late-onset post-natal depression, coupled with grief at losing a baby. But there was no point. He wouldn't listen, nothing would change.

There was a rustling noise as Georgia peeled off her washing-up gloves and dropped them into the bin – concealed in a cupboard, naturally. Nancy found herself seized with the desire to slip into the room next door and see whether Georgia had gone full Surbiton and hidden the television in some kind of awful cabinet.

'We should put Lila to bed,' said Georgia, across the room. Her tone was weary. Clearly, she had done this before, more often than Nancy had realized. She made a mental note to thank her for it later. Georgia was a martyr – deep down she'd be glad that she'd been allowed to do all that good work. But it wouldn't do to look ungrateful. None of the men moved. Brett looked embarrassed. Thankfully he had the sense to realize he couldn't help. Neither Charlie nor Roo even seemed to consider it. Roo was rooted in his seat, one leg casually flung over the other, refilling his own glass, and Charlie's. Nancy watched as he hovered the bottle over the glass nearest to Brett. How many times had he forced Brett to refuse alcohol that evening? It must be giving Roo a manly kick every time. Brett wasn't an alcoholic of course. He and his friends had landed on the concept once and been taken with it. It made them seem more exciting, more like their idols. No British twenty-something would give up booze because they'd blacked out a couple of times or had a slightly heated discussion with a policeman. But Brett was precious. He was the kind of man who openly talked about having feelings and allergies.

She looked down at the ring on her left finger. She'd managed to put off introducing him to her parents this weekend by treating her parents to a trip to the South of France. She'd told Brett with a long face that they would be away. He'd cuddled her and told her that it sucked but it didn't matter – they'd meet soon.

The idea of him sitting around the same table as them, earnestly talking about his writing and the off-Broadway play he had written (so off Broadway it was in New Jersey) made her cringe. They would be polite, but he would bore them. They wouldn't say anything, they would claim to be pleased for her. Once, when she had been at Oxford, she had brought home a boy whom her father had found googling 'Mon-ay' in the hall. He'd waited until they had broken up to reveal the story, but even so, each time one of her parents regaled a table with the anecdote, always thinly veiled with the intro of 'We're so pretentious, we're such a cliché!', it was a humiliation. Eventually she would find someone who could manage a dinner party in her parents' kitchen. And then she would take him home. But it wouldn't be fair to put Brett through that horror, especially as she probably wouldn't go through with the marriage anyway.

It would be easy enough to end it. She would claim that her trip to London had made her realize how much she wanted to be back there, and that she wouldn't feel comfortable asking him to move, so while they had had something wonderful, it had to end.

'Are you coming?' asked Georgia. Nancy stood up, sending a look which said, 'Calm the fuck down, you're not supposed to seem stressed.' Georgia gave the tiniest nod imaginable and wrapped a smile across her face. 'She'll be in the bathroom. Sometimes she falls asleep in there and then it's a nightmare to get her out.'

THEN

Lila

The canopy of the tent was uneven. They hadn't pitched it properly. Unsurprising, given the dark and the drizzle and the fact that none of them had ever slept in a tent before. Lila could feel the warmth of Georgia and Nancy either side of her, swathed in their sleeping bags. Each time someone moved there was a faint rustle. Lila couldn't help but ask herself: were there really people who did this for fun?

'What are we going to do tomorrow?' came Georgia's whisper.

Closing her eyes, Lila wondered how many times they had lain in the same dark room, whispering. In so many ways it was just like it always had been. Only before, the worst punishment for being caught was being sent to the isolation dorm. Up in the eaves of the ancient boarding house, every gust of wind sounded like a scream. It only had one bed in it, the walls were completely bare. Everyone said it was haunted. Lila had found herself there once. The girls had been giggling and shrieking and Matron had marched in, forgone the requisite verbal warning and sent Lila straight upstairs. Nancy had volunteered to go instead. 'I was making the noise,' she had lied, 'I'll go.'

Matron hadn't believed her; even then Nancy didn't look like the kind of girl who giggled or shrieked. Lila had sat, wrapped in the unfamiliar duvet, with her back against the corner wall, her eyes frozen open, waiting for it to be light, waiting to be safe, when Nancy had crept up the stairs. They had slept, the two of them squashed in one tiny single bed, until the morning when the light stripped away the shadows.

That was what Nancy did. She was your worst enemy until you needed her and then suddenly she was the best of best friends.

Was that still true, Lila wondered. Would it still be true tomorrow morning when everything became real?

'We need a plan,' Nancy breathed, her voice almost nothing. She was lying on her back, looking upwards, her face solemn in the dark. 'In case they don't believe us.'

Lila lay still, listening to the other girls breathing, to the faint snuffles coming from the other tents. They must be asleep. All the booze, all the walking.

'We could run away? Maybe by the time they found us they'd be so worried that we wouldn't be in trouble?' said Georgia. No one replied. It was a stupid suggestion. As if they'd survive a week on their own. 'What would happen if . . . ?' Georgia trailed off. Her voice was very small and very frightened. Lila wished she hadn't asked the question.

'The problem is Heidi,' said Nancy. 'She hates us.'

'She hates you and me,' said Georgia, her voice was harsher now and Lila could see her frown in the half-light.

303

'That's true,' said Nancy. 'She doesn't hate Lila.'

The silence rang out between them. 'We need sleep,' said Nancy eventually. 'We'll be able to think more clearly in the morning.'

Lila murmured her agreement. 'Night,' she whispered.

'Night,' said Georgia.

'Night,' said Nancy.

Lila stared into the darkness, listening to her friends' breathing become slower, waiting until they were unquestionably asleep, so asleep they wouldn't stir as she slipped away from the tent, phone in hand.

It was true, that expression about it being darkest before the dawn. Lila had watched the tangle of sleeping bags and rucksacks and walking boots grow darker and then slowly illuminate as the sun rose behind the clouds and light seeped through the tent.

Lila watched Nancy's eyes flicker under her lids. Her hand seemed to be searching for a pillow which didn't exist. It was strange, watching someone wake up, watching them try to work out where they were. As she came to, Nancy sat up. She looked affronted. Lila realized that in all the time she'd shared a dorm with Nancy, she'd never seen her asleep. She was always the last to lose consciousness and the first to wake up, lying on the floor doing her sit-ups before the others had even opened their eyes.

'How long have you been awake?' asked Nancy.

'A while,' said Lila. Georgia began to murmur. She was always the slowest to wake up, the least willing to get out of bed, trying to bribe the others to smuggle her some toast from the dining hall so that she could snatch another fifteen minutes of sleep. 'What time is it?' she whispered. 'What's that noise?'

All three of them paused to listen. It was a heavy whirring, like a washing machine on a superfast spin.

'What is that?' asked Nancy, repeating Georgia's question.

'A helicopter,' said Lila, fiddling with a bit of skin on the side of her finger. It wasn't long enough to get a proper grip on, so she couldn't quite manage to pull it off.

'A helicopter?' said Georgia, her eyes wide. She sat up and began to scrape her hair into a bun, as if having her hair tied up would make her more able to cope with whatever was about to happen.

'Why would there be a helicopter?' asked Nancy. Her voice was low and slow, but she was grabbing for her socks, pulling them on, as if she was getting ready to run.

'I called the police,' said Lila. The bit of skin was too short. She put her finger to her mouth and tried biting it instead.

'You did what?' asked Georgia.

'I called the police,' she repeated.

'What did you say?' asked Nancy super slowly, as if Lila didn't speak English.

'I told them the truth,' she said. She watched her friends' faces flood with horror. 'I told them that Heidi pushed Miss Brandon.'

NOW

Georgia

'Lila?' Georgia called through the wooden door. 'Lila, can you unlock the door, please?'

There was no answer. Classic. If she had passed out with her head cradled in the loo bowl, they would have to wait for her to wake up, which could be hours. 'Lila, please,' she tried again.

'Shall I try?' asked Nancy.

No, Georgia wanted to say. No, you shouldn't try because it will probably work and I can't bear the fact that she'll listen to you when she doesn't listen to me, just like she always did, in spite of the fact that I'm the one who's actually been a friend to her lately.

'Sure,' said Georgia.

Nancy stepped forward and knocked gently on the door. 'Li? Can I come in?'

There was no reply. Pleasure swelled in Georgia's stomach, covering the gnawing feeling that had been there all evening. 'Lils, Georgia's got a key, we can unlock the door from out here, but it's a pain to dig it out and I've told her she's overreacting. You're coming out, right?'

Georgia didn't have another key, and Nancy had said

nothing of the sort. But of course it worked, because it was Nancy and everything Nancy ever did always worked. There was a flushing noise and the door handle turned. Swaying in the doorway, her black eye make-up etched down her face like smudged charcoal, was Lila.

'I'm fine,' she moaned, her head tipping forward as if it was too heavy for her neck. 'Fine.'

'I know,' said Nancy. 'We're going upstairs to chat for a bit. Come with us.'

Lila didn't say anything.

'We're going to hang out upstairs, grab some time away from the boys,' Georgia heard herself say. 'Come on.'

Lila didn't move.

'Or you can stay down here,' said Nancy. And we'll talk about you behind your back, said the unspoken words between them. Lila lurched forward. If she was sick again, especially on the carpet, Georgia decided she wouldn't clean it up. Roo could pay for a fucking professional to come round.

They walked behind Lila, who moved slowly, one hand on the banister and the other on the wall, swaying from side to side and dragging her feet up each step. It was an irritating, affected way of walking and Georgia was sure that if she tried she could walk properly. Eventually they reached the second spare room, next door to where Brett and Nancy were sleeping.

'Put her in my room,' said Nancy. 'In case she needs to yak in the en-suite.'

'Charming,' said Georgia, but she did as she was told. 'You don't mind swapping rooms?'

Nancy shook her head. 'We're happy anywhere.'

Even when it was only the two of them, her oldest friend wouldn't drop the act. She thought back to Nancy at the start of the evening, her little eighteen-plus performance. The boys downstairs had been convinced, believing that they were accidentally party to a spontaneous new couple who couldn't get enough of each other. Georgia knew better.

Lila crashed on to the bed, still fully dressed. The soles of her feet were filthy – black from walking around outside with bare feet. Georgia tried not to think about the smears they would leave all over the fresh white sheets.

'Should I take her necklaces off?' asked Georgia, looking at the mess of tangled gold chains around Lila's neck. Nancy shook her head. 'Let's just get her changed.'

Georgia took off Lila's top, replaced it with one of Nancy's T-shirts, peeled off her jeans and folded them on a chair, marvelling at how anyone could be so tiny, and dressed her in some pyjama bottoms. She could feel Nancy's eyes on them. She took more care than usual, careful to make her actions look as if they were motivated entirely by love, trying to act as if the routine came naturally to her. It had, once upon a time. But this had happened again and again and again. It was too much to ask of one person.

Lila flopped backwards and Nancy, kicking off her shoes, lay down next to her. Georgia followed suit, because this was clearly what they were going to do. Lie next to each other, Lila in the middle as always, pretending to be close. Were all friendships like this? Were all failings and confessions seen as weaknesses to be exploited? Or were there actually people who could tell their friends something embarrassing or sad without knowing it was bringing them joy?

'What's going on, Li?' Nancy said, stroking Lila's long hair. 'You're a bit of a mess.'

Lila nodded.

'Why?'

'You know why,' she murmured, crushing the heel of her hand into her eye, smudging the mascara even more. 'I told you.'

'Is that it?' Nancy asked. 'You're not using that as a distraction from Roo?'

'Roo? What do you mean, Roo?' asked Lila.

What was Nancy playing at? Georgia watched her stroke Lila's arm.

'Nothing,' said Nancy. 'I only meant that it seemed like you weren't having an easy time.'

A silence filled the room. Georgia took a long breath, trying to catch the scent of the diffuser she'd chosen for in here. Pink Peppercorn, it was called. But Pink Peppercorn wasn't covering the smell of stale smoke and sick and alcohol from Lila's skin. There was no way Nancy's words had been accidental. Nancy didn't have accidents. She didn't let things slip. Every word she said was chosen.

'That's not what you meant,' Lila slurred, pulling herself up to a sitting position.

'She didn't mean anything,' said Georgia, trying to calm Lila down.

'How do you know?' Lila asked.

Georgia hesitated. Nancy had been right. They had to

have this conversation. They had to know how bad it was. Whether Lila might tell their secret.

'It's probably nothing,' said Georgia.

'Tell me,' said Lila again, her voice cracking. 'Tell me what's happening.'

'Tell her, Georgia,' said Nancy. 'She deserves to know.'

'Know what?' said Lila, panic rising.

Georgia took a long breath, her eyes focused on the ceiling. 'It's probably nothing. But Charlie saw Roo at the Harbour Club a few weeks ago, with a woman.'

Silence again. Silence was lovely.

Silence was safe.

'What were they doing?' asked Lila, her voice calm.

Georgia waited a moment. She thought that it would hurt to tell Lila, but it didn't seem to hurt at all. 'Kissing.'

The three of them stayed still and silent, shoulder to shoulder. Georgia wasn't sure how much time passed.

'I don't care,' Lila slurred.

'You should,' said Nancy.

'I don't. We never have sex any more.'

'That doesn't mean he can cheat,' said Nancy. Georgia wondered how often 'never' was. Did she mean truly never? Or just rarely?

'He'd be better off without me,' said Lila quietly.

Neither Georgia nor Nancy said a word. 'He'd find someone else,' Lila went on. 'Someone who's better at all of it.'

A long pause. 'No one would be better than you,' said Nancy flatly.

'I'm not good at it,' said Lila. 'Any of it. I wasn't

supposed to – I shouldn't have—' Her words were becoming more and more jumbled and tears were slipping from her eyes again, black tears which would stain the pillowcases. How many times had Georgia's cleaner held another pillowcase up, sighing about the stains from Lila's mascara?

'What do you mean, "shouldn't have"?' asked Georgia. 'What did you do?'

Lila murmured a reply that Georgia couldn't hear. 'What?' she asked.

'The woman from the Harbour Club,' said Lila weakly. 'I'm so tired.'

'What about her?' asked Nancy.

'She's Roo's friend from uni. She's called Venetia.' She locked eyes with Nancy. 'I want to go to sleep for a while. I never sleep any more.'

Lila said the woman's name with a contempt that Georgia hadn't heard in her voice for years.

'You're not sleeping?' asked Nancy.

Lila shook her head. 'Not since I lost the baby.'

Nancy sighed. 'I could – no, no, you've had too much to drink.'

Lila sat up slightly. 'What?'

Nancy looked frustrated. 'I've got shit-hot American sleeping pills in my handbag. But you can't take them with alcohol. At least, not as much as we've been drinking tonight.'

Lila's face crumpled.

'Just lie down,' said Georgia. 'If you lie down, you'll drift off.'

'I'll wake up in the middle of the night,' whimpered Lila, like a little girl. 'I always wake up.'

Nancy cocked her head to one side. 'Could she perhaps have one or two? She's probably sicked up most of the alcohol anyway.'

'Absolutely not,' said Georgia. 'It's dangerous.'

'Are you sure?' asked Nancy.

'People take overdoses by accident all the time, Nance. Don't you read the papers? It's dangerous. You fall asleep and you don't wake up. Doctors over here don't even prescribe the stuff you can get in the States any more.'

Lila was staring at the ceiling.

'I went to see her once, you know?' she said sleepily. Her lashes butterflied against her cheeks. Georgia touched her arm. She couldn't be allowed to fall asleep. Not yet. Not until they knew she wouldn't talk.

'Who?'

'Heidi. I went to see her.'

NOW

Nancy

Nancy took a slow breath. This was no time to panic. Before long she would be home, back at work, back in her apartment, thousands of miles away from here.

'You went to see Heidi?' she asked, keeping her voice gentle. 'When she was in prison?'

Lila shook her head, but stopped abruptly, as if it was making her feel even more sick. She retched. Nancy watched Georgia to see whether she'd react to any potential damage to the sheets. To her credit, she didn't. Perhaps it wouldn't be the first time that Lila had been sick in the spare room.

'No,' she murmured. 'At her flat. After she got out.'

'Why?' asked Georgia, her chin resting in her hands.

'I needed to.'

'Why did you do that?' asked Nancy. It took a superhuman effort to keep her tone light.

'I'm sorry,' she said. Her head was lolling sideways on the pillow.

Georgia looked nervous. Her eyes kept flicking back and forth to the door, as if one of the boys was going to burst in. They weren't. There was no chance. Brett wasn't stupid enough, and the other two were having too much fun trying to let Brett's coolness rub off on them. Pathetic as it was, Nancy could feel Georgia's nerves. Perhaps they were contagious. Every word that slipped from Lila's lips seemed to seep into the fabric of the room, into the world, poisoning it, putting them all in danger.

'What was it like?' Nancy heard Georgia ask.

It was a stupid question. Nothing Lila said was going to make any of them feel any better, and feeling guilty wasn't going to change what happened, what happened back then, what happened to Heidi. None of it.

'Shit,' whispered Lila, her eyes closed. 'Sad and shit. They were making her take all these pills. She didn't have any stuff. Nothing.'

'She must have had something,' Georgia pressed. Nancy blinked. Perhaps this wasn't weakness. Perhaps it was guilt.

Lila was trying to shake her head again. 'She had a picture of us, some clothes and some stuff in the bathroom. That was it. And she was so happy to see me. So so happy.' Lila paused. 'God, I feel terrible, I didn't even go to her funeral.'

Tears slipped out of the corners of Lila's eyes, running down her face and into her hair, leaving inky trails across her skin.

'She said she understood why I'd done it. Why we'd said what we said. She said she didn't mind.'

'We didn't *do* anything,' said Nancy flatly. 'We were kids. Besides, it was her fault that woman was even up there. You know that.'

'That's what she said.'

'What else did she say?' asked Nancy.

'She asked if I'd pushed her, if I'd done it,' said Lila in a tiny voice. Georgia held herself still. Sixteen years and not one of them had uttered a single word about that day. Not one of them had ever asked the others what role they had played. It was the rule.

'I didn't,' said Lila, her voice almost too quiet to hear.

'It's ancient history, Lila,' said Nancy gently, from the other end of the bed.

'Two people are dead, because of us,' snapped Lila, her voice hard, a million miles from her usual breathy tones. 'She killed herself in that shitty flat because of what we put her through.'

Georgia looked up, trying to breathe, trying to process the information. It wasn't Lila. Lila hadn't pushed Miss Brandon.

'No one meant for it to happen,' said Georgia, unable to think of anything else to say, leaning forward to stroke Lila's hair. Lila smacked her hand away. Georgia snapped it back, shocked.

'You know that's not true,' said Lila, pulling the duvet over her tiny body.

Georgia said nothing.

She had always wondered what would happen if anyone found out what they had done. When she was waiting for trains or when the film was about to start at the cinema the question would suddenly lodge itself inside her mind and squeeze out everything else.

She wasn't stupid enough to consider googling it on

her phone, or her laptop, even at work. But very occasionally at an airport she would wander around a shop full of laptops and tablets and her fingers would start to itch.

Manslaughter. Perjury. Murder.

All she had ever wanted to know was how long the sentence would be. How many years she'd lose. Sometimes she would work herself into a worry loop about what might happen if someone started digging into Charlie's personal life. Even if nothing came of it, even if they thought that she had done nothing wrong and it had all just been a terrible accident, his career would be ruined. He'd shouted at her for nearly an hour when she had forgotten to renew their television licence, years ago. 'You don't understand,' he had told her. 'I have to be pristine. That's how it is now.'

And her parents. Her father with his gnarled, twisted bones and her mother who never complained. What would they do without the money she silently transferred to their account every month? The thought was too horrible to entertain. She pinched the skin between her index finger and thumb, trying to distract herself with the pain.

Nancy crossed the room to the window and stooped to get something from her handbag on the armchair. She unscrewed a tube of hand cream and rubbed it into her palms, perfectly calm. 'Anyone want hand cream?' she asked, holding out the tube. Lila said nothing and Georgia shook her head. What was Nancy playing at? How was this going to fix anything? Nancy needed to talk to

Lila, put the fear of God into her, explain that she would lose Inigo if she kept acting like this, do something. Anything to seal Lila's lips.

'The pills are in here, Lila. Like Georgia said, don't touch them tonight – with the amount you've drunk this evening. But when you wake up tomorrow you can take a few home with you, OK? Then you'll get a couple of nights' sleep and this will all seem better. I promise.'

Nancy looked down at the Cartier watch she'd worn on her left wrist every day since her twenty-first birthday. 'We should go back downstairs, Gee. Let Lila get some rest.'

Georgia stroked Lila's hair, like she was a child, and stood up. 'You're lucky you're drunk, Li. If you weren't, you'd have to come downstairs and listen to Charlie and Roo prattle on about rugby. We'll have to rescue poor Brett.'

Lila said nothing. Her gaze was still focused on the ceiling. Georgia followed the line of her eye to the light fitting. It was an antique, a chandelier which she had found in an East London junk market and had lovingly restored. Every tiny crystal caught the light inside it and turned it to rainbows. She was glad that Lila had noticed it. It was perfect to fall asleep under.

'You go down, George. Check on the boys.'

'What?'

'You go downstairs. I'll stay with Lila for a while, until she falls asleep.' There was something in Nancy's voice. An ice which told Georgia that to disobey, to stay lying on the bed, would be a terrible mistake. Obeying Nancy was what they did. It was the glue that held them together. The only thing all three of them had ever agreed on. It was what had always kept them safe.

Georgia dragged herself up, away from the softness of the bed and the warmth of Lila's body.

'Sure,' she said. 'Night, Li,' she added, stroking her friend's hair. 'Sleep well.' She heard her voice catch.

Closing the door, she sank down on to the top step and gripped the white spindle which held up the rail, gripped it until it hurt the fleshy palm of her hand. It would be bliss to stay there, to stay sitting. Not to have to go downstairs, not to have to keep pretending that everything was fine. And part of her, the part she liked least, wanted to try to listen. To know what Nancy was going to say to Lila, how Nancy was going to succeed where Georgia would have failed.

When she was little, sitting on the stairs was a punishment. Being removed from whatever was going on and deliberately excluded, forced to sit and listen to everyone else having fun. Funny, that what had once felt like a punishment now felt like the safest place in the world.

NOW

Georgia

'Nance,' Georgia whispered as Nancy's long dark figure, like a shadow, slipped out of the bedroom and on to the landing.

Nancy paused between the door and the stairs. 'What are you doing? Why aren't you downstairs?'

'I was waiting for you.'

'That wasn't what I told you to do.'

'I'm sorry,' she dropped the heavy weight of her head into her palms, looking at the carpet through the gaps in her fingers.

Nancy shook her head. 'It's fine. Let's go.'

Georgia hesitated on the step. 'Are you sure?' she said.

Nancy leaned against the banister. Georgia focused her eyes on Nancy's face, refusing to allow herself to look at where she was standing, how close the heels of her shoes were to the edge of the landing, almost between the spindles of the stairs.

It was amazing how much Nancy's face could change. Sometimes, when she was trying to seem sweet, she was pretty. Beautiful even. But tonight her features were angry in the half-light. The perfection of her face was in the angles, angles which were harsh now.

'Am I sure about what?'

'Leaving her.'

'She's fine,' said Nancy. 'Come on.'

The banister was almost perfectly aligned with Nancy's hips. Had she always been this tall? She'd always been above average height, and people didn't grow in their twenties, she knew that, but only half of her body was below the banister. That couldn't be right, surely? The whole of her torso, her head, they backed on to nothingness, just open space. Even the wall behind her was stark because Georgia hadn't been able to find anyone who would put a ladder on those stairs to hang a picture.

Words bubbled inside Georgia's throat, forcing their way out into the air. 'Lila didn't push her.'

'What?'

'Lila. You heard her. She said she didn't push Brandon.'

Nancy paused at the top of the stairs. Her chest was blotchy. She looked down and, as if realizing where Georgia was looking, wrenched up her top. 'We should go down.'

But Georgia didn't seem to be able to make her legs move. 'Don't you care?' she whispered. 'Not at all?'

Protecting Lila had been the glue that had held them together for the last sixteen years. The silent, unspoken knowledge that their eyes had been on each other when that scream came. The scream that would rip through Georgia's mind at three o'clock on a Tuesday afternoon when she was shopping or in the middle of a friend's baby's christening.

'Of course I care,' Nancy snapped. Georgia pulled backwards, surprised at the venom.

'I don't understand,' said Georgia. 'If it wasn't her . . .' Georgia took a long breath. 'Was it you?'

She stared into Nancy's face, watching it for a reaction. It flushed with genuine shock. 'No,' she said, after a moment. 'I was looking at you. When it happened. I didn't see . . .'

Georgia nodded, her head heavy. She had been looking at Nancy. She could still see her white face and her black hair, stark against the grey sky. 'But if it wasn't Lila . . .' she went on.

'Then we must have been right all along. It must have been Heidi.'

Georgia barked a sort of half-laugh, outraged at Nancy's desperate clutching at straws. 'You know it wasn't Heidi.'

'There were only four of us up there. Who else could have done it?'

'What if it wasn't any of us?' Georgia replied.

Nancy looked confused. She shifted her weight from one leg to the other, her gaze over Georgia's shoulder aimed at the stairs. 'What?'

'What if no one pushed her? What if she fell?'

What if, she thought, unable to turn the words in her head into speech, what if none of this ever needed to have happened? What if they had simply called an ambulance and Heidi hadn't taken the blame and we'd all just been able to get on with our lives and only seen each other once a year because we weren't so cripplingly afraid that someone would say something and bring down everything we've spent our entire lives trying to build?

'We need to go downstairs,' said Nancy. 'Come on.'

'But . . .' Georgia trailed off. There was no end for that sentence.

'But nothing,' said Nancy. 'I'm fixing it. That's what you wanted, right? That's why you made me come here? Now all I need from you is to put on a smile, go downstairs, sit at that table and keep everyone's glasses full. Got it?'

Georgia nodded. She took one last look at the white door to the bedroom, framed by yellow light, and then she gathered her thoughts and twisted them up into a tight ball, shoving them to the back of her head. There was nothing more to say. She couldn't lose everything over one obscene mistake from the past. They both knew now. It had all been a mistake. They had dedicated their lives to guarding a vault which, in the end, turned out to be empty.

A breath.

A glance in the mirror hung above the stairs.

A smile.

It was too late now.

There was nothing she could do.

THEN

Nancy

'In my many, many years at Fairbridge Hall, I have never had cause to hold such an assembly. It is with a heavy heart that I stand before you girls today.

'You will all know by now that a member of staff, a member of our community, tragically lost her life earlier this month, during a house expedition. You will also know that a pupil at this school has confessed to being responsible for Miss Brandon's death.'

Mrs Easton looked down at her note cards, swallowing. Nancy hadn't ever seen her struggle like this. She never used notes usually. But then, this one was a first.

'It is impossible to say what led to the choices made by Heidi Bart. We will never fully understand how such an act of violence could have taken place. What we do know is that it is time for us, as a community, to try and heal. Many of you loved Miss Brandon. She was a brave, talented and intelligent woman. She was a housemistress to some of you, and English teacher to others. While she was only with us for a short time, she made an enormous impact on the school and those of you who were lucky enough to encounter her will, I am sure, remember her for the rest of your lives. A memorial for Miss Brandon will be held in the chapel later this week, and a book of condolences will be made available in your boarding houses. Any memories that you would like to share there will be given to her parents. We hope that this will provide them with some comfort at what is no doubt an extremely difficult time.'

Nancy glanced at her watch. Two hours. The car would be arriving in two hours. She could practically feel the sun on her skin and taste the cocktails already. The flight was nine hours. She counted in her head, two until they left, an hour to the airport, hardly any messing around once they were there because they were going first class . . . sixteen hours. In sixteen hours, they'd be lying on sun loungers in their bikinis with no parents, no work and no one to tell them what to do.

'While this is an extraordinarily tragic situation,' Mrs Easton went on, 'I would ask that you do not give in to the temptation to gossip. If you wish to discuss Miss Brandon, or any of the circumstances surrounding her death, your form tutors are always available to you, as are our team of counsellors. The way in which we will rebuild from this tragedy is to move forward. With every sports match you play, every test you revise for, every choir you sing in, you will make Miss Brandon prouder. We do not allow grief to defeat us, instead we use the inspiration of the person we have lost to power us forward.'

Mrs Easton looked earnestly around the room. Someone coughed into the silence.

'Please stand, and turn to page three hundred and forty-two in your hymn books.'

'I win,' Nancy breathed under the noise of four hundred girls getting to their feet. 'I said she'd only say tragic twice.'

Georgia rolled her eyes. 'I was sure it would be more.'

The grand piano on the stage of the concert hall droned out the school hymn and the room was filled with music. They were so nearly free.

It was only going to be a short break to help them recover, what with everything they had been through – the police, the questioning, all the eyes on them. The press coverage. The holiday mustn't look like a reward, that was what their parents had said. It had been the school who had suggested a little time off to clear their heads and reflect. Nancy was quite sure that Mrs Easton hadn't meant for them to go to Jamaica for three weeks, but Lila's father had offered the house, Nancy's parents had said they would cover Georgia's flight, and it seemed sensible. Her parents didn't have time to be running around after her, and, as they had told her on the phone, she and Lila and Georgia were so close. They needed to be together. Even the missed lessons didn't matter. Their exam boards had been entirely convinced by their extenuating circumstances. They'd all have extra time and if the stress became too much they would simply be awarded their perfect predicted grades.

All in all, thought Nancy, as she got to her feet to watch Mrs Easton exit assembly, things seemed to have worked out rather well.

NOW

Georgia

'Did you put my troublesome wife to bed?' roared Roo as Nancy and Georgia walked back into the kitchen. Georgia's fingers felt slippy. Where was her glass? She took a slow breath. It would be here somewhere. She mustn't look flustered. Everything was going to be fine. Absolutely fine.

Nancy was laughing, 'We did. Not for the first time. You're useless, Roo, sitting down here pulverizing your liver and letting us do the hard work.'

Roo wrapped his arm around Nancy, squeezing her into him. She was too tall. She didn't fit under his shoulder. Nevertheless, they both seemed to have committed to the act.

'Come and sit down, Nonce,' he laughed, using the nickname he'd tried to give Nancy years ago, which had never caught on. 'We need to plan your wedding to young Brett.'

Roo swept Nancy back to the table and sloshed wine into her glass. Georgia began to collect dirty glasses. How had the six of them managed to get through so many? She placed them in the left side of the huge porcelain sink, taking the detachable tap off its stand and sluicing them. As she did so, she felt arms wrap around her waist. Charlie. The warmth of his torso was reassuring.

'You did an amazing job this evening,' he whispered in her ear. 'But I wish they'd all fuck off so that we could have the place to ourselves.'

Georgia dropped the tap and turned to face her husband. 'Me too,' she whispered. 'We never did christen the kitchen.'

Charlie looked as if every single one of his Christmases had come at once. She laughed, and resolved to say things like that more often. She reached up and kissed him, hard and deep. Perhaps it was silly. It was certainly out of the ordinary. But she was drunk and everyone else was drunk. And she wanted to feel close to him in that moment. From the kitchen table, Roo and Brett cheered. Charlie stuck his middle finger up, laughing. Pleased that they all thought he and Georgia were so blissfully happy.

'Come and sit down, you soppy sod,' shouted Roo. 'Bring the port over, too. And not the cheap stuff – I'll know if you're trying to fob me off.'

Charlie laughed and rolled his eyes at Georgia.

'I'll go down to the cellar,' she said indulgently. 'You go and sit down. I have a feeling this might be a late one.'

NOW

Georgia

Georgia's stomach ached from pretending to laugh. Roo had told a long, self-indulgent story about paying a secretary in his office – who everyone hated – to photocopy her tits, and how she had subsequently been fired. Leaning forward to refill her wine glass she felt a squeezing soreness. No, she realized. It wasn't from the fake laughing. It was the bruises. With a feeling like falling forward she realized that she hadn't had her injection that evening.

Charlie had probably had too much to drink to inject her. Would waiting until the next morning throw the whole process off? Probably. The idea of the eggs she had worked so hard and suffered so much to produce just floating into her stupid body and being washed away in another crimson tide of disappointment was too much to bear. Not to mention the money. What if missing the jab ruined everything and Charlie wouldn't pay for another cycle? He'd been difficult last time, making worrying noises about waiting and saving up, like he thought this was all one big indulgent extravagance. She would have to do it. It would be a matter of minutes. Georgia looked around the table, planning to tell Nancy where she was going, to ask her to keep Roo and Brett distracted. But Nancy wasn't there.

Never mind. Everyone was drunk. Roo wouldn't remember the next morning, and anyway the chances were Lila would spill the IVF beans next time she got pissed anyway. Georgia wasn't sure why the idea of Roo knowing was so repulsive to her, but it was. He'd probably make jokes about rotten eggs or Charlie standing too close to a microwave as a child.

Under the table she reached for Charlie's hand. 'Injection,' she mouthed.

He looked away. She squeezed again. 'Injection,' she whispered this time. 'Wait a minute,' he replied.

Georgia slipped to the fridge, took the vial from inside the sealed box, behind the orange juice that she used as a decoy, and pressed it into her palm. The boys were listening to Brett, rapt by his storytelling.

'Please?' she simpered into Charlie's ear, standing behind his chair and using the sweet voice he loved. He rolled his eyes, but got up.

'Excuse us for a moment,' he slurred. 'Brett, I want to hear the end of this story when we get back.'

Roo started making a barking noise, banging the table with his hand. 'Taking your wife UPSTAIRS,' he yelled.

Georgia painted a smile on her face, determined that after tonight she would never have to play nicely with Roo again. 'We're getting some more wine from downstairs,' she said. 'We're not teenagers any more, we can wait until we go to bed these days.'

She paused outside the kitchen door, her eyes adjusting to the brighter light. 'Let's go in the bathroom. Quick.'

'Do you really need me for this?' he asked sulkily. He hated needles and he hated injecting her, but it needed to be now and last time she'd tried to do it herself she had sat on the bed for an hour trying to force herself to shove the needle in.

'Yes, I do. Come on.' She yanked at his arm, pulling him towards the downstairs loo underneath the stairs. A flicker in the corner of her eye distracted her. She looked up. Standing perfectly still on the stairs, back against the wall, was Nancy. Georgia opened her mouth to ask her what she was doing. Before she could speak Nancy pressed her index finger to her lips. Georgia shut her mouth.

'Are we doing this or not?' asked Charlie, who was facing in the other direction.

'Yes,' she replied firmly. 'We're doing this.'

In the yellow warmth of the loo, Georgia bent over, putting her hands on the wooden lid of the loo seat. She trained her eyes on the spines of the books in the bookcase. Silly books lived in here, the kind of books that people who didn't know what to buy them – people like Charlie's siblings – had given them for Christmas. Charlie had wedged last weekend's *Sunday Telegraph* into one of the shelves. How had she missed that when she cleaned up earlier?

Dipping her head to remove the offending object from her eyeline, she felt the blood and booze rushing between her ears and willed Charlie to get on with it. He always took so bloody long, doing it fastidiously, as if it was more likely to work properly if it took half an hour.

'Come on, darling,' she said, trying to keep her voice light but already acutely aware of how long they had been missing from the gathering. 'We're missing the party.'

'One second,' he said, 'just let me—'

A noise, unlike anything Georgia had ever heard, came crashing through his sentence. A huge, blunt slam followed by echoing silence, and the tinkle of glass hitting stone as Charlie dropped the vial of hormones.

'What the fuck was that?' asked Georgia. But she knew. If she was honest with herself, she knew.

She knew as she watched Charlie's terrified face, as she saw him fumble with the gold doorknob, as she followed his hulking body into the hall and heard his horrified gasp for oxygen.

The kitchen door was flung open and the others charged out to meet them. Georgia heard their footsteps stop abruptly. She saw Brett throw his hands up around his head and drop to his knees.

Her body was bent like a swastika. Georgia felt awful for thinking it, but that was what it looked like. Legs at angles that legs shouldn't be. Arms splayed out either side of her body. She was so beautiful. So white and broken and beautiful. Charlie threw his arms around Georgia's shoulders and pulled her to his chest as they stood, silently watching the slow red puddle that seeped from behind her head, ringing it like a halo in a medieval painting.

'Lila,' whispered Roo after what could have been a minute, or could have been an hour. 'Lila.'

NOW

It was a good picture. Lila would have liked it. It had been taken on their honeymoon. She was squinting at the camera, a smattering of freckles over the bridge of her nose. Her pointed chin was cradled in one palm, and her wedding and engagement rings glinted in between all the other rings she liked to adorn her fingers with. She looked happy. Peaceful. As if life had given her everything she had ever wanted. Georgia supposed she owed her a pretty final portrait, if nothing else.

The type font was elegant, too. *Camilla Brear (née Knight)*.

Georgia and Nancy had chosen it. Actually, they had chosen almost everything. Roo was in no fit state to help. Georgia couldn't have predicted how he would go to pieces. All those rows, the way Lila spoke about him. It had seemed like they hated each other. But as he sat in their living room, ignoring the toddler when he cried, and patchy grey stubble puncturing his face, she wondered if perhaps he genuinely had loved Lila.

'I don't understand,' he kept repeating. 'I don't know why she would do this.'

It had felt cruel to tell him that she had known about the affair, that she had told them both how she had found hairs on his clothes, followed him to the club and watched as he pressed some twenty-two-year-old up against a locker. But it had to be done. Now he knew it was his fault. She hoped he wouldn't ever tell Inigo. That would be unnecessary. He certainly wouldn't tell anyone else. He was too wracked with guilt for that. Instead he'd tell them that Lila couldn't get over losing her baby, that she was drinking heavily. Depressed.

Inigo had been staying with her and Charlie. Roo's parents were too old to take him, and there could be no question of Lila's stepmother Clarissa helping out. Roo had made noises about wanting to keep Inigo with him, but he was drinking. Drinking a lot, actually. Georgia had pretended not to notice all the bottles lying around when she visited. But they were rudely present, declaring Roo's mental state for anyone to see.

Georgia had snapped a picture, then neatly stacked the bottles in the recycling bin, and asked Charlie to have a word. Inigo, at least, didn't seem to have noticed any change to his life. Perhaps Lila had been around less than any of them had known. He slept through the night, mostly, his chubby hands clasped around the Peter Rabbit which Georgia had given him as a baby. Charlie had seemed a bit uncomfortable to start with when the John Lewis van had drawn up and unloaded the furniture for Inigo's new room. But, as Georgia had explained, he needed somewhere to sleep. It could all go on eBay after Inigo went home, but without Lila, Roo would need them to babysit more often. It made sense, for now, for him to have a bedroom with them. It was purely practical. A few nights ago, Georgia had come down the flight of stairs from their bedroom to the first floor and caught a glimpse of Charlie over the crib. He was stroking Inigo's downy head and whispering something. Georgia had said nothing, she hadn't wanted to interrupt. But the sight of them together, of Charlie fathering a tiny person, had filled her chest with a warmth she couldn't remember experiencing before. 'Let's make a baby,' she had whispered to him later that night, reaching under the covers for him.

Charlie had seemed surprised, as if there was some strangeness in wanting to do it so soon after Lila's death. She had started to say that Inigo would need someone to play with, a sibling. But she had stopped herself.

'Roo looks terrible,' Nancy whispered to her. 'He should have made an effort, for her father at least.'

Classic Nancy. Brutally, cruelly honest, even now.

She looked over the crowd of people in black, searching for Roo, checking to see that he was looking after Inigo properly. He seemed to be. Perhaps he had managed to make it this far through the day without drinking.

'It was a lovely service,' she said. 'The vicar managed to make it uplifting, in spite of everything.'

Nancy snorted. Why couldn't she play nice, just for today? A little respect, a few tears. But no, she had to do it her way, turning up as the ceremony started, wearing navy instead of black because it didn't wash her out as much.

'Bullshit. Nothing uplifting about it.'

Georgia cast her eyes around, trying to see if anyone in the slow procession towards the house had heard. It seemed not.

'Why is everyone walking so slowly?' complained Nancy again.

'Because they're sad,' she hissed.

'I didn't realize sadness impeded your ability to walk,' said Nancy, but at least she'd had the decency to lower her voice. 'I have to leave for the airport at four.'

They'd be back in Boston tomorrow, their lives entirely untouched. They wouldn't have to sit across the Sunday lunch table from Roo every weekend, watching him numbly push food around a plate and down his glass of wine three times faster than anyone else. Grief was boring, she was starting to realize. In film and on TV it was all screaming and shouting and deep conversations about the person who was dead. But not in real life. In real life it was slow and dull and it turned people who were once good company into zombies.

'Is that her dad?' Georgia asked Nancy. 'I haven't seen him for years.'

Not since university, in fact. They'd stayed at Lila's father's house after some party in South London. It had smelt like milk and been full of prams and soft toys. A time-warp. It wasn't the house of someone who had a grown-up daughter. And now, he didn't. His arm was linked with Clarissa's. She wasn't ageing well. She'd had something done to her face. It looked pillowy. It was a shame. She had been beautiful, once.

'George?' asked Nancy.

She looked up. 'Yes?'

'Are you OK?'

Georgia nodded. 'Fine.'

'No regrets?'

She paused for a moment. 'I don't think so.'

'Good.'

Georgia watched their breath float away on the blue air. 'Why do you ask?'

Nancy smiled, her teeth brilliant white. 'Just checking.'

Acknowledgements

I wrote the later drafts of *Perfect Liars* when I was staying with my grandmother, who was dying. One of the real gifts of getting my first book deal was that it afforded me the flexibility to spend time with her over the last two months of her life.

During those final few weeks we had a lot of conversations, as you do when someone is dying. One of the things that she told me she hated (though not as much as she hated what the *Daily Telegraph* wrote about the Kardashians) was books with long acknowledgements.

I was inclined to agree with her until I sat down to write mine and realized quite how many people it takes to make a book happen.

Without Darcy Nicholson and the team at Transworld there might have been a book, but it wouldn't have been this book. From the moment I met Darcy I knew she was my person and that I needed to work with her. The entire team at Transworld has been a gift.

Before Darcy there was the team at the Eve White Literary Agency, most importantly Eve herself. Eve discovered my writing in the Royal Holloway Creative Writing

Anthology when I was twenty-three and the idea of writing a book still felt like a complete dream.

Similarly, I owe an enormous debt to my MA creative writing group, most especially Monica, Gail, Rebecka, Samantha, Sophie and Max.

Before I wrote books, I wrote articles, and it would be enormously remiss of me not to thank the people who taught me how to do that. Claire Cohen, Emma Barnett and Radhika Sanghani, then the team running the *Telegraph*'s Women's section, took a chance on me when I'd never published so much as a blog post. I am grateful to them every day.

Similarly, the Lifestyle team at metro.co.uk – Miranda Larbi, Ellen Scott and Lisa Bowman – have been unfailingly flexible, kind and understanding when writing this book made me unreliable, annoying and a pain in the arse to work with.

Friends, also, were a huge part of getting this done. Chloe, Pete, Catherine and my beautiful goddaughter Ivy. Natalie, Hannah C, Emma, Jon, Catherine, Ian, Madeline, Jelly, Alicia – you are the most incredible cheerleaders.

The Coven: Liv, Emily, Grace, Mel, Kathy. You're the best/worst friends a person could have. You were supporting me even when you didn't know it. Mostly with wine.

The Mayfield girls – Flick, Becka, Aimee, Georgie, Carol, Lexi and all of the rest of the class of '09 – always so unfailingly kind and supportive.

If I was a little scornful of people who wrote long acknowledgements, I was very judgemental of those who decided that their acknowledgements were a place to thank people they hadn't seen for several decades. But again, I was wrong.

There are teachers who taught me that, despite being dyslexic and having terrible handwriting, I could probably achieve quite a lot if I stopped being so sodding lazy. So even if they never see this: Miss Upton, Miss Halliday, Mr Filkin, Mr Kilbride, Mrs Thompson, Miss Cornish and Mr Oxborough, I am so grateful.

A foray back into childhood brings me neatly to the part that I couldn't have avoided even if I'd wanted to. My mad, wonderful, brilliant family – all the Reids, the Mears and the Sillars, but most especially Tim, Charlotte, Lucy and George.

No two parents have ever believed in their children as much as Tim and Charlotte believe in us. The emotional and logistical support that they've given me is truly astonishing. You could not find two more generous human beings. With parents like them, it's no surprise that my divine siblings Lucy and George turned out so bloody great.

Lastly, I would like to thank my husband. When I was twenty-three I sat at our kitchen table and told him that I wanted to be a writer. He said that he would support me in any way that he could.

I don't think he knew then that what would follow would be two years of stress about money, stress about writing, stress about agents and submissions and contracts and finally, *finally*, a book. Neither of us ever had any way of knowing that it would be OK. Sometimes I was quite convinced that it wouldn't be. But he always seemed sure.

Thank you, Marcus. Thank you for being a broke twenty-something in your thirties for me. Thank you for all the holidays you skipped and things you went without so that I could make terrible money following my enormously impractical dream. I love you.

(Sorry, Granny. Miss you.)

Loved *Perfect Liars*? Share your review online.

And you can keep reading for an extract from
Rebecca Reid's next novel

TRUTH HURTS

What's more dangerous, a secret or a lie?

Available to pre-order now
Out August 2019

AFTER

'Ready, Mrs Spencer?' he asked.

No, she thought. *Not ready at all*. She nodded. 'Yes. Go ahead.'

It was a noise like nothing she had ever heard. A bang would be the easiest way to describe it, but it was more than that. Shattering. Cracking. Hundreds of years of history and memories collapsing as the wrecking ball swung into the house. Her home.

She watched the honey coloured walls fold in on themselves, watched as the ball smashed through room after room. The crowd behind her gasped with each swing.

It looked like a doll's house now. You could see right in, the rooms rudely naked without the front of the house. It was almost comical, the huge porcelain bath of the blue bathroom exposed to the elements. And then, with another swing of the ball, that was gone too. Poppy tried not to wince, to look like this was what she wanted. She had to put on a show for the people who had come to watch.

This was entertainment for them. She'd dressed carefully that morning, choosing the beautifully cut trench coat and velvet-soft jeans as protection against them just as much as the autumn air.

They think I want this, Poppy told herself. *They think this was my choice.*

Clouds of beige dust filled the air, her home reduced to nothing.

Odd to think that once upon a time she had worried about stains on the sofa or marks on the carpet.

'Are you all right?' The man with the clipboard seemed confused by her. Maybe the purple stains under her eyes were too much of a contrast with the size of the diamond on her left hand. She nodded again. 'Yes. Fine.'

'Most people don't like to watch demolitions,' he said. His suit was cheap. Shiny. The kind of thing Drew would have despised.

'No?'

'Upsetting, I suppose. Seeing your home go.'

Poppy pulled her jacket around her. 'It's the right thing to do.'

Those were the official words. The words she had said to the local council, to people in the village who asked about it. To the local paper when they rang to discuss her generosity.

It was a gift to the community, she claimed. A lovely, grassy park full of climbing frames and swings, somewhere for local children to play together. A way of changing a tragic place into a place of enjoyment. Of hope. And no one seemed to question it. After all, how could Poppy really be expected to go on living there, after what happened?

CHAPTER 1

'Right, they're now officially five hours late,' Poppy said into the phone.

'Have you called them?' Gina's voice, though hundreds of miles away, was comfortingly familiar. Poppy could see her, tangled up in her bed, curls tied up on the top of her head. For the hundredth time that week she wished she were here with Gina, instead of the Hendersons.

'No, I hadn't thought of that, I've just been trying to reach them with my mind,' she sniped.

Gina didn't answer.

'Sorry,' Poppy said. 'I'm just pissed off.'

'I can tell.'

'It's the third time this week.'

'You need to say something to her when they get back.'

Poppy raised her eyebrows at the phone. Maybe Gina's boss, who adored her, might take kindly to being told off by the nanny but Mrs Henderson made Cruella de Vil look like Julie Andrews.

'Have you started playing that game where you work out how much they're actually paying you per hour?' asked Gina. 'That's when you know it's bad.'

'We're down to £3.70,' she said. Eighteen hours a day, six days a week, for four hundred quid. She'd done the calculation on her phone after the kids had gone to bed.

Gina hissed through her teeth. 'That's bad. My worst was the Paris trip with the Gardiners. Seven kids, fifty quid a day. And they made me keep the receipts so they could check I wasn't buying my lunch with theirs. I actually lost money that week.'

Poppy used her finger to hook a piece of ice from her glass of water. It slipped, falling back in. She tried again, craving the splintering of the ice in her back molars. It slipped again. 'Why are rich people so stingy?' she asked.

'I don't know, babe,' said Gina, yawning. 'I need to hit the hay.'

'No-o,' Poppy whined. 'I've cleaned the kitchen twice. I've laid the table for breakfast. I need you to entertain me . . .'

'Go to sleep.'

Gina was right, of course. The youngest Henderson, little Lola, would be awake in four hours, and if Poppy didn't snatch a few hours' sleep before then she'd find herself snappish and short-tempered all day, taking the children's parents' shitty behaviour out on them. Which wasn't fair.

'OK, OK. Abandon me.'

'Call me tomorrow, tell me all about how you calmly explained to them that you need notice if you're going to be babysitting later.'

'Yeah, yeah, yeah. Night.'

Gina made a loud kissing noise and then the line went dead.

She could go to bed. Of course she could. But if Mrs Henderson came back sober enough to realize that Poppy had slept on the job, she'd lose her temper. Her husband might earn a million quid a year in the city, but she wasn't above docking Poppy's pay over crimes like needing sleep. Poppy tipped her head back, looking up at the sky. The stars were incredible here. It was hard to believe that it was the same orange sky she looked out over every night from her tiny room in the Hendersons' London house.

She had hoped that the cool air out here by the pool would wake her up. It wasn't working. She could feel her eyelids pulling downwards. She picked up her glass and walked barefoot, back in to the house, sliding the huge glass doors closed and locking them behind her. She padded upstairs, putting her head around Rafe's bedroom door first. He slept, just as he always did, perfectly still and clutching a plastic gun. His round face and rosebud lips betraying none of the aggression that would fill the house once he woke up tomorrow morning.

Damson next, Poppy's favourite. She had decided years ago that parents weren't allowed to have favourites, but nannies definitely were. Damson slept like her brother, perfectly still. Her iPad was in the bed next to her, an audiobook of *The Secret Garden* still being read out. Poppy leant over to turn it off and gently stroked the little girl's cheek. Damson hadn't been allowed a single ice cream all holiday because her parents had decided that those cheeks were too round. Damson hadn't questioned it, or made a fuss, but watching her stoic little face while her siblings wolfed down gelato hurt Poppy's heart.

Last, Lola, curled into a little ball in her huge white bedroom. Poppy had spent every day of the holiday so far worrying that Lola would touch something white with chocolatey hands. Thoughts of childproofing didn't seem to have been high on the agenda when they had booked this place.

The blankey that Mrs Henderson insisted Lola adored was a puddle on the floor. Just yesterday, Mrs Henderson had posted on Instagram about how Little Lola had told the first-class air hostess that she could have a cuddle with blankey during turbulence. The story, like everything else that woman posted, couldn't have been more of a fiction. As Poppy bent down to retrieve an old cup from the bedside table, a beam of white light pressed through the cream curtains of Lola's bedroom. So, they had finally come home. She glanced at the watch on her left wrist. Twenty past two. They'd said they would be home at eight.

'Oh Poppy,' husked Mrs Henderson, looking up as Poppy came into the kitchen. 'Could you undo this?' She held her wrist out. On it was a delicate, sparkling bracelet with a fiddly clasp. Poppy looked behind her, scanning the stark white living space for Mr Henderson, wondering why he hadn't been asked to help. Mrs Henderson seemed to see where she was looking.

'Mr Henderson decided to stay on at the party. But I couldn't bear to wake up away from the children, so I decided to come home.' She gave Poppy a wide smile.

Five years working for the Hendersons had taught Poppy to read between the lines. This was a warning shot.

'You know, Mrs Henderson,' said Poppy, as she unclasped the bracelet. 'The kids were worried. You told them you'd be home by eight.'

Mrs Henderson raised her eyebrows. 'I'm sorry?'

No, you're not, thought Poppy. *And I'm damned if I'm going to make this easy for you.* 'The kids. You said that it was just a drinks party. That you'd be home by eight. Kate and Damson didn't want to go to bed because they were worried about you.'

Taking one heavy jewel from her earlobe, Mrs Henderson smirked. 'Poppy, I don't expect to have my movements policed by you.'

Poppy leant on the kitchen counter, trying to keep her cool. 'I realize that, I'm just saying, they were worried. And I did call a couple of times but you didn't pick up . . .' she trailed off. Mrs Henderson was taking a bottle of San Pellegrino from the fridge and walking towards the staircase. 'Mrs Henderson,' Poppy heard herself saying, louder than she had intended, 'please will you listen to me?'

She turned at the foot of the stairs. Not for the first time, Poppy drank in the thinness of her limbs, the depth of her tan.

'Poppy,' said Mrs Henderson slowly, as if English was Poppy's fifth language. 'You're tired. I don't think you're entirely in control of what you're saying. Go to bed.'

'I'm tired because I get up at six with Lola every day and you won't let me sleep when I'm here alone with them.'

'I do not pay you to sleep,' said Mrs Henderson, in a

349

voice that could freeze ice. 'I pay you to look after my children.'

'And I do look after them! I do a hell of a lot more looking after them than either you or your husband do. But you can't just waltz home six hours late without so much as a phone call.' Her volume had climbed even higher as she spoke and Poppy realized that she was shouting. At the top of the stairs, Damson appeared.

'Mamma?' she said, to her mother's back.

'Now look what you've done,' said Mrs Henderson.

'Everything's fine, Damson,' said Poppy, forcing herself to smile. 'Just go back to bed, OK?'

'Where's Papa?' she asked.

'Out,' said Mrs Henderson, without turning to look at her daughter.

Poppy could feel the anger rising like bile. She grappled to keep a hold of it. She didn't do this. She didn't lose her temper, or tell people how to raise their children. She joined families, she looked after the kids and she didn't interfere. That was her job. That was the only way that this ever worked. 'Go back to bed, Damson,' said Poppy gently. 'I'll see you in the morning. We're going to look at the rock pools, remember?'

Damson seemed satisfied. 'Night, night,' she said, trailing back to her bedroom.

'Now that you've woken the children up and disrupted my evening, have you finished?' said Mrs Henderson.

Poppy sank both rows of teeth into either side of her tongue, focussing on the sharp sting of pain. Of course she wasn't done. She wanted to tell Mrs Henderson that she was a bitch, that her children weren't fashion accessories, and to let her know that Mr Henderson had slid his hand down the back of her jeans at Lola's birthday party last month. But Damson's worried face had put paid to that.

'Yes,' said Poppy slowly. 'I would just really appreciate it if in future you would call me to let me know that you're going to be late.'

'In future?' laughed Mrs Henderson, starting to ascend the glass stairs. 'Poppy, you're fired.'

'What?'

'You didn't think that you could talk to me like that and still keep your job?'

It was hard to find words. It was as if there were too many of them, all fighting to exit her mouth at the same time.

'Fired?' she repeated, quietly.

'Yes, get out,' said Mrs Henderson, as she reached the top of the stairs.

'Now?' asked Poppy, astounded that even Mrs Henderson could be this vile. 'You want me to go now? I have nowhere to go. What about the kids?'

Mrs Henderson shook her head. 'I think you've done quite enough to upset the children.'

'Please,' said Poppy. 'I'll go in the morning? Let me say goodbye to them.'

Mrs Henderson smiled. 'I don't think that would help anyone.'

'What about my stuff?'

'The maid will pack it. I will let you know when you can come and pick it up, at a time when the children and I are out, so that you don't cause any more distress. And you can arrange to collect your things from the London house when we're back.'

Poppy gave herself a fast, angry talking to. She had nowhere to go, fuck all money and it was the middle of the night. She shouldn't have lost her temper, she shouldn't have picked a fight. Forcing her mouth to form the words, almost choking on the humiliation, Poppy put on a gentle voice. 'Mrs Henderson, this is mad, I'm sorry I said anything. Let's just go to bed, let's talk about it in the morning—'

She shook her head.

'Please?'

Mrs Henderson smiled. 'No.'

Rage, pure hot rage, swelled up in Poppy's stomach. 'Fine.'

Marching across the kitchen, she grabbed her handbag and, hoping Mrs Henderson wouldn't notice what she was doing, swept the car keys she'd dropped on the side into her hand. Reaching the door, Poppy realized to her panic that her feet were bare. The only shoes by the front door were the strappy gold sandals that Mrs Henderson had kicked off on arrival. Sighing, she yanked them on to her feet. They were still warm and slightly damp from Mrs Henderson's feet. Slamming the front door behind her she bleeped the Range Rover keys and slid into the driving seat, thanking her lucky stars that she hadn't drunk an illicit beer earlier, though there was no way Mrs Henderson had driven home sober. But, Poppy thought, as she took the car in a sharp U-turn and out of the drive, the rules were different for people like her.

CHAPTER II

Pepito's was on the side of the road and full of Spanish teenagers, but it was open, and it was still serving, which was all that mattered. Poppy found the last empty table left outside, ordered herself a beer and then, because tonight had gone to hell anyway, asked the guy at the table next to her if she could cadge a cigarette. She drew the smoke into her lungs, sighing and revelling in the burn at the back of her throat. The cigarette glowed orange at the end. She liked watching the ash creep up. The beer was cold and had a thick wedge of lime shoved in the top. It was what she needed. It was a shame that she could barely afford this one, let alone another one. Steadying herself, she pulled her purse open. She had twenty-two euros in cash. A credit card which had a hundred quid left on it, and less than fifty pounds in her debit account. The Hendersons owed her several hundred in expenses – she'd paid for Rafe's sailing lessons and lunch for all four of them all week. Mrs Henderson always had a lax attitude to repayment, what were the chances that they'd bother to pay her back now? Would they even honour her final month's salary?

First things first, she pulled out her phone.

Got fired. Sitting in a bar, working out my next move. Back in England asap. Can I crash on your sofa? she wrote, and pressed send.

Gina wouldn't be awake, but she would see it in the morning and she'd definitely say yes. Gina had a sweet deal, a 'nanny flat' in the basement of the house her bosses lived in. Was there any chance she could ask Gina to lend her a couple of hundred quid to get her home? Probably not. Gina was just as broke as she was. Poppy ran her finger down the list of contacts in her phone, scanning for someone she'd forgotten about who would lend her money. There was no one. Her eyes settled briefly on 'Mum'. No way.

Next, she typed out a message to Damson, who had been given the most recent iPhone for her eighth birthday. Would she see it before her mother intervened? It was worth a try.

Darling Dam, I'm so sorry that I didn't say goodbye. I'll miss you lots and lots. Give Lola a big squeeze from me and tell Rafe that I'll miss him too. PS. Don't worry about the argument earlier. Sometimes grown-ups have fights but it's no one's fault and everything is OK. All my love, Poppy

Writing the penultimate line was almost impossible. She had to force her fingers to press the buttons. But it mattered. Damson needed to think that her mother was on her side. She was going to end up fucked up enough as it was. Poppy couldn't be part of that.

What next? Grimly, like looking down at a cut, knowing that once you saw the blood it would start hurting, she searched for flights on her phone. Ibiza to London in the middle of summer with twenty-four hours' notice was, unsurprisingly, ruinous. The cheapest one, with two stops and a final destination in Manchester – two hundred miles from home – was three hundred quid. She slumped forward, letting her forehead touch the cool table. She'd have to sleep in the Range Rover on the side of the road, and then beg her final salary and the money the Hendersons owed her when she dropped it back tomorrow. Oh God, she'd have to go back in Mrs Henderson's shoes. Despair swelling up in her chest, she scanned the restaurant for a waiter. The money situation was bad enough as it was. Another four euros couldn't make much of a difference at this point.

'*Uno mas, por favor,*' she said, gesturing to the empty beer bottle in front of her. She looked down at her sundress, wondering if enough smiles and cleavage might get her a free drink. The thought that finding someone here to go home with would be a lot less unpleasant than sleeping in the car crossed her mind. The waiter smiled back at her, but didn't seem to be listening. She got up, squeezing through the drunken crowds and ordered her drink at the bar. Stepping back on to the terrace she saw that her table had been taken by a man in a blue linen shirt, sitting with his back to her.

'*Lo siento,*' she said, realizing that she was rapidly running out of Spanish words, '*Es mi—*' She gestured to her handbag, which she had left on the table.

The man turned to look at Poppy. He had green eyes, curly dark hair and an irritating smile.

'You got up,' he said. His voice was cut-glass English.

Poppy rolled her eyes. The last thing she wanted this evening was to get into another argument with a Henderson-type.

'Never mind,' she said, reaching over to grab her bag. As she leant over she caught the smell of him – the scented ironing water some maid had used on his shirt. The expensive aftershave. It smelt good.

'You could join me. If that's the extent of your Spanish I can't imagine you're going to be making conversation with anyone else in this place.'

'Seeing as it's my table,' said Poppy, pulling out a metal chair, 'you'll be joining me. Not the other way round.'

He smiled. 'A shame. If you were joining me then I would have insisted on paying.'

Poppy felt her lips curling into a smile. 'In which case, perhaps I was mistaken.'

He let out a low laugh. 'Not bothered about pride. I like that in a person.'

'In a *woman*,' Poppy replied without thinking.

'No,' he said. 'In a person.' He stuck his hand out. 'I'm Drew.'

'Poppy,' she said. His hand felt cool in hers.

'Poppy,' he repeated, smiling at her. 'Is there any chance that you're at all hungry?'

She'd been too angry and worried earlier to eat, and thinking about it, it had been hours since she'd had anything. She nodded. 'Fucking starving.'

'What do you want to eat?' he asked.

'Everything,' she replied, swigging from her beer.

Drew gestured for the waiter and, though Poppy wouldn't have admitted it for all the money on Ibiza, she was a little impressed by how fluent his Spanish was.

'What did you order?' she asked as the waiter walked away.

'Everything,' he smiled.

TRUTH HURTS by Rebecca Reid

Poppy has a secret.
Drew has nothing to hide.

Theirs was a whirlwind romance.

And when Drew, caught up in the moment, suggests
that he and Poppy don't tell each other anything about
their past lives, that they live only for the here and now,
for the future they are building together, Poppy jumps
at the chance for a fresh start.

But it doesn't take long for Poppy to see that this is a
two-way deal. Drew is hiding something from her. And
Poppy suddenly has no idea who the man she has
married really is, or what he might be capable of.

Poppy has a secret.
Drew has nothing to hide.
Drew is lying.
Which is more dangerous, a secret or a lie?

Available to pre-order now
Out August 2019